One Last Time

ABOUT THE AUTHOR

Helga Flatland is already one of Norway's most awarded and widely read authors. Born in Telemark, Norway, in 1984, she made her literary debut in 2010 with the novel *Stay If You Can, Leave If You Must*, for which she was awarded the Tarjei Vesaas' First Book Prize. She has written four novels and a children's book and has won several other literary awards.

Her fifth novel, *A Modern Family* (her first English translation), was published to wide acclaim in Norway in August 2017, and was a number-one bestseller. The rights have subsequently been sold across Europe and the novel has sold more than 100,000 copies. *One Last Time* was published in Norway in 2020, where it topped the bestseller lists.

ABOUT THE TRANSLATOR

Rosie Hedger was born in Scotland and completed her MA (Hons) in Scandinavian Studies at the University of Edinburgh. She has lived and worked in Norway, Sweden and Denmark, and now lives in York where she works as a freelance translator. Rosie was a candidate in the British Centre for Literary Translation's mentoring scheme for Norwegian in 2012, mentored by Don Bartlett. She has translated Agnes Ravatn's *The Bird Tribunal* and *The Seven Doors* for Orenda Books, as well as Helga Flatland's *A Modern Family*.

One Last Time

Helga Flatland

Translated by Rosie Hedger

**ORENDA
BOOKS**

Orenda Books
16 Carson Road
West Dulwich
London SE21 8HU
www.orendabooks.co.uk

First published in Norwegian as *Et liv forbi* by Aschehoug Forlag in 2020
First published in English by Orenda Books in 2021
Copyright © Helga Flatland, 2020
English translation copyright © Rosie Hedger, 2021

A catalogue record for this book is available from the British Library.
ISBN 978-1-913193-69-0
eISBN 978-1-913193-70-6

This book has been translated with financial support from NORLA

Typeset in Garamond by typesetter.org.uk

Printed and bound by CPI Group (UK) Ltd, Croydon CR0 4YY

*For sales and distribution, please contact info@orendabooks.co.uk or visit
www.orendabooks.co.uk.*

In the middle of your life, death comes calling,
Here to measure you up. You forget
His visit and life continues. But still
He sews your suit in secret

Tomas Tranströmer

1

I bring the blade of the axe down on her neck. Drop the head into one bucket, the body into another, hear the way her claws scrape slightly against the plastic before silence falls once again. I head into the barn and fetch the next one, clutch her tight to my breast as I walk, feel her tremble there, the quiver of her pulse beneath her feathers, I whisper quietly to her before turning her over, holding her by the legs until she calms down. Quickly I lay her on the chopping block, stretch out her neck, deliver a hard blow to the head with the blunt end of the axe, and in one swift gesture I spin it around in the air and swing it back down again, slicing off her head with the axe blade.

I've forgotten to close the barn door, one of the hens has escaped and is standing in silence just outside. She gazes at me. She looks distraught, possibly confused, as if she can't believe what she's just witnessed, I feel for her, wonder if I should return her to the others and save her for last, or if she'll simply wander around, dreading the inevitable for longer than is necessary. Gustav would have laughed at me, told me I'm crediting them with feelings they don't have, feelings of my own.

'Come on, old friend,' I whisper, crouching down on my haunches, feeling an aching sensation in my knees, throughout my whole body, need to call Sigrid, take out the grain feed in my pocket, lure her in, she whips her head first to the left, then to the right.

I don't even particularly like hens, and this flock has long since stopped laying, I've only kept them for nostalgic reasons – and to maintain the illusion of some sort of working set-up. A farm needs animals, Viljar had said when he was last here. I agreed with him to some extent, but keeping five hens that no longer lay for the sake of grandchildren who visit four times a year is no longer reason enough.

The hen can't resist temptation in the end, wanders over and eats out of my hand. I stroke her feathers and let her finish the grain before butchering her.

2

'Sigrid? Your mother rang,' Aslak says as I step in the front door, he's lying on the sofa with his back to me and picks up my phone as if to show me the conversation, but without turning to look at me. 'Something about some hens, I think.'

'What do you mean, you *think*?' I ask, taking off my shoes and coat.

'Well, it was definitely something about hens, but I didn't grasp exactly what it was all about, to be honest with you,' he says.

'Well done,' I remark dryly, sinking into the chair beside him, can't face saying any more than that.

He chuckles, turns around and casts a glance in my direction.

'That's what happens when you forget your phone. You look tired,' he says, a comment I take as an acknowledgement.

I am tired. So tired that every conversation, every gesture, every thought is an exertion.

'Well, it's Friday,' Aslak says, as if to wrap up my thoughts, he smiles and pats my thigh. 'Viljar wants tacos, but don't blame me, all this stuff about everyone having tacos on a Friday night must be something he's picked up at preschool. Do you know if Mia's coming?'

Mia is with her father, and clearly not planning on joining us. Aslak looks so hopeful that I can't face breaking it to him that she hasn't been in touch for several days now.

'Aren't you going to get changed?' I ask him instead, nodding at his work trousers. 'Given that it's Friday, and all that?'

❖

I put off ringing Mum, head on up to see Viljar, who is sitting inside the little tepee in his room with his iPad resting in his lap.

'Hi there, buddy,' I say, sticking my head inside the tepee and kissing his cheek, my lips brush against salty, damp crumbs around his mouth, I realise his face and hands are bright orange. 'Have you been snacking on cheese puffs before dinner?' I ask loudly.

Viljar nods, his gaze still fixed on the screen, *Peppa Pig*. Aslak has no doubt given him the whole bag, some form of compensation, I think, if not, then it's intended as some sort of dig, it can't be anything else, but I've stopped trying to get my head around whatever it is he's trying to achieve. I suspect that he doesn't know anymore, either. I tease the bag from Viljar's clutches, fortunately without objection.

'Just one more episode,' I say as Peppa and the rest of her family break out in the same absurd laughter that concludes each episode, family morale always perfectly intact, and Viljar casually, competently scrolls down the list of episodes.

I take a shower, wash my hair twice, lather myself in antibacterial soap I brought home from the office, scrub my body, under my nails, can't get clean enough, there's still bacteria on my skin and in my hair from all those patients with their rasping coughs, open sores, itchy crotches and overburdened souls. Some days it is as if their problems consume me, I can't get a foothold, they just take what they want and leave. Days like that leave me powerless to argue, I dole out sick leave and prescriptions, refer people for MRIs and CT scans, send them to cardiac experts, all as my self-confidence plummets and my anxiety soars.

When I come back downstairs, I see that Aslak has fallen asleep on the sofa, I suppress the urge to wake him, to shout that if anyone should be sleeping on the sofa it's surely me, but I leave him be, I don't have the heart to complain or to start an argument when I haven't the ability to say what I really want or feel. An argument that will reveal, above all else, the fact that I don't really *know* what I want or feel. He's lying with his arms crossed behind his head, I notice that he's wearing his gold chain again, the one he received as a confirmation gift, the same one he stopped wearing when we moved to Oslo.

The carrier bags on the kitchen countertop are packed full, milk and sour cream and mince, the cartons and packets are wet with condensation. I wonder how early Aslak actually left work, how long he's been lying on the sofa while Viljar has screen time in his room, a concept that Aslak refuses to acknowledge. He makes his way into the kitchen as I'm browning the mince, stands behind me and wraps his arms around me, kisses the nape of my neck. It's a rare occurrence, I turn around and lean against him for a moment, sniff at his left armpit. I miss the smell of him when he used to get home after a day of lugging around and slotting together enormous planks of wood, the smell that conveyed strength and a primitive sense of security. He established himself as a furniture maker when we moved to Oslo and only ever smells faintly of wood oil and detergent these days.

I was the one who wanted to leave, I was the one who wanted to come here, I was the one who wanted this life.

He holds me for a while, tightens his grip before sighing and letting go, starts setting the table. I try calling Mia for a second time, silently pray that she'll pick up the phone, can't go making many more unanswered calls to her phone without her reading something into it, two missed calls could still just mean that I want to talk to her. I used to attempt to get through to people over and over again until I got hold of them, it took me a while to grasp the idea that doing so could be considered invasive or alarming, perhaps I didn't really grasp it properly until the day Mia lost her temper with me. If I don't pick up the phone, surely you realise that I'm busy, nobody rings five times in a row unless it's some sort of emergency, she said, why the hell do you always have to be so intense?

She doesn't pick up, of course, and I can picture her, sitting in Jens and Zadie's kitchen, relaxed, smiling, the three of them making dinner together, the conversation flowing, all in English of course, for Zadie, something Mia thinks is a great learning opportunity, particularly useful since she's planning on moving to London to study next year. I resist the temptation to leave her an irate voice-mail, bemoaning the deep injustice around the fact that Jens, finally a fully-functioning adult at the age of forty-five, should find an obliging daughter, primed and waiting for him after all the years of hard work and love that Aslak and I have invested in her – particularly after the last few hellish years, which have featured endless rounds of upset and confrontation, arguments that have left me dumbfounded at what the unfamiliar individual before me is capable of thinking and bellowing. Where does this come from? I've wondered, it bears no resemblance to my own darkness, my own sense of rage, it bears no resemblance to me at all. Mia has been so controlled, so precise, at times so cunning and cold during confrontations, that on occasion, in the wake of our arguments, I've had to look at pictures of her as a young girl to remind myself that I still love her. This is all Jens, I've tried telling myself and Aslak several times, this is his doing, his genes, his absence.

But it bears no resemblance to Jens, either. He's chronically evasive, incapable of making a single decision, of standing for anything other than his own impulses. I met him when I was nineteen, when he turned up in the village as a junior doctor – attractive only due to the fact that he was an outsider, that he offered something different, something new, an alternative to everything small and spent and cramped. And attractive because he had the ability to drown things out; he was excessive, transparent. I think you've been waiting for me, Sigrid, he remarked to me over his fourth beer on the night I met him. It was only later that it occurred to me that he was probably high on all sorts of opiates at the time, but it hadn't mattered, there was no fight left in me, I was snared, trapped. After his foundation years ended he stuck around – because of me, I thought, because we'd settled on something without ever making it explicit, a life and a future together. I didn't realise how aimless he was, how flighty – didn't realise what I've since repeated to myself hundreds of times: that he was fragile, dependent, damaged, that he needed picking up, craved constant recognition or admiration or intoxication simply to keep himself afloat. Without the slightest hint of embarrassment, he would tell me about glowing praise from adoring patients, or commend his own skills and attributes in such an explicit manner that I misinterpreted it as an expression of sheer self-confidence and a statement of truth. It was a new experience for me, to find myself so wholly absorbed by another person in such a way, never able to get enough or be close enough. A yearning for him could flare up within me at any given moment, I could find myself pining for him, for more of him, even at times when we couldn't possibly be any closer, when there wasn't a millimetre of space between our bodies.

When I was five months pregnant with Mia, a complaint was made against him. A colleague discovered that he had issued a huge number of prescriptions for addictive medication, and in the space of just a few days, Jens decided that he needed a change of scenery. I've never told anyone that the person who drove him to the airport to travel to Bangladesh with an aid organisation was me, pregnant, furious and infatuated.

❖

Mia calls me back after we've finished our tacos, after I've sung Viljar's obligatory lullabies. Aslak and I are watching a film, each sitting on our own sofa. It's so long since I last objected to spending our weekends in front of the television. At the very beginning of our relationship, more or less without thinking I tried to pressure Aslak into following the same routines that Jens and I had followed when we had been together; I can't recall us spending a single evening watching television in all the years we spent together, I only recall conversations, sex, sorrow, arguments and reconciliation, all played out in an all-consuming vicious circle. We must have had more settled days, but I remember us as if in constant motion. Aslak's sense of calm and stillness forces different shapes to emerge, different patterns, another life altogether. And had Jens not moved back to Oslo a year ago and invaded my life, invaded Mia's, I wouldn't be spending yet another evening impatiently comparing him to Aslak.

'Hi, love,' I say as I answer the phone, keeping my tone bright and breezy.

'Hi, you called me?' Mia says.

'Yes, it'd just be nice to know if we should include you in our plans for dinner or not,' I reply.

I sit there on the sofa, pulling at a loose thread along the seam of one of the cushions, where Aslak's work trousers have chafed against the fabric every day after work without fail. He pauses the film.

'I know, but if you don't hear from me, then surely you realise I'm not coming,' she says, and I try to listen out for Jens in the background, sounds, conversations, something to indicate what they're up to, I hope they're watching TV.

'It'd be nice to hear either way,' I say. 'I hardly see you these days.'

This is close to crossing a line I promised myself I'd never cross with my children; I promised myself I'd never make them feel guilty, never leave them with the feeling that they owe me anything.

'You saw me two days ago, Mum,' Mia says, sounding more re-signed than plagued by a guilty conscience.

'But will you be staying there all weekend?' I ask.

'I don't know, Dad and Zadie might be going out somewhere tomorrow night, so I think I'll come back home if they do,' she says, and the fact that she still refers to Aslak and me as home trumps both the fact that she's started calling Jens 'Dad' and the desire to ask where he and Zadie might be going.

'That'll be nice. We'll see you tomorrow, then,' I reply, and out of the corner of my eye I see Aslak straightening up.

'Sure, maybe. Grandma rang me a while ago, by the way, but I didn't get to my phone in time, and now she's not picking up when I try to call her back.'

'She's called us too, but it's nothing urgent, Dad says it was just something or other about the hens,' I tell her.

Aslak shuffles around on the sofa. There's a brief pause.

'OK, so, I'll see you tomorrow or Sunday, then,' Mia says. 'Bye.'

'OK, bye then,' I reply.

Aslak looks at me as I hang up.

'I'm sure she'll be back tomorrow,' I tell him, trying to smile, in that moment remembering Mia as a baby, lying on Aslak's chest, the way he would gently blow on her head to help settle her.

It's not unusual for Mum to call Mia, they often chat, probably more often than I speak to either of them on the phone. But there's something about the timing, or perhaps it's just me. Perhaps I'm always on my guard when Mum calls, and perhaps the relief that it's never anything serious erases my memory of the anxiety I feel at receiving each call. Either way, it's unlikely that Mum would have called to talk to me about the hens. I try calling her back once we're in bed, but she doesn't pick up. I check Facebook before bed, as I often do, to see how long it is since she, Mia and Magnus were last online. Mum was active nineteen minutes ago, I relax my shoulders. I register the fact that it's also nineteen minutes since Jens last logged in.

I lie there and listen to Aslak breathing and the distant alarm in the city that I've never become accustomed to, it still disturbs me, even though I object when Aslak complains and says it's impossible to sleep with the windows open in the summertime. Rubbish, this is one of Oslo's quietest neighbourhoods, I told him during one of our first summers here, pushing open the window that looks onto the garden, you won't find anywhere quieter than this if you want to live in the city, I continued. I'm not the one who wants to live here, he replied, closing the window.

I was the one who wanted to move to Oslo when I was done with my foundation training, when I was done with my studies and everything that had gone before them, done with village life, done with my feelings for Jens, done with Dad, done with Mum's invasive loneliness. Aslak and Mia had to adapt to my needs, as he put it years later, not sounding angry or accusatory, more as if he were simply acknowledging the fact. I can't carry an eternal debt of gratitude to you, I shouted at the time, not that he's ever asked for gratitude, not once. But over the past year I've felt his need for some sort of assurance on a daily basis, payback in the form of some kind of commitment that I can never leave him. In the worst moments, my jealousy of Mia – her rebellion and freedom, the way she's pulling away from Aslak – leaves me livid, and in that same instant, guiltily I grieve.

Mia has landed a job with a production company while she takes extra study credits, earning her own money for the first time in her life – the momentous discovery of economic freedom has propelled her need for independence. She arrives on Sunday morning, the previous day's make-up smudged beneath her eyes, wearing a pair of jogging bottoms she's borrowed from someone or other, too unflattering and far too baggy to belong to one of her female friends. She takes a seat at the kitchen table and helps herself to the bacon I've made for Viljar and Aslak. It takes all my strength not to tell her that I wasn't counting on her being here for breakfast.

It must be nice having a grown-up daughter when you're still so young yourself, you must be like friends, my own friends have said to me on more than one occasion. I've agreed with them, definitely nice, really nice to be a young mother to a daughter Mia's age, yes, it *is* a bit like being friends, definitely. But I don't want to be Mia's friend in any way, shape or form. I don't need to know where she spent last night, for example, not as long as she seems happy in herself. Mia, for her part, is still working out where the line is, occasionally she shares uncomfortably intimate details with me about her newly discovered and constantly expanding adulthood, while other weeks she's silent and stand-offish with me. I want her to be able to tell me anything, I thought to myself when she was a child, that's the sort of mother I want to be, and to remain, but in practice a line has appeared when it comes to Mia.

She looks happy, she looks like Jens, like him and him alone, as she fortunately laughs at one of Aslak's many jokes. He's trying too hard; I hope he's able to strike a balance. I've witnessed numerous situations over the past few months, Aslak so happy and hyped up at any interaction between them, the fleeting moments of attention that Mia has graced him with, that he crosses a line only Mia and I can see, and then she unexpectedly utters some condescending comment, in the worst case involving Jens, as if it were coincidental.

Throughout her upbringing, Aslak has been the one to have meaningful conversations with her about Jens, and to be asked the most questions about him. You can't say things like that, Aslak told me when Mia was six years old and wanted to include Jens in a picture of the three of us. She wondered what colour his hair was, I shrugged, said she could decide for herself. She was confused, of course, looked to Aslak. He's got the same colour hair as you, he said. And the same colour eyes, he added hastily, without looking at me. She doesn't need to know every little thing about him, I remarked later. She's going to find out what she wants to know about him sooner or later, and I don't want to be the one standing in the way of that, Aslak replied. His approach worked well until Jens moved to Oslo, until he came and cast Aslak and me in a different light, gave her something to compare us against.

The change is vague and irrefutable, I can't find the words to articulate it, but neither do I dare pushing her further towards Jens, and both Aslak and I find ourselves unwillingly tiptoeing around her. It drives me mad, a fire rages within me, fuelled by a thousand comments and bellowed requests for her to turn her music down, to clean the bathroom as we agreed she would, to let us know if she's coming home for dinner, not to throw coloured socks in with a white wash, not to forgive him, not to idolise him, not to disappear in him.

The past year has offered an uncomfortable taste of what life will be like when she moves out, I've felt myself struggling to breathe whenever I think about it – that she should be so far from me, and that I'll be left to discover what Aslak and I are without her.

'Did you manage to get through to Grandma?' Mia asks as Aslak and I clear the table, she's sitting on the bench with her legs tucked up beneath her.

'No, I'll call her later, but it's nothing to worry about,' I say.

'Sure,' Mia replies, 'but I'm the sort of person who can't help but worry.'

'Oh, you *are*, are you?' I reply, chuckling.

'Oh, whatever,' Mia replies, 'you know what I mean.'

We've had this conversation many times before, I can't help but remark on the need that she and her entire generation has to assert their own characteristics and personality traits. I'm a very empathetic person, a young girl who turned up in my office with a broken arm said to me once. I nodded as I looked at her arm, unaware of the context. Hmm, yes, is that hard for you, I replied, unsure. Not really, she replied breezily, things just hit me *hard*, if you know what I mean. I see, I replied, sending her off for an x-ray.

There's something uncomfortable about being told what I should think about you, I've tried explaining to Mia. It fell on deaf ears. It's more uncomfortable having someone see you the wrong way, she replied with a shrug, and perhaps she's right.

Monday arrives with such a normalising force that I almost burst into tears on the train to Ellingsrud. The autumn darkness unites us passengers in a fellowship that I never feel on bright summer mornings, a sociable silence, perhaps a sense of mutual sympathy, an acknowledgement that we are among those who have been roused from their slumber at six o'clock in the morning to make it to work on time, in spite of the bleak November darkness and biting cold, no sign of snow. I am part of this fellowship, my shoulders pulled up to my ears as I blow into my hands, but there's no month that I like more. No events, no annual celebrations, no emergencies, just the uninterrupted and tranquil darkness that eats away at the days in ever greater chunks.

The forty-minute commute to work and back has become the highlight of my day, a comfortable intermediate moment when I'm able to escape demanding patients and equally demanding relatives. As I step off the train, I try to call Mum for the third time, but get no reply, and for the first time since Friday I allow myself my usual worry for her, a feeling that is of such a constant and fixed size within me that it could be an aching body part in its own right, occasionally tamed, but ever present.

I spend a disproportionately long time seeing my first patients, as usual, spend far too much time with Ingrid. She's ninety years old, and always carries a bag of boiled sweets, which she hands out to patients in the waiting room and staff on the front desk; she always strokes my cheek before she leaves, like some sort of universal grandmother figure. Her presence is so comforting and mild that I just want to keep her here with me, to suppress any thoughts of the day to come. Afterwards I'm struck with guilt on behalf of my next patients, guilt at having shown favouritism, and I spend much longer than necessary carrying out a gynaecological examination and signing off on a driver's licence.

Just as I'm about to fetch Frida, who I know has already been sitting in the waiting room for an hour and a half, as she always does, Mum finally calls. Just before I manage to pick it up, Frida opens the door to my office. I reject the call.

'Frida, you need to wait for me to come and get you. We've talked about this, haven't we?' I reply, trying to take a pedagogical approach without coming across as patronising, an impossible balance, particularly when Frida behaves like an impatient child.

'But my appointment was at ten past, and your last patient left ages ago,' she replies.

'Go back out to the waiting room and wait to be called, please,' I say, but Frida doesn't believe that I'm being serious, she hovers in the doorway, uncertain. 'I mean it,' I tell her, turning to face my computer screen, swallowing.

'I think I'm about to have the baby,' she says.

'You're not,' I tell her, still facing the screen, clenching my teeth until she finally closes the door.

I sit there for a few minutes and stare at her medical records without reading them, then make for the waiting room and call her back in. She's already crying before she reaches my office, but I've grown used to that, her tears no longer knock me off balance, and I know that if I give her so much as a glimpse of hope or care beyond the professional boundaries, she'll eat me alive, skin, hair, the lot.

I gave her a hug on one of the first occasions that I met her, didn't know how to handle her depression and fear – and her expression intimated her belief that, once again, even after years knocking around a system that couldn't accommodate her, she'd found someone who could help her. I'm going to help you, I thought at the time, still in the belief that I could. There are still days when I think I can, days that I believe the fact I'm here is help enough, someone stable she can talk to, with clear boundaries between us established over time.

It was difficult to like her the first time she turned up in my office. She was clingy and full of complaints, headstrong, with a medical record that she knew by heart, an endless list of hospital admissions, medication, social-security measures, a patchy record of attending psychiatric appointments, and an unreasonable number of GPs she had worked her way through. She's been my patient for seven years now.

'So, how are things?' I ask once she's taken a seat, passing her a box of tissues, as usual.

'I think I'm about to have the baby,' she says again. 'Please,' she continues.

She hiccups as she leans over her knees, her stomach pushing against her thighs, clasps her hands behind her head, rocking back and forth.

'You're not going to have the baby just yet, you're only twenty-four weeks pregnant,' I tell her. 'But we're past the halfway mark now, Frida, you can do this.'

I curse myself at my use of the word *we*, still make fundamental mistakes in my eagerness to help, to give her a sense of solidarity, when the most important thing is that she knows above all else that she's alone in this, nobody is going to come and save her. Nobody apart from me, that is, and the thought sends me into a panic, the idea that I'm all she's got.

'I can't do it, I want it gone,' she shouts at the floor. 'It's eating away at me.'

A terrifying number of her thoughts remind me of those I had when I was pregnant with Mia, I remember how fear and loneliness manifested itself in absurd feelings and notions of being consumed. In Frida's medical records, I've written that her thoughts are a sign of illness, that she's imbalanced, on the verge of psychosis.

'Nothing's eating away at you, there's a lovely, healthy baby growing inside you,' I tell her, feeling that I'm choosing all the wrong words, the thing growing inside her is the very thing that it's impossible for her to relate to, I remember that, but I don't have any reserve energy to spend on finding the right way to approach her today, I'm already running over half an hour late after seeing only three patients. 'Shall we take your blood pressure, then we'll measure your bump after that?'

Frida gives in, straightens herself up, rolls up her sleeves. Her slender lower arms are covered in criss-crossing white scars. I didn't mention them the first time I saw them, I remember her anticipation as I rolled up her sleeve, and her subsequent disappointment at my lack of reaction. The memory pains me, I could have offered her that satisfaction, I've thought to myself since, after getting to know her, growing fond of her.

Often I see myself when I look at her, recognise myself in her, she's living out so many of my own inclinations, the things I need to control, to keep in check. I can't get enough of seeing how she pushes the limits of every chart, boundless in her approach to the world around her.

I stand at the kitchen worktop in the break room and eat a yoghurt for my lunch, feeling like time passes more quickly if I don't sit down, and the smartwatch Aslak gave me for Christmas has already reminded me umpteen times that I need to get moving. The two other doctors I share a practice with are sitting with their phones in their hands as they eat, in spite of the fact that we decided long ago that lunch would be device-free time, a 'tranquil oasis' in our day, a half-hour period during which we could chat and keep one another up-to-date on things, share our experiences and any potential frustrations.

I take the rest of my yoghurt into my office, call Mum. She picks up straight away.

'Finally,' she says.

'Hi to you too,' I say.

'I've been trying to get hold of you all weekend,' she says.

'Hardly, you've tried calling me once. If anything, the opposite is true, I've tried calling you back several times now,' I reply.

She falls silent for a few seconds, I can hear the sound of the kettle in the background, picture the kitchen at home, Mum in her yellow cardigan, her green teacup.

'None of you picked up when I called, in any case,' she says. 'I was starting to think there might be some conspiracy in the works.'

She chuckles briefly.

'I wouldn't worry about that, I haven't heard from Magnus in weeks,' I reply. 'Was there something in particular you wanted to discuss?'

'No, it was really just about the hens, I told Aslak when I spoke to him that I wanted to speak to you all before I butchered them, Viljar is so fond of them, and...'

Mum has had chickens ever since Dad became disabled and they'd had to slaughter the cattle and sheep, she insisted that a farm needed animals and promptly acquired twelve birds. I remember seeing headless chickens running around the yard at home after Mum had beheaded the first brood. She had invited her natural-sciences class along to give them a chance to learn about the circle of life, the fact that the chicken breasts they had for dinner didn't simply materialise in the supermarket freezer aisle. They don't come from tough, old birds like those either, Mum, Magnus said to her, but Mum carried on bringing students to watch the birds being butchered right up until a few parents complained to the headteacher on behalf of their traumatised children.

Viljar has, as far as I know, never had any kind of special fondness for Mum's chickens, quite the opposite, in fact, he's shown clear and somewhat troubling signs of a general phobia of birds, the root cause of which I haven't bothered to investigate. To claim that she's thinking of Viljar is just another way of making me feel guilty.

'It's nice of you to think of Viljar,' I remark. 'But obviously you have to do what you think is best when it comes to the chickens, Mum.'

'Well, it's too late now in any case,' she says. 'I slaughtered them on Thursday.'

3

'But if you already slaughtered them on Thursday, then I'm not sure I understand quite why it was so important to get a hold of us on Friday,' Sigrid says.

I fill the tub on the kitchen countertop with the boiling water from the kettle, don't know how to carry on the conversation, shouldn't have chosen such a roundabout approach involving the hens, should have gone straight to the heart of the matter, as I'd intended to on Friday, but all weekend I've imagined Sigrid and the impossible prospect of having to bring more of me and my issues to the fore.

'No, I meant Friday, I slaughtered them on Friday,' I tell her. 'But that's enough about all that. How are things with all of you?'

'Good thanks, but I'm at work just now, so if it's not urgent than perhaps we can talk this afternoon instead,' she suggests, she sounds hesitant, no doubt keen to avoid committing herself to yet another conversation.

I always think something might change when I speak to her, I don't realise it until the call is over, I'm always left with a sense that something has been left unsaid. I often feel frustrated for days following our conversations, at the reproach in her tone and her pauses, the brief moment of silence she leaves before she answers, as if to give me time to say more.

'Of course,' I tell her. 'Of course we can speak this afternoon.'

I carry the tub outside, only got as far as plucking the birds roughly and removing the innards on Friday before I had to concede defeat and place the half-prepared carcasses in the freezer.

I hauled my body onto the sofa after that, where I lay for hours, exhausted. The chickens are piled up inside the freezer out in the barn, which is already full of game that I haven't managed to bring myself to eat, but which I found myself equally unable to dispose of after giving in and placing Gustav in a nursing home.

I can't imagine I'll eat any of the chickens either, but it feels significant, turning them into food in this way, no detours or unnecessary carbon emissions. I fetch one of the headless carcasses from the freezer, try to avoid reading any of the labels on the rest of the meat, Gustav's sloping handwriting, *Elk Tenderloin 2009*, the last year he'd joined the hunt, when the others had practically had to carry him out to his post. They had honoured him with tenderloin steaks from one of the elks they'd shot, something that left him feeling more embarrassed than having insisted on joining the hunt in the first place. He was wheelchair-bound by the following year.

I give the frozen chickens a better clean, my fingers in their yellow rubber gloves growing stiff with the cold, but I refuse to give in, need to finish the job before Sigrid calls me back; I am struck with a sense that everything has to be in order before I tell her, I realise that I probably ought to go and see Gustav first too, get all of my tasks out of the way.

Gustav is sitting by the window when I arrive, as usual, looking down on the farm and on me. His hair is grey, almost white, and still thick in contrast to his slender frame. I am occasionally surprised when I see him as he truly is; the fact that he no longer looks the way he does in my mind's eye, my memories.

'Hello, you,' I say, leaning over and giving him a hug. 'Didn't they shave you today, either?' I ask, stroking his stubbly cheek.

He lifts his gaze and looks at me, starts to laugh, he still has a surprisingly good set of teeth, strong and white. He's always taken care of his teeth, he used to say that you could tell a lot about a person from how well they looked after their teeth, and he followed a strict routine when it came to brushing and flossing every morning and evening. Even after he could no longer remember how to turn on the shower, he carried on cleaning his own teeth.

I release the brake on his wheelchair and wheel him to his room, can't bear to sit there being gawked at by the carers or other patients. I think you're supposed to call them residents, Mum, Magnus said when he was last here. He was sitting at the table in the corner with Sigrid and me, we talked around Gustav, as always ends up being the case when they come, we've never been able to find a method of communication that includes him. I can't talk to Gustav the way I do when it's just the two of us, and I don't imagine Sigrid and Magnus can, or want to, either. Why should I call them residents? I asked. The only reason they live here is because they're ill, and ill people receiving treatment are, by their very nature, *patients*, I continued. Sigrid nodded, but I've heard her refer to her own patients as users or something along those lines on numerous occasions, something intended to confer a more equal status upon them. I've confronted her about it, why on earth would any patient want to share an equal status with their doctor, that would certainly leave me feeling deeply concerned, I told her the last time we spoke, you've gone there seeking help, that's the whole point. That requires some sort of hierarchy. Sigrid said nothing, just flashed Magnus the same knowing look she so often does, self-pitying, almost pleading, seeking reassurance, as if I had attacked or criticised or offended her during the conversation, during every conversation.

Either way, I feel less confident about my own arguments now. Referring to myself as a patient does, on the one hand, offer a certain passivity, a safe denial of liability, but on the other hand it is a role I cannot completely identify with, it's perfectly possible that I might end up feeling more like a *user*, some sort of participant with a greater degree of control.

The other residents are much older than Gustav on the whole, and on numerous occasions I've felt that the situation must be accelerating his cerebral atrophy, finding himself surrounded by stooped, ailing individuals. Whenever I make my way across the car park towards the entrance to Gustav's final fixed abode, I allow all my thoughts about how awful it must be for him to live here to wash over me.

Today things feel slightly more straightforward, I even manage to make a little small talk with Gustav on our way to his room, smile at the carer I usually do my best to avoid because I can't bear the disapproval I see in his expression. Once Gustav and I are alone in his room, my shoulders relax. I take off my cardigan, park his chair by the headboard of his bed then lie down there, my head on his pillow, breathing in his scent. I inhale deeply, exhale slowly, reach out a hand and stroke his face once again, take his hand and squeeze it in mine, unable to hold back my tears. For the first time since Thursday, I cry. I suddenly feel so sorry for Gustav, it's unbearable to think how awful it must be for him.

'Don't mind me, I've been dealing with the chickens all day,' I remark as I look up at him, try to squeeze out a chuckle as I wipe away my tears with the sleeve of his jumper. 'I know you've never understood it, but you can become fond of them.'

He pulls his hand back, but there's nothing aggressive about the gesture. I take it once again. Carefully place it on my chest, over my T-shirt, my own hand on top of his. I lay my head back and relax, feel myself beginning to nod off until I suddenly feel him squeezing my breast. I turn to face him, smile. I shuffle upwards in the bed, resist the temptation to move his hand to other parts of my body, still recall his wild fury when I sat on his lap one Sunday a few years ago. And his reactions on the countless occasions that I've touched him in ways that no longer have any place in our life. Sometimes I think that my touch is to blame, my body against his, that it awakens memories, a desire for which he has no outlet – or perhaps that the damaged nerve endings in his brain confuse desire and anger. But more often than not it is the way that he pushes me away, squirming free, that serves as a reminder of just how much he blames me, perhaps even loathes me, for giving up on him and moving him in here. A long time has passed since I last dared expose myself to such rejection, but today I find that I can't help myself, I squeeze his hand where it rests on my breast, need to feel his presence, which is, in many ways, much less complicated now than it was when he was in good health.

I consider rehearsing my conversation with Sigrid, but decide against it. Even though Sigrid and various other doctors have stressed the fact that he no longer remembers any of us, occasionally I catch a glimpse of something within him, a gesture or expression that doesn't fit in the context of his illness – and since no one can know for certain exactly what he picks up on and what passes him by, I've decided to proceed on the basis that he understands more than we think.

'I had a long chat with Sigrid a little while ago,' I tell him, getting up. 'She wanted me to say hello and to tell you that she misses you,' I continue as I roll his chair into the bathroom, parking him in front of the mirror and finding his razor.

I stand there for a moment and look at us, see our roles reversed, myself sitting there in a wheelchair in a nursing home, malnourished and unable to function, Gustav standing behind me, strong and capable, ready to assist me with my every basic need. Never, I think to myself. I won't do it, I won't end up like this. I cover Gustav's face with white foam, shave his cheeks and chin and throat with steady sweeps of the razor, he closes his eyes. When I'm finished, I feel restless, want to leave the home and the sense of illness that surrounds us.

'I'm not sure I can stay for quite as long today,' I say without looking at him.

Gustav stares at a point in the distance somewhere beyond me, out of the window, perhaps his gaze is locked on something else altogether.

'I'm sorry. I'll see you tomorrow,' I tell him, stroking his head, my hand sweeping upwards and through my own hair, I run my fingers through it.

I stop halfway and grip the hair in my hands, feel the resistance as I pull before letting go. I remember my mother cutting her hair short the day she turned forty, long hair does old women no favours, she said. I don't know what she meant by that, whether she thought it improper somehow, or simply impractical. Either way, I didn't heed her warning, my hair is still long and thick, strong.

A fine dusting of snow covers the landscape as I drive into the yard back at home. I turn off the engine and sit there for a while without moving, staying where I am until I hear Kant barking from his kennel. I make my way around the garage and fetch him, he needs a walk, but I need to be careful about how I expend my energy, prioritise fetching a few armfuls of wood to make sure I have enough for this evening and early tomorrow morning. It's a new experience for me, not having sufficient energy to carry out simple routines – and even though it's been explained to me, I still can't understand the reason for my listlessness, don't know quite why my arms and legs feel so heavy, why it feels like moving through treacle when the cancer itself is in my abdomen.

We've found cancer in your colon, the doctor said. I'm embarrassed by how surprised I was to hear it, the fact that I almost stared open-mouthed at him, but it was my first reaction. Perhaps I've thought myself some sort of exception to medical rules, given that I've never been properly ill, I've always had a body that's worked as it should, I've been almost *too* robust and well, always ticked every box when it came to constantly shifting public health guidelines. Or perhaps I've felt that there ought to be some sort of justice in the world, that Gustav's illness made me immune somehow, that he bore the brunt of things for me and everyone else around us. Either way, I can't seem to recapture that feeling, it disappeared in the new reality that was revealed to me.

I've been practising my conversation with Sigrid. I've revealed my cancer diagnosis to Kant in at least ten different ways over the past few days. It doesn't make things any easier, I'm still dreading it just as much as I ever was, don't know how to express myself in such a way that I get across the fact that I don't expect anything of her. You don't need to come home, obviously, I've told Kant, but I've immediately regretted uttering the words.

I've also apologised during my conversations with him, something I know I won't manage with Sigrid. I know that she feels I owe her an apology for her whole childhood, as if I've damaged her, damaged the foundations for another life, different choices. It feels so unreasonable that I struggle to think about it rationally. Whenever I speak to her, I feel overwhelmed by the accusations that lie quivering beneath the surface, barely concealed, expressed only through half-finished sentences I'm supposed to comprehend without hearing in full, through self-pitying sighs and long-drawn-out pauses; I picture the expression she always wears when Magnus or I, or anyone else for that matter, mentions something with the potential to remind her of her childhood, a knowing, long-suffering look. I dig my nails into the palms of my hands during conversations of that nature, they leave marks in the skin. I feel certain that Sigrid's memories of her upbringing grow more painful and terrible every time that I fail to apologise, but I've realised that it's useless to try to dispute her memory of events, or to integrate them with my own, at any rate.

Never any waterproofs, Sigrid said four years ago, I spent every rainy day at primary school wet through, she continued. She and I were sitting in the kitchen, Aslak and Viljar had gone to bed, and Sigrid had mooched around restlessly all evening, waiting for an opportunity, as I later realised; we were discussing the teaching of New Norwegian in schools, as far as I can recall, or at least we were until she suddenly came out with all that about waterproofs. It wasn't true, of course, I'm sure I nagged her about wearing her waterproofs on many a rainy day, but even as I grasped what she was trying to say, a familiar defence mechanism flared up within me, I shook my head, my pulse thudding in my temples. I don't need this, Sigrid, I said. I was so cold, freezing all through primary school, do you know what it was like sitting through a whole day in class with wet socks, ice cold, not daring to take them off for fear that someone might see? She looked as if she were about to burst into tears. See what? I shouted. She stared back at me. See what? I repeated, calmer this time, not waiting to hear her reply. Honestly, Sigrid, you more than anyone saw what looking after Gustav involved, how much I've sacrificed. If you spent a few days with wet socks at primary school, obviously I'm sorry about that, but you're hardly the true victim in all this, I told her in as measured a tone as I could muster. She said nothing, waited a few seconds before getting up and leaving. I woke that night and remembered at least one occasion when Sigrid had been at high school and I had urged her to wear her boots, she had flown into a rage with me, stormed out the door and into the icy rain in her trainers and denim jacket.

She doesn't call until half past ten at night, I'm woken all of a sudden by the sound of my phone ringing, I've nodded off in front of the telly.

'Were you sleeping?' she asks when she hears my voice, seems surprised, almost sceptical.

'No, no,' I reply. 'I was just marking some assignments.'

Silence falls for a few seconds.

'Sigrid, there's something I need to talk to you about,' I say, then swallow, rest a hand on my stomach, feel the cancer cells within, the way they're taking shape at furious speed deep inside me.

She says nothing, but I hear her taking a deep breath.

'I don't know if I've mentioned it, but I've not been feeling myself for a while,' I begin, knowing full well that I've avoided mentioning to anyone the nausea and listlessness that I've been trying to ignore for weeks on end, the fact that I've had to perch myself on a rock and rest halfway up to the little cabin just three hundred metres from the house, the fact that I've suddenly discovered that my trousers no longer fit me around the waist, that they've become roomy around my thighs and bum, and the way that I've blamed November, a month that always leaves me feeling disheartened with its sudden, sweeping, monotonous darkness.

Sigrid still says nothing. I hope that she's breathing.

'I thought it must be something to do with the time of year, the fact that it gets so dark so early in the day, you know how I can't stand the darkness,' I tell her, hear my self-pity from Sigrid's perspective, stop myself mid-flow. 'But then I booked a doctor's appointment, I didn't want to bother you with it, and of course all you'd have been able to tell me was that I ought to see my doctor for some tests...' I continue, sensing that Sigrid hears only criticisms and attempts to make her feel guilty.

She clears her throat. I give her a moment to speak, but she remains silent.

'And then I was sent for a check-up that revealed I have colon cancer,' I say eventually.

'Are they going to operate?' Sigrid asks without hesitation.

'Yes, next Tuesday,' I reply. 'And they're optimistic, Sigrid, they said they hope I'll make a full recovery.'

'I see. But they haven't found any evidence that it's spread?' Sigrid asks, still sounding calm, I feel a hint of disappointment.

'No, they didn't mention anything along those lines,' I tell her. 'But the most important thing for me at this moment in time is that you and Magnus don't worry too much. It'll be OK.'

'No, Mum, the most important thing for now ought to be preparing yourself for what's ahead,' she says.

I have to let her react in her own way, but the cool composure in Sigrid's tone awakens some sort of desperation within me.

'Of course I'm preparing myself ... but I am a little scared, I have to admit,' I tell her, hearing a tremble in my voice.

I realise once again that my expectations have been too high, expectations of this conversation, Sigrid's reaction, and that part of me has also slightly relished the prospect of telling her, the idea that it might force something out of her or compel something to come to light between us, somehow.

'I'll need to speak to Amir and Camilla, but I imagine that I might be able to move my patients around and be with you by Monday at the latest,' Sigrid says, the fear immediately releasing its grip around me.

'There's no need for you to come home, obviously,' I whisper, almost without uttering a single sound. Gratitude overwhelms me, and fortunately Sigrid doesn't catch what I say, or perhaps simply chooses to ignore it.

I wake on Sunday with a stomach ache. Ever since telling Sigrid and Magnus about the cancer, establishing myself as formally unwell, I've woken in pain every day.

I make my way to the bathroom, take two paracetamols, turn the heating up yet another notch, shivering as I pull on my dressing gown, it's baggy over my chest and stomach, I wrap myself up in it before I catch sight of too much of my body in the mirror. I pull on my boots and call for Kant, then step outside. It's still dusky, I tread carefully to avoid slipping on the icy ground, blindly feeling every rock and bump in the path on the way down to the water, but I'm no longer able to trust my legs or my sense of balance or any other vital bodily function. Down by the jetty, I look out across the water; the high peaks surrounding us have been topped with a forgiving layer of snow, they look calm and obliging against their backdrop of darkness, and I feel rage pounding through me.

When I called Magnus, initially he was upset, then angry, where's the justice, he shouted. I chuckled, told him that unfortunately the world didn't work that way. No, but it should, it bloody well should, he shouted. It was distressing yet satisfying to hear his reaction after Sigrid's detached response, and since my conversation with Magnus, something has smouldered within me. Nothing to do with any sense of injustice, that would be too vague and intangible, but more a sense of having been let down, or that my body has let me down, to be more precise. Suddenly a split has formed between my body, and my mind and soul, me against it, embroiled in an impossible war.

Almost every day for the past forty years, I've set out from the jetty for my morning dip, in summer I swim two hundred metres to the furthest buoy and back again, in winter just four strokes out and four back again. It was Gustav who first invited me to join him for his regular morning bathing routine, he firmly believed that it was the best and healthiest possible way to start the day, regardless of the season. The first time I spent the night here, on the smallholding his father had left him, I was sure he was joking when he told me he was going out to bathe. It was New Year's Day, so cold that the ice had crept all the way to the shore. Gustav jumped in, straight through the thin surface layer of ice, waving at me from the water, the steam rising from his body, his breath visible in the frosty air, I'm not going anywhere until you join me, he called.

Every morning we've woken up here at home, we've had a morning swim before coffee, before breakfast, before engaging in conversation. Gustav insisted on his morning swim right up until the point he was so ill that he could no longer walk. For a long time, I had to support him on his way down to the water's edge, holding on to him as he climbed down the ladders, and even afterwards, when he was in his wheelchair, I'd wheel him down to the jetty wrapped in blankets with nothing but his pyjamas underneath, where he sat seething as I dived into the water.

I concede the first battle of the day to my body, carefully climbing down the ladder into the water rather than jumping in, feeling the cold envelop me, happy that my instincts remain intact, my body longs to retreat to safety, I launch into my obligatory swimming strokes, dunk my head beneath the water before returning to the ladder once again, the cold is like nails boring into my scalp, it feels like a punishment and a victory all at once.

❖

I sit in front of the fire afterwards and eat breakfast in my dressing gown, my laptop on my knees. This loss of appetite is so unfamiliar, it's intensified in recent days, the cancer might well be to blame, though it could just as easily be my fear in the face of it. I don't feel nauseous, but the idea of chewing something, swallowing it, anything at all, repulses me; I know now that a mucus-coloured tumour is growing within me, bleeding within me, and that everything I put inside me is destined to pass it by.

I know, too, that I have to eat, that my body yearns for nourishment, and over the past few days I've gone back and forth between feeling that it's getting what it deserves and making genuine attempts to conjure up a feeling of hunger, remembering what it was like to arrive at the mountain pasture, having carried several kilos of rock salt on my back all the way up the steep mountainside, for instance – and afterwards, the waft of bacon and cheese and thick slices of bread fried in butter over the fire. It does no good, I've given up, I've eaten nothing but natural yoghurt all the weekend, dusted with a symbolic scattering of oatmeal for breakfast and dinner alike.

It helps to distract myself, and I ignore the idea that I should avoid eating in front of the telly or computer, which I settled on after Gustav moved out, when I felt so stiflingly lonely. Even though it was unbearable having him at home towards the end, and all I longed for was to eat my meals in peace rather than face his aggressive outbursts, I've occasionally felt that it would be worth it simply to have some company at mealtimes.

Magnus has sent me research articles published in recent years, progress is being made at breakneck speed, he writes in one email, this looks promising, he writes in another. I hesitate when it comes to clicking on the links. Don't google it, promise me that, my GP said last Thursday, if there's something you're wondering about then call me – although your daughter's a doctor, isn't she?

That's helpful in situations like these, he continued, smiling at me, I wondered what sort of relationship he has with his own grown-up children. I haven't googled it, I haven't read the articles Magnus has sent me, apart from the first one, which left me feeling so anxious that I couldn't sleep. I lay there, dwelling on the research going on in laboratories all around the world, all the various break-throughs, people dressed in white coats celebrating their successful efforts, none of which would benefit me, I had the feeling that my cancer had appeared a few years too early for all that.

I can't bring myself to call Sigrid to ask even one of the many thousands of questions that have cropped up over the past few days. She's messaged me a few times, asking if she can speak to my GP, among other things, if I would withdraw my right to confi-dentiality, as if it were an obvious thing. I didn't dare ask what that might involve, if she'd be allowed access to all of my medical records, I flinched at the thought of what he might have written up in his notes over the years, particularly after Gustav's first relapse – how much did he take down of everything that had poured out of me? The fact that I'd wished we hadn't had children? That I'd wished someone would come along and shoulder the responsibility for me, take them away from me? Or in the years after that, my self-pitying approach to everything?

She'd only be given access to anything relating to the situation at hand, my GP told me when I called, chuckling under his breath, I'm not planning on telling her about everything else, he added, confirming that there was a great deal he himself wouldn't reveal to Sigrid if he were me. When we ended the call, I realised that I also ought to have asked what would happen to my medical records if I were to pass away, and in that moment, for the first time, I had the overwhelming sense that I was going to die. Not the vague knowledge that everyone feels from time to time, that you might be knocked over by a car or perish in other unknown circumstances, and not a sense of the constant, distant fact that we will all die one day – but an awareness of something surrounding me, overpowering me.

I have no idea what Sigrid has discussed with my doctor, whether she's been told something different to me, whether they've discussed what to tell me and what to omit, what with it being important to keep my hopes up and all that – making it pointless to tell me how unlikely it actually is that I'll pull through. There's no point embellishing the truth, I told the doctor when I received my diagnosis, right before I was about to leave, and it suddenly seemed impossible to step through his office door, as if opening it and stepping out would be akin to opening the door to a reality I didn't dare face, and instead I started to spin things out. We'd been sitting there for over an hour, discussing my clinical pathway and all of the possible outcomes – that is to say, both possible outcomes – and his tone took on a conclusive edge. I'm not embellishing anything, I promise, he replied, but I do need to see my next patient now. You can call me whenever you need to, he said.

Late in the afternoon, Kant and I both hear Sigrid opening the front door downstairs, followed by her footsteps in the hallway, I'm so sure that's what I can hear that I make my way downstairs to greet her. She's not there; the door is closed, the floor is spotless, there is no sign of her at all. Just as I turn around to go back upstairs, I hear her shouting something or other to Aslak outside, then the door opens.

'Hi,' she says, looking surprised to find me already standing there in the hallway, ready to greet them.

'Your *vardøger* arrived a few minutes ago,' I explain, putting what I just heard down to the old, premonition folk tale, and chuckle under my breath as I head over to her. 'I was sure I just heard you coming through the door, but it must have been your spirit. Hello, my girl.'

I wrap my arms around her, embrace her for slightly too long, she reciprocates for a few seconds before taking a step back.

'So, cancer's made you superstitious too, eh? she says with a smile.

'Too?' I reply.

She doesn't get a chance to say anything else before Aslak and Mia step through the door behind her, carrying a reassuring quantity of luggage, Viljar squeezes past them, runs in my direction, I only just manage to crouch down before he throws himself at me, his tiny arms flying around my neck and clinging on tight. I let him stay there as long as he likes, feel his breath by my ear and savour the smell of dungarees and Viljar and car and cheese puffs.

'Oh, it's so good to see you,' I whisper into his hair.

All of a sudden, he spots Kant and lets me go, I'm knocked off balance, have to support myself with a hand on the floor behind me. I catch Sigrid's gaze locked on me, scrutinising, but she says nothing.

'Hi,' Aslak says as I get up, and he too embraces me generously. 'Bloody hell, this is an awful situation, Anne. How are you feeling?'

I've made up my mind not to complain; at no point in time, regardless of what happens, do I want to be the sort of person who complains about things. I'll be honest and factual, but I refuse to complain.

'Thank you, I'm actually feeling alright. Just a bit tired, I say, and receive a quick hug from Mia too, she's so like Sigrid that I can't help but smile.

'Hardly surprising if you're eating as little as you appear to be,' Sigrid says as she leans over to untie her bootlaces. 'And don't be afraid to turn up the heating too, it's ice-cold in here.'

'Hardly surprising that you think it's cold when you go around in flimsy shoes like that, rather than a proper pair of winter boots,' I remark with a laugh, even though Sigrid's choice of clothing and footwear and make-up and attitude and manner of speaking are all plainly intended to demonstrate her distance, from the village, the farm, me.

4

I have to swallow hard to suppress the sobs I feel in my throat and chest as I lean over to take off my boots. The smell of the house, the sight of Mum.

I haven't been here since Christmas last year, took Aslak and Viljar on an unsuccessful trip to Italy over Easter, then in the summer I beat Mum to it by inviting her and Magnus to the cabin we have down south that we barely ever visit. As we drove over the mountains on our approach into Mum's village, I remembered why I haven't been here for so long. The resistance I feel is physical, I feel pain in my neck and my back, begin to feel nauseous. But what *is* it about the place? Aslak has asked me. It's everything, I've told him. The atmosphere, the people, the memories. Which memories? he asked me once, he wanted to try to understand when he realised that moving to Oslo wasn't just something done on a whim for a set period of time, that his hope that the four or preferably five of us should live on his farm was beginning to crumble. Oh you know, everything that happened with Dad and Mia and ... I said, stopping myself before I included Jens in the tangle of memories. Not to mention all the stupid things I did, I added with a laugh, trying to redirect both him and the whole conversation. I'm sure you were no more rebellious than the average seventeen-year-old, Aslak said, refusing to give up. It wasn't a case of rebellion, I said, rebellion requires you to have something to rebel against. Aslak's face took on the same resigned expression it always does when I say anything negative about Mum. You know she forgot pretty much every one of my birthdays, I said.

Mum has forgotten at least five of my birthdays, in any case, I particularly recall the day she forgot I was turning fifteen.

Magnus's birthday is exactly a month before mine, and on that day Mum and I got up early, stoked the fire in the kitchen and made him waffles before he woke up. She mixed the batter, and I cooked them, while she helped Dad with his morning routine. She ran down to bathe while I set the table, returning with a little bouquet of liverwort she'd found growing along the pathway, placing them in an eggcup on the table.

We've never had birthday traditions, but the morning I turned fifteen, I still woke with a sense of anticipation. I lay there for a long while, listening out for sounds from the kitchen or Magnus's bedroom. Eventually I got up to a silent house, an empty kitchen. I found Mum in Dad's room, where she was lying on the mattress beside his bed. It only makes things worse, she said one night when I awoke to find her cleaning the hallway just outside my bedroom door, no doubt in the hope of waking me – lying so close to him yet feeling so far away, it's like torture, my body calls out for his, she said, I stood there in my nightie, freezing cold, no idea how to respond.

She only woke when I closed Dad's bedroom door, following me into the kitchen as I stood in the middle of the room, no idea what to do with myself. Oh, it's awfully cold in here, she said, wrapping her arms around herself, I don't suppose you could run out and fetch some wood for the fire, she said, then I'll get it going. I still remember going out to the woodshed and wondering how I might remind her what day it was without having to spell it out, whether I could devise a way that would help her realise before it was too late. I took my time fetching the wood to allow Magnus time to get up before I returned to the house, but his window remained dark. Eventually I went back inside, Mum had put the coffee on, I could hear her in the bathroom downstairs. Can you watch the coffee while I go down to bathe, Sigrid? she called out as the front door slammed closed behind her.

❖

Aslak took over the conversation once we'd all made our way inside, he's so fond of her. He's listened and tried to understand whenever I've told him about how she disappeared, retreating into both Dad and herself when Dad fell ill, but he doesn't grasp the severity of it. And it doesn't sound that terrible when I say it out loud, either, particularly not after seeing the consequences of a truly awful upbringing like Frida's. But the comparison doesn't help where my feelings are concerned, they're just as strong, at times completely paralysing.

'Are you hungry?' Mum asks us, leading the way upstairs, everything about her is so familiar, so intimate, and I want to embrace her, to hold her tight, to be held, all while I long to return to Oslo, to keep her at a distance.

'I could eat,' Mia says behind me.

'That doesn't make any grammatical sense, Mia,' I remark without turning around.

Aslak laughs, of course. The last time we were here, between Christmas and New Year last year, Mia decided to stay behind with Jens and Zadie. It's such a long drive, she said, and since I spent Christmas Eve and Christmas Day here with you, surely it's only fair that I spend the last bit of Christmas with them? Her use of the word 'fair' was enough to force me to abandon the conversation and I left matters to Aslak. I spent the rest of Christmas, and all of the past year, for that matter, attempting to compensate for Mia's decisions, I've been close and loving and fun to be around, while Aslak has become more distant with me all the while, more demonstrative and demanding. That's how I've felt up until this past week, anyway, when he's been strikingly present, and I've found myself wondering which of us is doing the most pushing or pulling, Mia, Aslak or myself. I decide in the end that

Jens is to blame, everything was fine before he moved back, I wish he'd stayed in Sudan.

Mum's house is far too big, I haven't ever reflected on the size of it until today, how many stairs and nooks and crannies there are, how many cupboards that Mum has to stand on a step stool in order to reach. I feel relieved when I remember that there are still handrails in the bathrooms and a ramp leading from the back door down to the slope. Mum can effectively live on one floor, she doesn't need to sleep in her bedroom upstairs, I see the house through new eyes as I look for more reasons Mum can continue to live here, on her own, nobody required to be here to take care of her.

She's going to be right as rain, I told Aslak on the evening that Mum told me about her cancer. I sat in the kitchen for what must have been half an hour, feeling numb after receiving her call, initially irritated that she'd felt unwell for so long without mentioning it to me, as if she were trying to prove something. After that I felt terrified, not first and foremost by the idea that she might die, but for everything she would go through, even though she's going to pull through – fear and pain and side effects, and one step closer to death all the same. And then I felt angry at myself, guilty, as I always did after conversations with her, for the way I'd responded, mulling over everything I ought to have said, I didn't even ask her what she was most afraid of, of course she's afraid. I pictured Mum in the kitchen at home, surrounded by her new loneliness, alone in an ailing body.

You know her, I can't even remember her ever having a cold, I said to Aslak. Of course, she'll be fine, Aslak said. Everything suggests she's going to be fine, I said. Absolutely, Aslak said. She's fitter than I am, I said, you know that she still swims every morning? Aslak nodded. And she sent me that picture from the cabin just a few weeks ago, so she can't have been in a bad way for long, I said. Aslak moved closer and stroked my back with his strong hands. She hasn't said a word, I said loudly, she never even mentioned it. He pulled me close. I couldn't see anything in those daft selfies she sends us to suggest that there was anything wrong, I said as I lay pressed against his chest, my voice cracked. Of course not, he whispered, of course not.

I take Viljar out to see the empty chicken coop before dinner. It makes a bigger impression than I had thought, not on Viljar, but on me. I've never felt any sort of attachment to Dad's sheep or Mum's hens, in truth I've never felt any sort of attachment to farming. But there is a sense of abandonment about the run, the empty nesting box and sheep pens, the lack of any sounds or smells, a sense of something having passed.

'Come on, let's go back inside,' I say after a few minutes, leading Viljar out of the cowshed, turning out the lights, closing the door, turning the key in the padlock.

'Have you spoken to Magnus?' Mum asks when we're eating.

'Yes, most days this past week,' I reply, Mum looks pleased.

The last time she visited us in Oslo, she lingered in front of the picture of Magnus and me on the mountain at home, we've got our skis on and Magnus has his arm around me, we're smiling the same smile, two sets of big, straight teeth. I must be about twenty-seven years old, judging by my hair. You know you haven't failed completely as a parent when your children are still such close friends as adults, Mum said as she smiled at the photo.

'I told him he didn't need to come home for the operation. It's better if he comes once you're back from the hospital so he can help out, once we've gone,' I tell her.

'Very true,' Mum says, looking unconvinced. 'How long are you thinking of staying, by the way?'

'Well, I've got the rest of this week off,' I say.

As always, I find myself unsure whether she's asking because she wants to have us here, or because she finds it tiring. I've previously come to the conclusion that it's a combination of the two, that she's ambivalent about this, too – that she's lonely, yet finds company unbearable.

'Lovely,' she says, and she looks as if she means it, in spite of the fact that Viljar spits out a chunk of meatball with an exaggerated expression of disgust at that very same moment.

'It tastes funny,' he says.

'It's elk,' Aslak replies. 'Did Dad bring you some meat?' he asks Mum.

'No, there was no need, but thank you. The freezer has been full of the stuff since Gustav moved out,' Mum replies with a chortle. 'I thought it was about time we ate some of it.'

Mia clears her throat, looks as if she's trying to work out how long the meat has been languishing in the freezer, but given that she likes to go on about sustainability and isn't the best when it comes to mental arithmetic, fortunately she doesn't say anything.

'That was lovely, Mum,' I say.

The kilometre-long gravel track leading from our farm down to the main road is shot with holes. Mum's never-ending task, completed every spring, is to fill them with porous gravel, only for it to be washed away in the autumn floods just a few months later, and she does the same thing spring after spring after spring. As I drive too fast over a deep crater in the road and my bumper hits a bump on the track just in front of me, I call Aslak to ask him if he can find someone who might be able to lay some more practical tarmac or gravel. I make the decision without thinking to ask

Mum, realise that it's probably one of many decisions I'll take on her behalf over the course of the next year, the next few years, the rest of her life.

We'll have to get used to the idea that we have parents who are starting to fall ill and grow old and die, a friend of mine remarked a few years ago. I thought it would be different for me, I've been well acquainted with sickness and death ever since Dad had his first stroke when I was seven years old – plus, I'm a doctor, constantly surrounded by illness. There's a difference between illness and ageing, I think I said to her, but I realise that it's only now that I feel that Mum has grown old.

I'm on my way to the nursing home, I felt a sudden need to speak to Dad, like the nightly conversations we'd had when I was in my late teens. He'd already lost the ability to speak by then and gave no indication that he had any grasp on the wider context of life. I was drunk, made my way to his room, where he'd almost always be lying awake, his gaze fixed on the yellow curtains, waiting for Mum to come and help him up again in a few hours' time. The first few times, I sat at the foot of his bed and yearned for him in silence, but after a while I started telling him how much I missed him, that he needed to come back. He didn't look at me, I still don't know how much he understood, but it made me so angry, and on the last nights I sat with him, I told him about my life, in such specific, intimate and honest detail that I later felt nervous that he might one day regain the ability to speak.

Dad looks younger than I remember him looking last time. He's sitting in his wheelchair at the dining table in the communal lounge when I arrive, wearing a green cap I've never seen him in before, I've never seen him wearing a cap or a hat or anything else on his head, he always maintained that his hair provided sufficient insulation.

'Got yourself a new cap?' I ask, and chuckle as I take a seat beside him.

Dad looks at me, there's no recognition in his expression, but neither is there any sign of distress. I take his hand, bring it to my cheek, he doesn't resist. One of the employees sitting across the table smiles at me.

'Anne brought it just the other day, I thought it was a favourite of his?' he says.

'No idea,' I reply with a smile, I've no clue whether Mum has just come up with an explanation on a whim or sudden impulse, just as she's done all my life, a need to supply Dad with a need of his own, but I can't imagine what possessed her to think that Dad would need a cap.

I feel the urge to take it off him, it looks out of place.

'I often tell Gustav how lucky he is to have so many visits,' the carer says, looking around the room as if to demonstrate the other residents' loneliness to me, they sit by the windows and in chairs pushed up against the walls, looking like withered plants, some dozing in their chairs, others gazing out at the grey November landscape or staring at the wall. 'Anne comes by most days,' he continues, as if it were generous of her, some sort of good deed.

'Yes, she loves to visit,' I tell him, smiling and nodding, just as I've smiled and nodded at others as they've heaped praise on Mum's endurance and strength for as long as I can remember.

When Dad had his first stroke, he was the same age as I am now. It's strange to think about, but much more difficult to get my head around the idea that Mum was four years younger than I am now when it happened. She set the benchmark when it comes to age, and that will always remain the case. When I fell pregnant with Mia, it seemed so strange to me that I'd have a child before I'd reached the age she had been when she had Magnus. As if some-thing was out of step.

She was thirty-six years old when, one morning out of the blue, Dad couldn't remember what he'd eaten for breakfast every morning for the past ten years, only to then throw up all over the table. I only remember the last part, his relentless retching, and how confused he looked afterwards. And I remember the ambu-lance, the fact that they came to him at the kitchen table, but I know that's a false memory, because if they'd done that, the sub-sequent years would have unfolded very differently. Mum didn't call an ambulance, not for several hours at least, I hadn't ever heard of anyone under the age of sixty having a stroke, she's said on nu-merous occasions since then. I was certain he just had a hangover, she confided in me once when I must have been in my early twenties, giving me a meaningful look, as if I should know or would want to know how to read between the lines into what she was saying. If she had been trying to tell me something, I let it go, I don't need any more of her descriptions of him.

I remember his face, his smile, his expressions, until half of his face was left paralysed, lending him a permanent air of sorrow. I remember us driving in his blue Volvo, him picking me up from preschool, hearing him making his way along the road, Talking Heads blaring from the speakers, windows rolled all the way down, his hair long, the bassline thudding through the village as he came to fetch me. The anticipation on his face when he arrived home with carrier bags filled with records or books he'd bought for Magnus and me, the way we'd sit in the living room and listen or read aloud, listen to this, Magnus, listen, listen to that flourish, that's a twelve-string guitar, hear that? He had us read aloud from work by Strindberg and Bjørneboe, read that passage once more for me, Sigrid, once more.

And Gustav, of all people, a neighbour said to Mum after his first stroke, he had such lust for life, he was so active, I mean, *Gustav*. As if it were a bigger surprise, all the more improbable, that illness should strike him, with his insatiable appetite for life, than someone less full of verve and vigour.

Mum has taken Magnus's old CD-player down to the nursing home, it's sitting on the bedside table in Dad's room, I wonder if she still plays music for him when she's here alone, if they sit like they used to practically every evening before he fell ill. Even long after he became unwell, she'd play Prince and Bowie for him, but she's never had much of an ear for music or literature, and without his sensitivity for the two, the habit eventually faded. He lost interest in music after his first relapse, and I remember when he could no longer read, I don't know if it was his eyes that started to fail him or whether he simply couldn't understand how the words related to one another, one day he simply threw a book across the living room without a word.

I wonder what he'd say about the fact that it's possible to look up a song or a book with just the click of a button nowadays, all from the comfort of home, whether he'd embrace the possibilities it offered or if it would all be lost on him – the physical search, trawling through music or bookshops, was something of an aim in itself. I played some music on my phone for him last time I was here, he liked that, he closed his eyes at least, but I wondered how much of it he really took in, if 'Road to Nowhere' reminded him of something, of him and me lying side-by-side on the living-room floor, both with our eyes closed, the song on repeat to help me learn to tune in to what's beneath the surface, as he put it, past my first and second and third impressions – whether it left him with any sense of something familiar, something good.

❖

Magnus has told me more than once that he thinks it would have been better if Dad's last stroke had killed him, possibly even if the third or second had done so, that having his body here, with its familiar face and skin and smile, no more than a physical cast without the ability to communicate, has evoked a greater sense of loss and desperation and guilt than if she had a graveside to visit. Magnus was older when Dad fell ill, he has more to miss, but he seldom says any more than that, what he thinks would be best for Mum. The second time he mentioned it I grew irritated, mostly due to his undivided concern for Mum. We were sitting in the car on our way home on one of the few occasions he'd actually come down to the nursing home. Surely it's equally important to consider what's best for Dad? I said. My God, the man's a vegetable, Magnus said, surprisingly short-tempered, he sits there, draining people of their energy, just as he has all his life. How can you be angry at him and not her? I asked him loudly. At least she's been there, Magnus replied, then turned away to stare out of the window on the passenger side. We drove in silence for a long while before he turned around to look at me again. We have to be allowed to question things, he said. I haven't heard you ask a single question, I replied, so I'm not sure I understand what you're getting at, to be quite honest. I'm asking why we keep him alive like this, and for whose benefit, Magnus said. What do you mean, 'keep him alive', I asked, he *is* alive.

I can't get into the groove of a conversation with Dad, I sit there for half an hour or so chatting to the carer while dutifully turning to Dad every once in a while, making trivial comments – I'm sure you'd agree with that, Dad – as if I were addressing a child. The carer, who's not much older than Mia, tells me this is a part-time job while he makes up additional study credits, he wants to study medicine. I don't mention the fact that I'm a doctor, hope Mum hasn't said anything either, as I've heard her tell so many others about me. The way she starts off by mentioning Dad becoming unwell, that I've had close contact with illness for much of my life, and that ultimately, after a few difficult years, I chose to become a doctor – followed by an expression that suggests the audience can draw their own conclusions. I'm better able to live with this version of events than with the actual truth of the matter, I've even used it a few times myself, when someone has asked me what made me choose medicine, but this happens very rarely – it's revealed itself to be a career that prompts very few of those types of question.

'Well then, I'd best be off,' I say to Dad, leaning in to give him a hug, but he squirms in the opposite direction, looks afraid.

'It's OK, Dad,' I tell him, placing a hand gently on his shoulder.

'He's seemed a little tense this past week, maybe a bit sensitive,' the carer tells me, he knows Dad much better than I do, but still I feel the need to assert ownership.

'He looks to me to be on better form than he has in a long time,' I remark.

I pick Mia up from the shopping centre on my way home. She's never had a relationship of her own with Dad, and I no longer attempt to persuade her to join me when I visit him. There is a unique sorrow in the fact that he never got to know her, and on the few occasions she has joined me, he's only ever seemed uneasy in her presence, turning away as I've practically thrust her in his direction. I've wanted to shout, look at her, Dad, look what I did, look what I made.

I drive slowly past the small white house Jens rented during the years he lived in the village. I notice Mia glancing in my direction, but she says nothing until we drive past the school.

'Crazy that you grew up here,' she says.

'So did you, in part,' I reply.

'God, yeah, I wonder what I'd be like now if we hadn't moved,' she says.

'Do you really think you'd be that different?'

'I might have been a real redneck,' Mia says, laughing as we're overtaken by a Volvo with lowered suspension.

'Not the worst thing a person can be,' I say, increasing my speed as I drive past the bus shelter by the petrol station.

We found her alone, passed out behind the bus shelter, the policeman said, he was the father of a boy in the other class in my year, Lars. I can't remember what Mum said, whether she said anything at all, in fact. I vaguely remember hearing her laughter echo through the hallway as I tottered upstairs, laughing at something he said, but I was fifteen and had drunk almost an entire bottle of vodka, so that might not actually have happened. She wasn't laughing the following day, in any case, she didn't say a word, didn't even mention it, didn't come after me when I ran past her in the hallway on my way to throw up in the bathroom. It was Magnus who knocked on the door half an hour later, who tended to my grazed knee, who spotted the dried blood on my inner thigh. He was seventeen at the time, spotty and inexperienced, I shrank beneath his gaze, helped him to avoid the question, relax, it was consensual, I said, now can you leave me to shower in peace?

Who'd have thought you'd end up a doctor, one of my college tutors said when I bumped into him in the shop a few years ago. Not you, apparently, I replied, smiling. He laughed. Don't say that, he said. We knew there was more to you, he said. More? I replied, still smiling. He started to look uncomfortable, no doubt regretted the entire conversation, but I held his gaze. Sure, more than you showed at the time, he said, his gaze faltering. I gave up, even though acknowledgements of that kind from former teachers or neighbours, or anyone else who knew me at the time, always awaken flickers of the same anxiety I felt when I was sixteen years old, a sense that nobody took me seriously, that nobody really saw me for who I was. In those moments, I sometimes regret becoming a doctor instead of going off the rails to such an extent that it would be clear my upbringing had harmed me, that my parents' abandonment had damaged me, that I had more significant spiritual wounds than anybody would expect from the doctor in her white coat.

I started studying medicine because of Jens. For a long while, perhaps even to this day, I thought that he left because he was bored of me, that I'd failed to live up to his expectations, that he was fed up of my vacuous life, even though it was his idea that I take a gap year after college, thereby ensuring that he was always the one with something to talk about, something to tell me, something to teach me.

I signed up to take the exam as an external candidate when Mia was three months old, I'd been absent from college so often that I'd barely passed maths and history, and I lacked credits in P.E., of all things. Jens had stopped calling, stopped writing, he was done with us, no explanation given, it was unbearable the way he'd said we'd talk later the last time we'd spoken, only to vanish without a trace.

It's all thanks to you that I got to study medicine, I've told Aslak many a time, it would never have been possible without you. And it's true, it wouldn't have been possible without his support, his time spent looking after Mia, his money. But more than any of that, it would never have been possible without the obsessive driving force I felt propelling me in the wake of Jens' betrayal.

❖

Mum is standing in the hallway when I get back, even though it's another hour before we need to leave for the hospital. She's wearing the same coat she's had since I was a child, she's become even more frugal since Dad moved into the nursing home, not out of necessity, she's got plenty of money, but more out of a sense of concern for something that I've never been able to get my head around. Now she explains it as something to do with the environment, but that's just an argument onto which she has latched her almost compulsive frugality. I smile for her and at her, she's grown so thin that her coat is several sizes too big. Underneath it she's wearing a skirt, I can't remember the last time I saw her wearing anything but her blue trousers. She's dressed up, I feel such pain for her that it becomes hard to speak.

'You look nice,' I say eventually.

Late yesterday evening, after everyone had gone to bed, I heard her rummaging around in her bedroom. I lay there for a while before getting up and making my way to her room. There was a pile of clothes on the floor in the middle of the room, and Mum was standing with her head in her wardrobe. Are you packing? I asked her. She jumped when she heard my voice, turned around. Are you still up? she asked me. I wasn't, but then I heard that you were, I replied. Yes, I just ... I thought that I'd best take these old things of Gustav's down the road, he doesn't have many winter jackets at the nursing home, she said. I nodded, even though the image of her standing there in her nightie at one o'clock in the morning, her actions and expression frantic, reminded me of too many similar nights when I was a child; things she simply had to finish, be it the laundry or the floors, watering the flowers or polishing the silver. That sounds like a good idea, I said, I can drive them over this week. Mum looked relieved, I don't know if it was the idea that the clothing would be delivered or simply that I hadn't objected to what she'd said. I sat on the floor and started folding Dad's old shirts and jackets.

'Shall we get going, then?' she says to me.

'There now, it'll be fine, you'll drift off in no time. Can you count backwards from one hundred for me?'

'One hundred, ninety-nine, ninety-eight, ninety-seven, ninety-three, no, ninety-four, ninety...'

I feel stabbing pains in my upper abdomen for the entire duration of Mum's surgery. I haven't slept, feel light-headed with fatigue and fear, I don't have any rational thoughts left.

If she dies now, I say to Aslak at least eight times, if she dies now, if she dies now, but I can't finish the sentence, and I'm scared that she's going to do just that, I'm scared that she's going to disappear.

My body feels unfamiliar, I feel sensations in extremities that don't exist, but not pain, more like a sort of quivering a millimetre or so above my skin's outermost layer.

Sigrid spent the whole journey to the hospital preparing me for the possible side effects and pain that I might feel, you'll probably feel like you've been through the mill, she said, and dizzy and nauseous. But they'll give you painkillers, and you mustn't be scared to ask for more if you're in a lot of pain, there's no point in playing tough at the hospital, Mum, she said, you have to promise me that. I promise, I replied. I mean it, Sigrid said, the doctors and carers won't be impressed if you ask for fewer painkillers than anyone else. I started to laugh, and involuntarily to cry, reflecting on the normality of the conversation, on Sigrid's insightful comments and her care. She kept her eyes on the road, both hands on the wheel, smiling before she began to systematically list the kind of thing I might expect to feel or experience.

She never mentioned any sense of yearning, but I woke with an acute feeling that I was missing someone, a pull from deep within, it reminded me of my yearning for Gustav, but it was impossible to make concrete. Perhaps it's my body's way of letting me know that something is missing, that I can't simply extract part of its finely tuned system without consequence. All the same, when I wanted to get up and move around a few hours after the operation, to take a walk along the hospital corridor to get my body moving again, as the physiotherapist put it, I also felt so much lighter, as if the tumour they'd removed had weighed several kilos. I took a long walk, felt a stinging pain in my abdomen, but still my legs and shoulders felt lighter, my head and body on a par once again. The physiotherapist was impressed.

Sigrid was here a few hours ago, making sure that I ate a few Ritz crackers. Have you been here all this time, I asked. Of course, Sigrid replied, plumping my pillow, Aslak and I. Mia and Viljar will come by tomorrow, and Magnus will probably be in on Thursday.

I can see through the window that it's grown dark outside, the city below us sparkles with festive optimism in the build-up to Christmas, I drift in and out of a peaceful sleep, both the cancer and operation itself now feeling like a small price to pay for this glimpse of closeness and care around me.

I've managed two walks up and down the corridor by the time Aslak and Mia arrive the following morning. I feel fitter than I have in a long time, almost restless – a positive restlessness I haven't felt for months now. Mia is the first to open the door, two steps ahead of Aslak into the room, I think there's a likeness there, there always has been, something in their expression, I remember how pleased Mia looked when I first mentioned it many years ago.

'Hi, Grandma,' she says quietly.

'You don't need to whisper,' I reply, smiling at her. 'It's just me in here.'

The other woman I'd shared a room with on the first night was gone by the time I returned, I didn't ask anyone where she went. Mia embraces me cautiously, she smells strongly of perfume and shampoo.

'How are you feeling?' she asks.

'Honestly, I feel better than I have in a long time,' I tell her. 'Is it just you two?'

'Sigrid and Viljar will be here soon, Viljar wouldn't get out of the car, so we went on ahead,' Aslak says, looking as if he's not quite sure what to do with himself now Mia's taken the only chair, he's about to perch on the edge of my bed but thinks again, getting up and leaning against the windowsill instead.

'Take a seat,' I say, chuckling.

I ought to feel nothing but gratitude for Aslak, for the way he picked Sigrid up after Jens left, embracing her and Mia, caring for them and showing them love, and doing all the things that I never managed myself. However, I've often found myself growing irritated by his overly modest approach to life with Sigrid, the way he's adapted to her, effortlessly sacrificing so much. Even when she is at her most self-pitying and intolerable, he simply shrugs, laughing or agreeing with her, and I find myself envying the way he lets her reproaches and expressions bounce off him.

We hear Viljar howling along the corridor before he and Sigrid enter the room, she's wrangling him firmly with both hands as he thrashes and squirms. As she slides him down onto the floor, he changes his mind without warning, wants to be back up in Sigrid's arms, but she ignores him, smiling and rolling her eyes at me.

'Hi, Mum,' Sigrid says.

My reply is drowned out by Viljar's ear-splitting wails.

'Hi there, Viljar, why don't you come and sit here for a while?' I ask, patting the bed.

He falls silent for a moment before throwing himself to the floor and continuing to cry, he's only wearing a thin cotton sweatshirt and trainers in the middle of November, I have to smile to keep myself from commenting on it, remember Sigrid's face the last time – and any previous time, for that matter – I mentioned something along those lines, almost condescending, as if I had anything to teach her, as if I had the right to comment.

'Just let him get on with it,' Sigrid says.

'Look, Viljar, have you seen what I can do to my bed?' I ask, finding the little remote control that lifts and lowers the bed. 'Have a look at this!'

Viljar doesn't offer me a single glance.

'I said to just let him get on with it, Mum,' Sigrid says, a little more firmly. 'Don't suppose you fancy doing something about this, hmm?' she adds a moment later, looking over at Aslak.

Aslak sighs, but picks up Viljar from the floor.

'Come on, Viljar, let's go and see what they've got in the shop,' Aslak says. Viljar calms down in his arms.

'Lucky that there's two of you,' I remark, smiling in Sigrid's direction, she doesn't return my smile.

'How do you feel?' she asks after a short pause.

'Good,' I reply breezily.

'I'll stay for visiting hours, if that's OK with you,' she says, pulling a bouquet of flowers out of Mia's bag, looking at her with a resigned expression, Mia shrugs.

'Yes, that'd be lovely. If you have the time,' I say. 'Ohh, and you've brought flowers, that's wonderful,' I continue.

I feel drowsy, drift in and out of Mia and Sigrid's bickering over flowers and handing things over and bags being too big before sleep defeats me.

I don't think I've thought much about what my body is made up of before now, I've taught natural sciences and talked about cells and cell division, I've explained in detail the functions of various body parts, internal organs and veins and muscles. I've plucked hearts and lungs and intestines from the human torso model in the classroom. Take a good look at our finely tuned systems, I've said to my students, it's hard to believe that there isn't more that goes wrong.

One day over these past years, cells in my body have started to divide in an uncontrolled manner, and for a long time they've developed in peace and quiet inside an intact mucous membrane. Had I seen the doctor this time last year, when I read in a magazine that women over sixty ought to have a full health check at *least* once a year, perhaps I'd have ended up on the operating table before the tumour had penetrated the wall of my bowel.

I picture it as a sort of animated film, small, hairy-looking cells with eyes and teeth, freed from the captivity of my bowel, looking right and left for the next best organ, stumbling upon a few lymph nodes en route and sinking their teeth in. And that, unfortunately, is where we are now, the doctor said as he stood by my bed an hour ago, we've found traces of cancer in a few nearby lymph nodes, and there have been some changes to your liver based on what we can see, which we need to follow up on.

Sigrid was sitting in the chair on the opposite side of the bed, but she must have stood up at some point in the course of the conversation, she was standing by the time the doctor said that they still had a lot of tests they wanted to do in any case, that they wanted to try to target the cancer with chemotherapy in the first instance, beginning as soon as possible, he said. I couldn't keep up, I'd felt so strong after the operation, healthy and strong, as if I'd been cleansed of my illness. Even though they'd explained that they'd check for any signs of the cancer having spread, I was convinced that I was fine, I didn't even consider the possibility that the doctor would say anything different when he stopped by. I can't remember if I said anything, but I do remember that he took my hand, it felt so intimate and sincere, we'll follow up on everything very closely, he said, and we still hope that you'll get through this. Sigrid said nothing, and even though I saw the looks she exchanged with the doctor, I still feel certain that I'm going to recover.

All the same, the news of the cancer's spread suddenly hits me. I lie in bed all the next day, unable to bring myself to get up, to try to eat, to take short walks up and down the corridor, to think. But it's important now that you don't give up, this is when you need to get moving, you mustn't give up, say the physiotherapist, the nurse, the doctor.

'You mustn't give up, Mum,' Magnus says.

He's standing at the kitchen worktop, chopping onions with his back to me, I listen to the irregular hacking sound as the blade hits the chopping board, wonder if he cooks for himself when he's at home alone, or if he gets by on takeaways and ready meals. It's strange the role our genes play when it comes to eating habits, my own mother said to me, though I didn't find it strange in the least. Perhaps she was getting at the idea that our sense of taste was dictated by our genes, I don't know, I never asked her, never asked her anything of any real significance, not even just before she died, when I found myself standing beside her bed, realising that I didn't know who she really was, who she had been. I always felt so invasive, as if I was overstepping a boundary. I've missed her intensely over the past few days, missed the relationship we could have had. I've missed the relationship I could have had with Gustav. With Sigrid, with Magnus, with Mia.

Magnus has taken a week's holiday from work, he arrived the day before Sigrid left for Oslo. They organised what they'd do between themselves, didn't bother to involve me in the decision, I feel cared for yet also diminished, but either way, I don't have the strength to oppose this sudden role reversal, and perhaps it's not all that sudden, really, perhaps Sigrid and Magnus have felt superior and overbearing for many years now. On Sigrid's last evening at home, the three of us sat around the kitchen table. Magnus and Sigrid both pulled out their iPhones and opened their calendars, whittling down dates to decide who would *have* me when, as Magnus accidentally let slip. He laughed when I objected to his choice of words. Nobody needs to *have* me, I said after sitting in silence for what must have been half an hour while they discussed dates and weeks and treatment plans, I regretted doing the same thing with Gustav's home help as he sat at the head of the table in his wheelchair. Magnus placed a hand on my shoulder and smiled, sorry, he said, I didn't mean it like that. But can you *take* her for the first week of February, he continued, looking over at Sigrid, the two of them laughed, I couldn't help but smile.

I've nodded in agreement with everyone who's clenched their fists on my behalf, ready to take this on, we'll fight this. Up on the barricades, down in the trenches, armed with denial, there's nothing else to fight with; deny the facts and statistics and a body intent on attacking itself. I'm going to fight.

The realisation that Mum is going to die hits me in different ways each day, it has done ever since the doctor at Haukeland University Hospital told us that the cancer had spread. Mum in her blue hospital gown, nodding as the doctor spoke, confused at first, then determined, and how I wished that I could have switched places with her in that moment. How I wished that it was me who was sick and Mum by my side, holding my hand and grasping a severity that I didn't have the qualifications to understand for myself.

You arrogant little shit, I thought to myself as the doctor stood there explaining everything they would do for her, everything they would put in place to make her better, all while sending me knowing looks, as if I was any old colleague he could rely on. My fury at his conceit engulfed the whole situation, my whole reaction, and it continues to engulf my feelings whenever it hits me that Mum is going to die.

I wait for a sense of emergency to take over. It never comes, there's nothing unusual or provocative about the fact that life should carry on as normal for everyone else, just like it did when Jens left, for instance – back then I'd felt furious and desperate at anything that reminded me of everyday life, at people who passed by, outside my bedroom window, as if nothing had happened.

All the same, it's tough keeping my emotions at bay, they threaten to cripple me several times a day, and I go to work and make dinner and meet friends and go to the gym and do laundry to keep them from gaining the upper hand. I anchor myself in Mia and Viljar, insist on a form of intimacy that only a four-year-old can tolerate. Mia seeks balance, understands my needs, perhaps, but can't face what she calls fussing, you need to stop fussing, Mum, she said a few days ago as I stood in her bedroom doorway and saw that she was packing a bag to spend the weekend with Jens. She'd been staying here since we'd returned from Mum's, and I felt uneasy, wronged, maybe, when she told me that she was going skiing and would be staying with Jens and Zadie this weekend. I practically tailed her as she made her way around the house, didn't even know what I wanted from her, other than some sort of acknowledgement. Mia put up with it for a while, smiled and replied to me calmly, right up until I stood there remarking on almost every single item of clothing she placed in her bag – then she turned around very suddenly and loudly told me to stop fussing. It was good to be put in my place, pulled off track. I fell silent. Mia looked as if she regretted it as soon as the words escaped her lips, came over to me and cupped my face in her hands, kissing my forehead – she's at least five centimetres taller than me – sorry, Mum, but it's just for the weekend, she said, smiling, I'll be back before you know it.

At the same time, and in the same way as I cling to Viljar and Mia, Aslak clings to me. He craves intimacy, there's something claustrophobic about his attentions, something needy, something that has nothing to do with me. It reminds me of when we first met, when the same attentions were a lifebuoy for Mia and me.

Aslak grew up on a farm just five hundred metres from our own, we went to the same primary school and secondary school and college, but I barely remember him, he only ever lingered on the outskirts of my reality, he was unimportant. He was one of those guys who was into cars and snowmobiles and who listened to Ace of Base, I saw those things as stark contrasts to anything any intelligent individual would be interested in, something that Aslak still occasionally accuses me of believing, and which I still do occasionally think to myself.

Sorry, I need to finish reading this Bourdieu essay first, he often replies, waving a fictional paper if I ask him for help changing a car tyre or fixing the dishwasher. Occasionally it makes me laugh, and occasionally it reminds me of the life I had imagined with Jens, the yearning I had for a richer life, a more significant life, for good conversation and wine and art, and the two of us out in the field, without borders.

I discovered Aslak when Mia was two months old, I was living at home with Mum and Dad at the time, since the house Jens and I had been living in belonged to the local county and was to be rented out to the next foundation doctor – how I hated her whenever I saw her through the window, traipsing through our rooms, eating at our table, on her way to Jens' workplace. Mia had taken the edge off some of the sense of loss, but still Jens was everpresent, a voice in the back of my mind, an ever-watchful eye over us.

Aslak stopped by to borrow an angle grinder from Dad. I overheard the conversation that he and Mum had in the hallway from where I was sitting in the kitchen, she had invited him inside in such a way that he had no choice but to accept, and had sent him to wait with Dad and me as she looked for the angle grinder in the garage – Sigrid and Gustav are in the kitchen, just head straight through.

When the doorbell rang and Mum went down to answer, I was sitting with my jumper pulled up and my breasts on display, my nipples sore, nursing Mia while Dad sat in his wheelchair at the head of the table wearing his bib, confused and cross and dribbling

– head on in, of course, Aslak. I was about to call down to Mum, to ward off the visit, but I didn't have a chance to speak up before I heard Aslak's footsteps on the stairs. I pulled down my jumper as he stepped into the kitchen. Hi there, he said. Mia, faced with such a sudden interruption to her feed, started wailing, and Dad, who couldn't bear Mia's crying or any sort of loud noises in general, grew unsettled. He started to rock back and forth, slamming the palms of his hands on the tabletop and groaning loudly. I stood up with Mia in my arms, it's OK, Dad, I tried to say, but Mia's wailing drowned out the sound of my voice. Oh dear, Aslak said calmly, offering outstretched arms in my direction. Do you want me to take her? he asked, nodding at Mia. I didn't hesitate, handed her over and wheeled Dad into the living room to sit by the window with a view of the water and mountains, there, I said, resting my hands on his shoulders, my cheek on the back of his head, that's better, isn't it, I added, and he calmed down after a few minutes, as usual. When I returned to the kitchen, Aslak was standing there with Mia on his chest, one arm under her bottom and the other carefully supporting her back and neck, he bobbed up and down and side to side gently. Mia had also settled down, only squeaking quietly into his jumper. The sight and the sense of loss moved me to tears. Oh gosh, Aslak said when he realised, taking a few steps in my direction without giving any indication that he was about to hand Mia back over to me. Things will work themselves out, Sigrid, he said, and I nodded, even though neither he nor I knew if anything was going to work itself out.

He returned the following day to drop the tool back off. I was the one to open the door when the doorbell rang. It was nice to see you yesterday, he said with a smile. I laughed politely. Ask him in, then, Mum shouted from the kitchen. Is Mia sleeping? he asked after making his way upstairs, he looked disappointed when I told him yes. Two days later he stopped by to check how things were going. I was surprised by how direct he was, how secure and grown-up he seemed, while I was just a child with responsibility for a child of my own.

Up until I got together with Aslak, I conjured up endless excuses for Mum to take Mia as often as possible, to prevent myself from making significant, irreparable errors or dropping her on the floor. I didn't have the energy to hold grudges or resist or engage any sense of pride – I had to disregard the promise I'd made to myself never to ask her for help.

She was angry when I told her that I was pregnant. Initially her reaction pleased me, the way she chided me and shouted at me about my future, about Jens – who I didn't even think she'd bothered to form an opinion on – about money and responsibility. The feeling changed in the space of a few short seconds when she asked if I had any idea how much time and commitment a child requires, how much attention and care. I smiled at her, struck by the preposterous notion that she should be the one lecturing *me* about commitment and care, then got up to leave.

We didn't speak until she heard four months later, no doubt via Magnus, that Jens had left. She rang my doorbell, I was lying in bed, spotted the back of her car in the mirror above the chest of drawers, crept further beneath the duvet, didn't open the door. She stood there ringing the doorbell for what must have been ten minutes, trying the door handle, I know that it must have cost her a great deal to be so persistent, to swallow her pride in that way, I was furious and both wanted her to leave yet also to break in and save me from the all-encompassing darkness Jens had left in his wake.

She gave up eventually, I gasped for air as I heard her returning to her car, tore off the duvet and ran into the hallway, out onto the doorstep, barefoot and in my pyjamas, locked eyes with Mum through the car windscreen. She'd started the car, she seemed to hesitate for a second before turning off the engine, opening the door and stepping out of the car. Come on, let's go inside, you're freezing, she said as she made her way towards me and noticed that my whole body was shaking.

She didn't ask me about Jens, didn't even mention him, she didn't say much at all, she seemed stressed and restless, probably because she'd left Dad at home alone. We had a cup of tea together in silence, I longed to tell her about Jens, about the nights filled with anxiety and remorse, the gentle kicks, to ask whether so much movement was normal, if I was normal, if my bump was normal – and I so wanted her to tell me that things would work themselves out, that she would make sure of it. She didn't say that, but she did tell me to call her if I needed anything, if I needed any help at all. Whatever it might be, she added before she left.

A friend was with me for the birth, we were both twenty-one years old, both terrified, she came straight from a party and before we'd even made it to the hospital looked as if she regretted joining me – but she lasted the course, held my hand, helped me to retain some grip on reality. I learned afterwards that Mum had been in the waiting room for the duration, never entering, or never asking to enter, I've never asked her about it, but she did come in afterwards as I lay in bed on the maternity ward with Mia at my breast, dazed and exhausted, I think Mum cried, but I could well have dreamt it.

She was the one who asked if I wanted to move back home until I found somewhere else to live, since I only had two months to vacate Jens' house, two months I'd feared more than the birth itself; the idea of being alone with a baby in my arms in all of those rooms. I nodded at her suggestion, and as we drove home from the hospital four days later, Mum, Mia and I, she'd already packed up and moved me out of Jens' house, tidying away any trace of me having been there.

It was difficult to tolerate her belated attention, the energy she was putting in on my behalf. My response was to give Mia the name I did, a name found in neither Mum's family nor Dad's. Magnus is named after Dad's father and his brother; Dad's father was so ill when his younger brother was born that my great-grandparents wanted to ensure that the name would live on, they didn't want to be the generation to break a tradition stretching back several hundreds of years. I'm named after both my mother's mother and Dad's great-grandmother, not to mention numerous aunts going way back, Mum has never needed to state outright that I'm mostly named after her own mother, not even when I've asked on several occasions. I was sure that Mum expected me to call my daughter Anne, but when I told her that I'd chosen Mia, she smiled. M, after Magnus, she smiled at the old-fashioned tradition, how lovely.

I was constantly terrified of hurting Mia in those first few months, I was furious at Mum for not taking her, not doing all the things I didn't dare to do, changing nappies, dressing her, placing her in her pram. I felt as if I might break her arms and legs whenever I dressed her, that I applied too much cream to her rash-covered bottom, that I fastened her nappy too tightly around her tummy, strangled her whenever I tied the cords of her hat around her chin, that she was too cold and too hot and too hungry and too full. Mum watched me with a critical gaze, can't you just do it, I said, holding Mia out in her direction several times a day, you have to do it, you *have* to, Mum, I can't.

Eight months later, when I moved in with Aslak, I was finally able to rest, safe in his aura of security, his self-assurance, in the way he held and bathed and rocked and embraced Mia.

Among the many pictures from over the years that spring to mind, all of which I have an eternal ambition to organise in an album, there is a picture of Aslak and Mia together. Mia is around nine years old, we're up at the glacial potholes on the mountain behind the cabin, the evening sun is low, it might be as late in the year as August. Mia and Aslak are sitting in the biggest of the pools, water up to their middles, it conceals their lower bodies, but I know that they're both naked, I remember it, that I thought about that fact at the moment I took the picture, the fact that I'd never have managed to do the same, to have someone else's child so close to me, their body and smell and breath and nakedness, not like Aslak was capable of doing so naturally, never asking any questions or problematising things in any way. I tried to explain it as having something to do with the fact he's a man, that there must be something biological about it, but it didn't make any sense, it was just an excuse not to engage more deeply with the heavy debt of gratitude I felt. That subsided slightly when Viljar was born.

It's three weeks until Christmas, possibly Mum's last. December is a busy month at work as luck would have it, I have a schedule featuring all the usual faces, as well as those who otherwise never see the doctor, but who book an appointment to have some low-level discomfort or mole checked out, but who mostly want to talk about how much they're dreading the festive season ahead. It's a feeling we can agree on, but I can offer my patients no comfort or encouragement beyond what I tell myself: it's just a few weeks, it'll pass.

Frida has an appointment every third Tuesday before lunch, and luckily on this particular Tuesday she waits for me to come and fetch her. She is perched on the edge of her seat with one leg shaking impatiently when I arrive, but I smile in recognition as I say her name, as usual. She flashes a smile back at me, seemingly proud and embarrassed all at once.

'What are your plans for Christmas?' I ask as I measure Frida's bump, I've been dreading posing the question, dreading the answer.

I know that Frida refused to see her most recent foster family last year, instead choosing to hang around somewhere down south in the company of her alcoholic father. When she told me about her plans, I had to suppress the urge to invite her back to ours for Christmas. In hindsight, I can see that it might not necessarily have been that much better for Frida to have experienced the awkward atmosphere between Mia and me last year, our daily quarrels about anything other than Jens.

'I've been thinking about going away somewhere this Christmas,' Frida says cheerfully.

I nod, even though I'm sure it's just a phrase she's picked up somewhere, something that sounds normal and tempting and unattainable.

'Mm, it can be nice to get away from things,' I remark, tightening the measuring tape around her bulging white belly. 'Where were you thinking?'

'Thailand, maybe. Or Bali,' she replies.

'I see,' I reply. 'That sounds lovely. Though you probably shouldn't be flying quite so far at this point in your pregnancy.'

Frida looks unsure for a moment before composing herself once again.

'Oh, I know, I'm just joking. But I might go to Tenerife with a few friends, we'll see.'

I nod.

'Lots of people want to get away at Christmas, you know,' I say after a brief pause.

She falls silent, looks at the floor. I regret speaking up, hope not to trigger the same reaction I experienced last time I tried to normalise her feelings, when I pointed out that it was very normal to go through mood swings during pregnancy. I sometimes forget that Frida isn't looking to have her mind put at rest, she's not afraid of being unwell, in fact she's afraid of *not* being sufficiently unwell for me to care.

'I was thinking the same thing,' she says. 'Away from all the baking and cleaning and gift-giving and all that.'

She's more in control today, sometimes she turns up in this kind of mood, with a need to appear more normal and balanced. I wonder what it takes for her to remain within those boundaries, not to let things rise up and spill over. I don't press her on the matter, it's a good sign that she has the energy to compose herself in such a way, in spite of everything.

'Are you still taking your Lamictal?' I ask her, want to acknowledge her efforts, know how she loves discussing her medication – plus, I'm only ten minutes behind schedule.

Mia calls on Sunday evening and asks if I can pick her up from Jens and Zadie's, she sprained her ankle on the ski trip. I don't ask why Jens or Zadie can't drive her home, I'm glad she's called, but at the same time I curse her and Jens for making me feel grateful that my own daughter should call me to ask a favour.

I haven't been to Jens and Zadie's house before, I've only ever driven past it once, very slowly, one evening right after they moved to Oslo, took a five-kilometre detour on my way home from the shop. I spotted movement at one window, couldn't tell if it was Jens or Zadie or simply a shadow, but it was enough to make my foot hit the accelerator and disappear. His presence is difficult for me to accept, the fact that he's here, in Oslo, after spending the past nineteen years forcing myself to accept the fact that he forms no part of my existence, shifting between despising him and suppressing any thoughts of him. The idea that he might saunter past a window in his own living room in Lindern with such a natural air, as if he belonged there, as if he hadn't a single regret in his life.

I have no intention of getting out of the car, but, still, I change out of my work clothes and apply some mascara before leaving. The house is large and rectangular with a flat roof. It looks like an enormous box, no doubt practical and easy to maintain, I suspect that it reflects Zadie's personality and appearance. I park on the driveway behind a small electric car that's charging, look up at the house, there are lights on in all the windows, but I can't see any sign of Mia, Jens or Zadie. Beeping the horn would be too much, so I wait there in silence with the engine running before switching it off when I realise that this is probably the kind of neighbourhood that disapproves of cars that idle, or petrol cars more generally, for that matter. I try calling Mia, but as usual she's not picking up the phone, she always has it on Do Not Disturb mode. Just as I pluck up the courage to step out of the car, she steps out of the front door, smiles at someone inside, throws her head back and laughs. After a lengthy farewell, she hobbles in the direction of the car. Before she manages to get in, Jens steps out of the house, he peers at my front lights, I hesitate for a moment before turning them off. He waves enthusiastically when he catches sight of me, smiling widely and lifting a finger as if to ask me to wait there, then disappears inside and returns wearing a pair of slippers.

I've met with Jens on four occasions since he moved to Oslo. Three times when he drove Mia home, and once at his office. He never warned me that he was thinking of moving to Oslo, didn't mention it at all before he got in touch with Mia. She came home one evening in October last year and told me that she'd met him, clearly unsure whether she should feel bad about it. The thought of him calling her or sending a message, the two of them planning to meet, her leaving home in her blue jacket and new shoes, shouting 'bye' from the hallway as she always did, only to meet up with him in secret, it was unbearable. I couldn't meet her uncertain gaze or respond with anything other than silence. In the end it was Aslak who broke that silence, asking whether they'd had a nice time. Mia shrugged, said it had been fine. A bit awkward, she added, with a quick glance in my direction. I still don't really know him, she said. The 'still' prompted me to look up Jens' office address the following day, I was so angry that my legs were shaking and my stomach was unsettled as I stepped in through the door. It was impossible to say everything I'd planned to when Jens got up from his chair and hugged me, my God, Sigrid, it's so good to see you, you look great, he said, smiling widely.

He approaches the car, I roll down the window as Mia climbs into the passenger side, he leans on the car door, his fingers inside the vehicle, so close that I can smell him. What do I smell like? he asked me several times when we were together and I lay with my nose to his throat or armpit. He was always satisfied when I told him he smelled of something undefinably spice-like, exclusive.

'There you are,' he said.

An impossible opener, I've no idea how to respond to that.

'Yep, here I am,' I reply with a low chuckle. 'Hi there.'

'Mia told us about Anne,' he says. 'I'm so sorry, Sigrid.'

I was always flattered by the way he used my name, dropping it into almost every sentence, knowing and intimate. After a while, though, I realised he did the same with everyone, even people he didn't know that well, that it was an easy way to disarm people – even so, I feel myself softening against my will, my face and body and willpower made pliable by the way he utters it, leaning into the car.

'Thanks, yeah, it's not easy. But we're crossing our fingers things will go well,' I tell him, hoping he hasn't said too much to Mia.

I haven't told her how unwell Mum is. I've told her the same as the doctor at the hospital told us, that the cancer has spread, but that there are lots of options, that cancer research is developing at such a rate, it's virtually impossible to keep up, that there are new treatments coming to light all the time, new reasons to hope. I've told her not to google things. Why not? Mia asked. Because you'll find a lot of general information, a lot of things that will scare you, but each case is so individual, one body isn't the same as another, there's a whole list of factors at play, I replied, as I so often do when it comes to my patients, I get fed up of having the word 'google' forced down my throat by people who come in telling me they've googled all sorts, from ingrown toenails to narcissistic personality disorders, making me feel like an interfering middle man, the thing standing between them and any actual treatment. I couldn't tell you if Mia listened to me or whether she searched and found statistics to tell her how unlikely it is that Mum will pull through.

'Of course, of course,' Jens says, and I feel glad to hear it. He straightens up as we both catch sight of Zadie passing an upstairs window, he pats the car door lightly with one hand, that hand, with its long, slender fingers and visible veins, on my stomach, my hips, I avert my gaze.

'Let me know if there's anything I can do, anything at all,' he says, nineteen years too late.

Mia smiles, contented.

'Thanks. Anyway, time for us to head home,' I reply, starting the engine.

'Good to see you, Sigrid, I've been hoping you'd stop by,' he says, holding my gaze. 'And thanks for coming, Mia, remember to keep that ankle elevated,' he continues, taking a few steps back and standing there, watching as I reverse down the driveway, almost ploughing straight into a passing car, I catch sight of Jens pulling a face and laughing.

Mia and I drive home in silence. I burn with curiosity, want to probe her about every last detail of her skiing trip with Jens and Zadie, but Mia is gazing out of the window, closed off to conversation. She's more distant than when she left, there's a buffer around her, I'm familiar with it, know just how impossible it is for me to break through.

'Dad thinks I should be off sick, because of my ankle,' she says out of the blue, just before we arrive home.

'Jens thinks you need a sick note?' I repeat.

'I can hardly walk,' she says.

'It's hardly as though you do much walking around at work,' I reply, doing my best to remain calm.

She doesn't respond, something that started in the past year, she simply ends a discussion with silence.

'Do you?' I continue, my tone gentler this time, driving the car into the garage.

She sighs and shrugs, opens the car door.

'I'll have a look at your ankle, obviously,' I call after her, 'but either way, you'll need to see your own doctor if you need a sick note.'

'Dad's already looked at my ankle, forget I said anything,' she says, then slams the door and hobbles towards the house, where Aslak is just finishing up preparing a vegetable lasagne for her arrival home.

'He's not *Dad*, his name's Jens!' I scream in her wake, just after she's closed the front door behind her.

Mum has been a better grandmother than a mother. Both Magnus and I agree on that fact, even though Magnus thinks it's difficult to judge, since we've only experienced her as a mother – plus the fact that it's simpler and more rewarding all round to be a grandmother than it is to be a mother. Exactly, I've replied, which is probably why she's better at it.

Mia and Mum have their own dialogue, independent of me, and once she was old enough, Mia often went to visit Mum alone. I'm not envious, but I've had to remind myself on several occasions that Mia deserves a grandmother more than Mum deserves another chance. Sometimes it seems as if Mum thinks she can take credit for my children, that she can use them to rectify the mistakes she made while raising Magnus and me. You're so hard on Grandma, Mia said once a few years ago, when Mum had been to visit and the atmosphere had been strained from the moment she arrived to the moment she left. It's not fair, Mia said, think of everything she's been through.

I've deliberately not told Mia about my upbringing, Mum's long-drawn-out breakdown after Dad fell ill, how blind she became to everything around her, how Magnus and I have always taken care of ourselves, for the most part, ever since I was eight years old – and I've deliberately not told her that Grandma first became Grandma, and tentatively my mum, only after she moved Dad into the nursing home.

I didn't really want children, she told me one night when I woke to the sound of the shower, and found her on the bathroom floor on all fours, scrubbing the tiles behind the bathtub. It was Gustav who was keen on the idea, he insisted on it and then he disappeared, just like that, she said. She turned to face me. I miss him so much, you understand, don't you, Sigrid? I must have been fourteen, it must have been after Dad's third stroke, in any case, the big one, the one that changed his personality, made him angry and short-tempered and challenging even when it came to things that had once worked for us, when it came to everything that forms part of the ingrained pattern of family life.

My memory is filled with hundreds of these nightly conversations with Mum, I remember her despair and my own conviction that if I just listened long enough, if I was receptive, that I could shoulder her burden, relieve her of something.

I was just a child, I told Mum on the one occasion I've attempted to confront her, thinking that some sort of head-to-head would offer me a sense of relief or liberation, given that completing my studies, moving to Oslo and getting together with Aslak had all failed to curb my feelings of unrest. It wasn't how I'd intended on beginning the conversation, but she was sitting at the kitchen table, looking serene with her teacup in one hand after telling Viljar a bedtime story – I'd lingered on the stairs and heard her laugh as she sat on the edge of his bed and told him how afraid I'd been of foxes when I was young, how she'd had to check behind every door and under every bed for them before shouting from the bedroom window to scare them away. I couldn't keep my thoughts or my words in check, and she looked surprised, but made time to sip her tea before responding. What do you mean? she asked me. I was just a child, I repeated, louder this time, my voice and hands beginning to shake. I heard what you said, Mum said calmly, I didn't know what more to say. And you weren't a mother, I said after a brief pause. You forgot to be a mother, you forgot Magnus and me, you disappeared. Mum sat there in silence, taking small sips of her tea, I resisted the urge to smack the cup out of her hands. Magnus had to make my packed lunches, I said as I realised that it was true, that Mum forgot to make my packed lunch almost every day because Dad's morning routine took so long. And it was up to me to remember my hat and gloves, I never had my gym kit or my skis when I needed them, I didn't bring my skis even once, I said, but I couldn't get to the essence of anything significant, to the sense that I had let her down, not done enough to help, not taken enough on, not been enough – or the constant need for her to tell me it wasn't true, that I was more than enough.

9

The shower plughole has become clogged with my hair. Magnus is sitting on the lid of the toilet and reading the instructions on the back of the bottle of plughole unblocker when I return from my morning dip, he's wearing his headphones, doesn't see me standing in the doorway, watching him. He's leaning over the bottle, half turned away from me, I feel as though he's spending a disproportionately long time checking the three illustrated points.

'Is the unblocker a little too complicated for this particular engineer?' I ask, laughing.

He jumps, looks up at me, and only then do I realise that he's crying. He removes his headphones, dries his eyes, but does nothing to hide the fact. I smile at him, then wander over and stand beside him, stroking his hair. It's just as thick as Gustav's, I allow my fingers to run through it slowly.

'I think a blockage like this would benefit from the entire bottle,' I say.

He sniffs, straightens up as if pulling himself together, holds up the bottle to show me the instructions that I can't read without glasses anyway, and which I can't be bothered to pore over.

'I don't think that would do us or your plumbing any good,' he replies.

I grow impatient in the face of his feebleness and his tears, shed out in the open like this, annoyed at the way he allows himself to sit here, crying, when I'm the one who's unwell, I'm the one whose body has been pumped full of poison.

'Well, I'm sure it causes cancer,' I remark, trying to laugh, and I take the bottle from him. 'Go on, I'll deal with it.'

'Now you're being daft, Mum,' he says.

Yes, I am daft, I grow dafter by the day. My mind is withering away, just like my hair and teeth and guts and healthy and un-healthy cells here, there and everywhere throughout my body. The nausea is so chronic and claustrophobic that I want nothing more than to be alone, but Magnus and Sigrid follow their meticulous routine, ever on the alert, and I'm too weary to object – their pres-ence feels oppressive and uncomfortable for much of the time, the fact they're so close. The fact that they're around to witness the relentless exposure of my skin and scalp and anxiety and inner conflict as the poison is pumped into my system.

'I can sort out a blocked pipe, Magnus,' I reply, trying to open the bottle, but the lid is on too tight, the muscles in my arms and hands have wasted away over the course of just a few short weeks. 'Could you go and soak the mutton, please?'

He takes the bottle, unscrews the lid and passes it back to me.

'Whatever you say,' he replies, and leaves the room.

I pour the entire bottle down the plughole, hear it hissing and watch as vapour rises; I inhale deeply before leaving the room, closing the door behind me.

I try to imagine how happy it would have made me if Sigrid and Magnus had suggested that we celebrate Christmas here as a family last year, but instead I find myself looking forward to it all being over and done with. I can't face it, I've told Gustav, resting my head in his lap. He's become more obliging since I fell ill, there's a kindness in his expression, a gentleness to his gestures, neither of which were there before. Obviously I understand that there aren't sufficient connections left in his brain to grasp the fact that I'm ill and all that entails – but I still convince myself that something within him sees the changes in me, senses the fear and the need to be close to him, and that he allows that in a different way than he has in a long time.

There's nowhere that I can be alone now that the house is so full of people, nowhere to hide. It reminds me of the period after Gustav's second stroke, when both my sisters came to help out, all while Magnus and Sigrid were here, there and everywhere, their tiny bodies taking up so much space, the pair of them there in every room I entered on the hunt for peace to think, quiet to gain perspective, space to scream.

I realise that this might be my last Christmas, even though I haven't 'given up', a phrase that everyone uses as a sort of collective term to describe anything resembling sorrow or anger or exhaustion in their eyes. You mustn't *give up*, Magnus and Aslak and Mia tell me whenever I allow myself a sigh or rest my head in my hands for the most fleeting of moments. I want to shout at them, to slam doors, want to tell them all to bugger off, but ever present is the knowledge that I have to leave them with good memories, pleasant ones, memories of me smiling warmly, happily, calmly, memories of Mum, of Grandma. I have no chances left, and it's so important, so critical, that *someone* might remember me with uncomplicated feelings of affection.

There is something forced about the whole situation, I tiptoe around on the periphery of Christmas preparations and traditions that were once mine, previously my mother's and her mother's before that, only for Sigrid and Magnus to adopt them with an exaggerated sense of authority. It's as if they've been ready and waiting all this time, and have finally been given the green light to forge ahead, to execute their coup. I can't be the memorable version of myself that I'd planned to be, I feel irritated and restless about being undermined in this way, made invisible, prevented from bringing anything to the table.

Now you're just being ungrateful, Gustav's scent seems to say as I lie there with my head in his lap, complaining. You should be glad they came at all. The ambivalence is suffocating, and on the morning of Christmas Eve, I make my way into the living room and see that the tree has been decorated, with angels and tinsel and tasty treats hanging in all the wrong places, Aslak making porridge and Magnus whittling sticks for criss-crossing at the bottom of the mutton dish while Mia lays the table, I make my way to the cart shed outside and dig out Gustav's old bamboo snowshoes. I perch myself on the chopping block, it's flecked with dried chicken blood and chain-saw oil. I have to catch my breath before strapping on the snowshoes, rest my index finger on a stretched hole in the leather strap for a moment, picture Gustav's back, his mustard-yellow anorak and green backpack, ahead of me all the way up to the mountain pasture; I pull the strap tight, buckling it using the innermost hole.

I make my way up the snowy path behind the barn, into the forest, up the mountainside, slow and steady, I'm not as ill as everyone's expressions and gestures would suggest.

I've hardly stepped foot outside since I started chemotherapy, the air is cold against the dry mucous membranes in my nose and mouth and throat, and my thin hair provides no insulation against the cold, I feel the wind against my scalp. I pull the hood of the anorak over my head as I reach the little wooden cabin that belonged to Gustav's father, find the key to the padlock beneath the rock. The cabin can't be any bigger than eight square metres, sparsely furnished with a table and two chairs, a little bench that folds out to form a bed, a wood-burning stove in one corner, and a bookshelf that almost blocks the entrance. It was Gustav who carried the bookshelf up here after Magnus and Sigrid were born, before he fell ill, when he decided that he needed a little sanctuary of his own. There are a few books on the shelves that he brought to read up here on those occasions that he needed *air*. I pull out one after the next, open them, the spines of most are stiff and creak at being opened for the very first time – a few, such as a slim volume by Strindberg, one I've never heard of, are barely still in one piece.

I'm overwhelmed by nausea, lie down on the bench, my pulse quickens, I try doing the breathing exercises Sigrid taught me. Every morning at precisely half past four I wake up to sweat running down my chest, my pulse racing, I gasp for air, so terrified that I begin to shake, each day it is as if I haven't ever experienced a fear quite like it, it feels new every morning, fatal. But the fear won't kill you, Sigrid said when I called her after the fourth morning I'd woken in the same way, are you taking the Imovane like I suggested? I take sleeping pills and tablets to relieve my nausea but nothing works, I told Sigrid, sounding desperate, nothing works for me, nothing really does the trick. You're not a medical anomaly, Mum, she replied, of course they work. But she called me the following morning at half past four, listen to me, she said as I hyperventilated, take a deep breath. I couldn't do it, gasped for air. Mum, you have to listen to me, take a slow, deep breath, can you do that for me, Sigrid said calmly on the other end of the line, I clutched the telephone as if it were Sigrid's hand, Gustav's hand, Mum's hand, finally managed to draw air into my lungs, that's good, Sigrid said, breathe in for three, hold for three and out for five, good, let's try that again, and I breathed in for four and held it for seven and breathed out for eight to the sound of Sigrid's monotone counting as tears and sweat ran down my cheeks and chest and my pulse slowed.

I awaken on the bench to Sigrid shaking me.

'Poor show, Mum,' she says.

'I know,' I say.

She helps me up, her actions stiff and aggressive, I'm so cold that my teeth are chattering, she removes her wool jumper and gives it to me before walking out of the cabin. It's started snowing, my tracks in the snow have all but disappeared.

'My God, what if I hadn't found you?' Sigrid says as she marches ahead of me down the path, so quiet and vehement that she can't possibly be expecting a response.

What if she hadn't found me.

Three days after Christmas, Mia is ready and waiting outside the bath-room door first thing in the morning as I emerge in my swimsuit. Sigrid has tried to put a stop to my morning swims, but I've objected, told her that for as long as I can walk, I'll continue to bathe.

Sigrid and Magnus have never wanted to join me, and it's never felt like any great loss to me, it's not a tradition that I've felt is im-portant to see carried on, this ritual embraced only by Gustav and me. I hesitate for a moment when I see Mia standing there in her bathrobe, want more than anything else to be alone with the water and the mountains and Kant – and Gustav – but I haven't the heart to turn her down, want to create memories, to leave her with something to remember me by.

I catch sight of her out of the corner of my eye as I remove my bathrobe down by the jetty, she glances at my ailing, frail frame, the loose skin that hangs from my arms and thighs and buttocks. I turn around and look at her, smile and lift my arms in the air, flex my muscles like a weightlifter. A look of relief flashes across her face, she laughs and removes her own bathrobe. Her body is familiar to me, she's inherited Sigrid's figure, slightly out of pro-portion, something Sigrid inherited from me. Hefty, muscular thighs, wide hips, and a slim upper body that borders on shape-lessness, with slender arms and a long neck.

I stand there in the cold for a moment and watch her as she removes her shoes and socks, wrapping her arms around herself, tiptoeing around and trembling with the cold until her straight, white teeth begin to chatter. There's something refreshing and comforting in the notion that there's so much of me in Mia, that it lives on in her, and will continue to do so – in her muscles, the way she moves, in her mind and her expressions.

'So, are you ready?' she asks.

I pull on my padded bathing cap.

'I'll race you,' I reply.

'That's fighting talk,' Mia replies with a chuckle before sprinting the two steps towards the jetty and readying herself for take-off, then jumping in with her arms wrapped around her knees, disappearing in the dark water with an almighty splash.

She swims underwater, back in the direction of the jetty, then emerges once again, her breathing quick and shallow in the cold, frosty air surrounding her, but she smiles at me.

'Come on, then,' she shouts. 'I'm not going anywhere until you join me.'

As we make our way back to the house afterwards, I see Sigrid's silhouette at the kitchen window; it disappears when she catches sight of us.

'You seem better today,' she says as we make our way into the kitchen, she's sitting with her back to the window, a newspaper spread out on the table in front of her.

Both Mia and I sit down on the bench in front of the stove in the corner of the room, I savour the particular sensation of wood-fire warmth on skin fresh from a swim, and I nod at Sigrid.

'Yes, I feel better, barely any nausea,' I reply.

❖

I drive past Aslak pulling Viljar on a sled five hundred metres or so from the house, on his way up the hill towards the shop, or perhaps en route to see his parents. I've told him that he mustn't feel duty-bound to stay with me for the whole Christmas holiday, he and Sigrid obviously ought to split their time between myself and them, but Aslak has waved a hand in the air and told me that they've got a full house, in any case. I dread the prospect of bumping into one or both of them in the shop or out on the street, dread having to answer for the fact that I've had the children and grandchildren to myself for the entire festive season, or worse still, that they might willingly grant me the company out of a sense of pity.

The whole village knows I'm ill. Even though I grew up here, even though I've been part of conversations out on the street or in the shop, at school and on the ski track, at parties and in the community centre, around kitchen tables and in cars, it still fascinates me to witness just how quickly news or a rumour can spread. This village could give Facebook a run for its money, Sigrid remarked on Christmas Eve when I mentioned that a neighbour had left a casserole on the kitchen table, it had been waiting for me when I'd returned from hospital after my operation, still warm. She's never appreciated the values inherent to this tiny community, the security that comes from the knowledge that someone is always looking out for you.

You're not looking out for her enough, Magnus said the day after Sigrid was driven home by the police for the first time. They'd found her by the petrol station, so drunk that she couldn't even explain herself. It was uncomfortable making eye contact with the district sheriff I'd met at parents' evening just two weeks beforehand. I didn't know what to say, I was exhausted after dealing with

Gustav's nightly wanders, furious outbursts, unpredictable and un-familiar patterns of behaviour. Just before Sigrid was driven home at around two in the morning, I'd woken to sounds from the bath-room, where I'd found him in the process of shaving his head. I had only just managed to persuade him to return to bed when I'd heard the doorbell. I felt nothing but shame and fury when I saw Sigrid, bleary-eyed as she swayed before me, yet more for me to be dealing with. She leaned against the wall behind the district sheriff, smiling in a manner that was almost mocking, defiant, and when she eventually managed to lock eyes with me for a brief moment, I remember suppressing the urge to hit her, to slap her face with an open palm, to slap it out of her, her egotistical need for atten-tion, her need to inflict us, me, with more to deal with. She's the one who should be taking a long, hard look around her, I told Magnus, nodding at Gustav who lay fast asleep on the sofa.

Sigrid texts me to ask if I can pick up some thyme for the turkey stuffing. I turn the car around and drive back to the shop even though I'm sure we agreed yesterday that we'd be having elk for dinner this evening. I miss the authority that came with sound health, it's impossible to regain, even when I'm feeling much better; in the eyes of Sigrid and Magnus and everyone else around me I am ill, and therefore submissive, at least until I'm declared healthy once again – or dead.

I see his car before I turn off the engine. Wonder if I should just carry on driving, sit here until he comes out or simply head straight in. I don't have the chance to think any further before he emerges through the new automatic doors. He spots my car at once, stops and sees me sitting inside. I climb out, smooth my jacket. Once he's about three metres away from me, he stops.

In the five minutes that have passed since I spotted his car, the fact I'm ill hasn't crossed my mind once. I've forgotten that I've got no hair beneath my hat, that my clothes are baggy and loose, that the bone structure of my face is more prominent, making me look like a witch, according to Viljar.

'Anne, my dear,' Erik says, and stands on the spot for a moment before approaching me, forgetting to set down his shopping bags, attempting to embrace me with a full carrier bag in each hand, they swing against my back.

I start to laugh.

'I wasn't expecting this,' he says as he lets go of me.

'Well, it's not such a surprise,' I reply. 'On your way up to the cabin for New Year's Eve?'

He nods, then gestures at his car, where I realise someone is sitting in the passenger seat.

'Yes, just for the night. But…' he begins, doesn't know how to continue, and I understand, it's like so many similar conversations I've had lately, with people I know far less well than I know Erik, wondering what they can or should ask when they bump into such a visibly ailing body.

'Colon cancer,' I tell him. 'I'm having chemotherapy, and they're hopeful that I'll make a full recovery.'

I don't mention the fact it's spread, that information is reserved for those who can deduce such things from a single glance of my bald head, who understand that chemotherapy is for those in the more advanced stages of the disease. Not Erik, in other words.

'Well, that's good to hear. But my God, talk about injustice, you don't deserve this,' he says.

'Well no, I agree with you there, it'd be much better if someone more deserving had been struck down with it,' I remark with a wry smile.

He looks a little confused.

'Oh? Oh no, I just meant...'

'I'm just teasing you. I know what you meant. Thank you,' I say.

He shifts his weight from one leg to the other, looks restless and impatient, glances over at his car.

'Listen, we'd best be setting off to the cabin if we're to make it up there before it gets dark. But let's have a coffee when I'm next around, catch up,' he says.

'Of course,' I reply, know that he won't be getting in touch when he's next around. 'Just let me know when you're back.'

'I will do, I'm thinking February or March. It's good to see you,' he says, leaning in slightly, but the carrier bags are still in his hands and he changes his mind halfway.

'Happy New Year,' I say.

I stand there and watch as his car makes its way out of the car park and disappears. I regret making my way out of my own car, the fact that he'll remember me like this. It's an unbearable thought that the one and only meaningful witness to my naked, healthy body after Gustav has now undoubtedly replaced every memory of it with an image of illness.

You don't fancy finding yourself a boyfriend, then? Magnus asked me three days after I moved Gustav into the nursing home. I'm still married, I replied, holding up my hand with my wedding ring in view, I hadn't been prepared for the question. Only on paper, he said. Isn't paper the most important thing in any marriage? I remarked. Everything else is perfectly possible without being married, I said. You know what I mean, he said, and it was true, I did, I'd already been in a relationship with Erik for two years by then.

10

The banks of snow lining the road are several metres high. It's New Year's Day, we're on our way back to Oslo. Viljar has fallen asleep in the backseat and Aslak is taking the opportunity to play Candy Crush on his phone, given that I've banned the playing of brain-dead games in Viljar's presence. Aslak thinks the reading and counting games I've downloaded onto the iPad for Viljar are ridiculous and pretentious, and I'm certain that the two of them spend hours playing Candy Crush and other sicky-sweet-looking, addictive games every day after preschool. I've given up trying to put a stop to it, and now I find myself most impressed by Viljar's ability to keep a secret, he shakes his head firmly in response to every question, regardless of my half-hearted promises of rewards or consequences.

The route over the mountain seems longer than usual, perhaps a result of the monotonous view of walls of snow instead of the usual aesthetic treat one is rewarded with when driving this way, over the tree line, rolling through the bare, violent mountain landscape that resonates more deeply within me than Oslo's insignificant natural surroundings, in spite of everything. Or perhaps it's due to the fact that Frida called yesterday, she'd been admitted to a psychiatric unit after yet another suicide attempt, for want of a more precise explanation.

I gave her my number long ago, with strict instructions that it was only ever to be used in the most severe emergencies – and she has abided by that, with impressively few exceptions. She's been admitted several times in the years that I've known her, but the last occasion was a while ago now. At our last appointment before Christmas, she was composed, played her usual role, picked up from various television series and blogs, and time spent on

Instagram. Frida observes and interprets the world more accurately than anyone I know, hers is an eagle eye, and she has an impressive degree of emotional precision in her hunt for people to care for her and provide her with attention. She had re-established contact with her ex-boyfriend, the father of her baby, who I don't know anything about other than the fact he comes from somewhere down south and tries to have himself sectioned a few times a year in order to secure himself a free ride back home. I can't even pick up my own socks, she told me last time, rolling her eyes. He's so attentive, making sure I don't eat brie or salami or drink coffee. Typical man, she said, flashing me a knowing smile, almost more pregnant than I am, eh?

It was more difficult to relate to the insistent normality than to the explosive way she tended to do things, and it pains me that I didn't see that, or worse, that I had so many concerns about myself – and Mum – that I didn't have the energy to try.

Her previous admissions have followed a different pattern altogether, a completely different type of behaviour. On the first occasion, she issued me with the precise date that she planned on taking her life, I'm going to die on the fourth of June, she said, and even though I knew it was unlikely she would follow through on it, I couldn't take the chance, so had her admitted to hospital. The idea that she, or anyone, should die on my watch was impossible for me to handle at first, and at the beginning of my career, in those first few months, I referred more patients than I sent home. In the end, a tired and no doubt overworked senior consultant at the hospital called me and declared me incompetent, told me to pull myself together, that we, the new generation of general practitioners, were a band of fragile wimps afraid of taking responsibility for anything, that the next patient I sent her way had better need more than a prescription for acid reflux medication or a pat on the shoulder. I started crying on the phone, exhausted with being new to everything and afraid of making mistakes, knowing all the while that my croaky, teary voice and sniffly nose confirmed every one of her suspicions about me, she hung up on me. But she called me back the next day, fortunately not to apologise, but instead getting straight to the point. Do you want to be a middle man? she asked me. I shook my head. Hmm? she asked. No, I replied quietly. So start using your training and actually *treating* your patients, she said, with what I took to be a hint of warmth.

It's not possible to cure Frida, but I've learned to look for the small changes, the small victories. Such as the fact she's managed to get through her pregnancy so far without hurting herself, that it's been more than a year since she sought out one ex-boyfriend she's particularly besotted with. The fact that she finally has a job, a position at Seven Eleven that she's managed to hold down for seven months.

'Why now?' I say to Aslak in the car, unable to shake my thoughts of Frida, I ask the question only in order to say something aloud, to break the endless chain of reflection and self-reproach.

I've spoken to Aslak about Frida on numerous occasions. He objected in the beginning, didn't you swear an oath of confidentiality, he said to me. You've no idea who she is, I replied. He later pointed out that I only ever break my oath of confidentiality when it comes to my most vulnerable patients, you'd never dream of telling me if some politician or celebrity turned up in your office with the same issues. That's because they don't have the same issues, I retorted, but he's right.

He glances up from his phone, takes a moment to gather his thoughts before he realises what I'm talking about.

'It's not your fault,' he says. 'People take their own lives at Christmas time.'

'She hasn't taken her own life,' I reply. 'And I'm not saying it's my fault, I'm just saying that it's a damn shame.'

I'm angry now, can't direct it anywhere but at Frida as I mull over how incredibly selfish she's being.

'No, but you know what I mean,' Aslak says.

'No, I don't,' I say, lying through my teeth. 'She's pregnant, she has a job, we had a clear strategy in place for dealing with Christmas. We had an agreement!' My voice cracks.

'You're taking it too personally,' Aslak says. 'This has nothing to do with your mother.'

I turn to look at him.

'Don't play psychologist. And don't let me keep you from your game.'

Darkness falls long before we arrive home. The house is so tidy and smells so strongly of various cleaning products that it's blindingly obvious that Mia has had a party or a visit of some sort the previous night. Thoughts of Frida and Mum, and everything else, that have accumulated during the journey all fade with the relief I feel that Mia hasn't spent New Year's Eve with Jens and Zadie. She is cooperative and cheerful, teasing Aslak about his flannel shirt. Throughout autumn and much of the festive season, almost everything about him has unleashed her irritation, on one afternoon in December she asked if he wasn't starting to tire of looking as if he'd just stepped out of the barn or cowshed. I could see that Aslak was taken by surprise at the time, but he did his best to laugh it off. I thought that kind of behaviour was behind her, I remarked probingly once we'd gone to bed that night. He acted as if he didn't know what I was referring to, continued reading the paper. I'm sorry, I don't know what's going on with her, I continued.

Then he sat up abruptly in bed, stared at me, and I realised that apologising on her behalf, as if I had a greater sense of responsibility for her, a greater sense of ownership, was much worse, much more cutting than Mia's original remark over dinner.

From the minute I open our front door back at home in Oslo, I find myself imagining what Mum is doing at any given moment, what she's doing as I wrap an arm around Mia, as I make cheese on toast for her and Viljar, as I carry a sleeping Viljar up to bed and pull the covers up over him, as I put the dishwasher on, as I place two frozen bread rolls on a tea towel on the kitchen worktop to defrost so Mia can have them in the morning since she's got an early start, as I brush my teeth, as I go to bed.

Mum wants to spend the next few weeks alone; she pooh-poohed any attempts we made to arrange visits. Magnus had booked holiday to be with her until she'd completed her next round of chemotherapy, but she pushed back to the point of being almost aggressive about it. There are limits to what we can decide on her behalf, Magnus said when we spoke about it afterwards, I mean, she's a grown woman. She's old, I replied. Middle-aged, Magnus replied, and still one hundred percent compos mentis, he added. After discovering Mum sleeping in Dad's old cabin on Christmas Eve in a temperature of minus seven degrees, I had my doubts about the last part, her actions suggested terrible judgement – even for her. But she seemed to improve over Christmas, both in terms of her form and her mood, and when we left this morning, she appeared almost well. Better than she's seemed in years, I remarked to Aslak as we turned off the driveway and saw her standing and waving exaggeratedly at Viljar. Aslak said nothing, he's been hinting at moving back to the village lately, just the odd comment here and there, sneaked into conversation with Mum and Magnus and Viljar – imagine how nice it is to live somewhere that gets snow all winter long, Viljar – and with craft and cunning he used Mum's illness as a means to strengthen his argument. Mia is moving out in the autumn either way, I heard him tell Mum one evening when Mia and I were sitting in the living room watching a film while Mum and Aslak sat together in the kitchen. Very true, Mum chirped.

I'm still suppressing any thoughts of Mia moving out, or postponing them at any rate, until it's definite, until she's been accepted into her university of choice. I'm moving out in the autumn either way, Mum, she's told me. I'm proud of her sense of independence, but still feel terrified that she'll leave me, we haven't spent more than a few weeks apart in our whole lives. When she left for a four-week trip to Asia last summer, I curled up next to Viljar in his bed for the first three nights.

Aslak hasn't mentioned moving to me, and I've ignored his comments, even though it's clear that they've been made with the intention of me overhearing them, the idea is so alien to me, more so after spending Christmas there, and even more so since Jens moved to Oslo and began his occupation of Mia.

'Do you think Grandma is going to die?' Mia asks me one evening towards the end of January.

We're on our way home from the gym, Mia dragged me along for a free kettlebell session, I was so pleased she asked me in the first place that I agreed without realising that it involved lifting and swinging hefty weights around for a whole hour, and all in a room full of people glowing with New Year's optimism. I thought you said gym muscles were vulgar, Aslak remarked before I left, he was leaning in the bedroom doorway, watching me change into my exercise gear, laughing at me as I struggled to pull up the tight leggings. Once, just after we moved to Oslo, while Aslak was standing topless in the garden, planing a headboard, I sat on the steps and watched him at work, studied the muscles of his upper body, and I felt a rare urge to touch them, to touch him – perhaps mostly out of a sense of recognition of what he'd given up, sacrificed, in order to move to Oslo with me. I placed my hands on his chest, my palms flat against his skin, smiled as I ran them slowly along his ribs, clasping them behind his back and pulling him close, kissing his neck and shoulders. I'm going to need to start working out if I want to maintain this, he said. Don't even think about swapping this for a vulgar gym body, I said, he laughed. There's something sad about the fact that Aslak remembers that moment well enough to mention it, but I smiled at him once I'd pulled on my leggings, gym muscles are better than no muscles at all, I replied, he fell silent, and I slapped my bum quickly to demonstrate that it was my own lack of muscles that I was referring to.

My body feels as if it's been beaten black and blue, I can't remember the last time I did any exercise, and I'm dreading the aches I'll feel in the morning, but I do at least have some idea of the challenge I set for some of my patients.

I don't know what to tell Mia. I'm sick of the loneliness that comes with being the only person without any real hope of Mum recovering, Christmas was unbearable in that sense. The knowledge that this was one of our last Christmases, the pressure that came with trying to make it as good for her as it possibly could be, to allow her to die with a sense of peace, filled with good memories, it was unrelenting – like a mantra I had to turn to at the start of any discussion or confrontation.

'Well, we all have to eventually,' I replied with a chuckle, buying myself some time.

'Don't joke about it,' Mia replies, stopping abruptly and standing stock still on the pavement, taking hold of my arm. 'I'm being serious.'

'I don't know, Mia,' I reply, and it's true, I don't.

'Dad says that the cancer spreading to the lymph nodes and the liver is a bad sign, that most people tend to die within the year,' she says.

'Which Dad was that?' I reply, even though I know that Aslak would never dream of saying such a thing to Mia.

Nevertheless, there is something gratifying about the fact that Jens can't simply waltz in from nowhere as a fully functioning, perfect father figure, that he, too, occasionally trips up, says the wrong thing, leaving Mia feeling so unsure of something that she has to come to me for answers.

'Now you're being stupid,' Mia says. 'Why won't you just answer my question?'

'I already have, I don't know if Grandma is going to survive the cancer, and Jens knows even less about it than I do, I can promise you that at the very least,' I tell her, feeling my pulse begin to race.

'He's a doctor too, he's treated plenty of cancer patients,' Mia says.

I drop the gym bag I'm carrying and grasp her shoulders with both hands. This conversation could go one of two ways, I take pains to make what is obviously the right choice, but I can't do it.

'My God, Mia, why do you defend him? Why aren't you angry with him, why aren't you furious?' I ask her loudly.

Mia remains calm, doesn't pull away from me, looks at me as if she's waiting for me to finish, only the corners of her mouth give the slightest hint of her true feelings, defiance above all else, perhaps, enough that I continue.

'You do know that he left when I was pregnant, don't you? You know that he left me all alone to look after you? That he hasn't cared a jot in nineteen years? That he let us both down? It wasn't just me he walked out on.'

She shows no reaction. Her apparent calm drives me mad, even though I know it's hard-won. I shake her as I speak, want to shake loose any feelings she has, she's nineteen years old and must be full of them, but her expressionless face leaves me feeling that I'm the one acting like an insecure teenager. My anger at Jens multiplies, he's ruined her, his psychopathic traits have rubbed off on her.

'Isn't it funny how everyone else is always letting *you* down, Mum,' Mia says, loosening my grip on her shoulder with her hand.

I send Jens a message the following day, tell him we need to talk, that I'll be heading over to his on my way home from work. He replies with two emojis, a thumbs up and a smiley in sunglasses, I can't help but laugh, even though I've criticised Aslak for his extensive use of emojis. The idea that you can't express what you want to say in words is ridiculous, I've said. Aslak hasn't stopped, quite the contrary, in fact, in protest he's started replying to almost every question I ask with an aubergine emoji. Just for laughs, he claims. I don't find it funny in the slightest, but I don't rise to it, and he doesn't stop, it's a stubborn and silly battle that neither of us wants to lose. Jens' thumbs-up and sunglasses smiley prompt something else, though, it comes across as intelligent, he's too sophisticated to use emojis, which is exactly why he allows himself to do so.

He opens the door in bare feet, surprisingly well-groomed feet given that it's the middle of winter, I wonder if he's been for a pedicure, cling to the only thought to cross my mind that degrades him in some way to prevent myself from being entirely overwhelmed by a feeling of being nineteen all over again. He comes around behind me to take my coat as I unzip it, hangs it up in a cupboard with a sliding door as he tells me all about his flexible working hours at the private drop-in clinic he works at. I remove my boots, which look large and clumsy as Jens places them on a shoe rack next to Zadie's high heels and narrow ankle boots. He throws out a hand, we make our way up to a mezzanine-level, open-plan kitchen area, so minimalist that the smooth, clean surfaces would be enough to trigger Aslak's annoyance, you should be able to see a handle or a door knob, *feel* it in your hand before you open a door, don't you think, you should *want* to open a door when you feel a perfectly formed door handle. Nobody wants to open a cupboard with no handle.

'Coffee, Sigrid? Tea? Wine?' he asks, gesturing towards his handle-less cupboards, all lined up behind him.

'I'm driving,' I tell him, smiling.

'You did once say that a little dram improves your driving,' he replies, laughing.

I'm surprised and flattered that he remembers, I once drove five miles to pick him up from a party after he missed the last bus home. I'd arranged a birthday party for a friend and had spent the evening drinking to drown out new, obsessive thoughts of Jens. We'd only met a few months beforehand, and I was so happy when he called me that I promptly left the party and walked four kilometres back home to fetch Mum's car, driving to the neighbouring village while well over the limit without giving it a second thought, until Jens had mentioned it. Did you leave your own party? he asked me as we drove back, did you drive five miles over the limit to pick me up? I shrank in my seat.

'And you once claimed that opiates made you a better doctor,' I reply, even though he's said no such thing, I don't know where that came from, a desire to shake him up, to lash out at him.

He looks surprised before bursting into laughter. He holds his palms up in the air.

'I stand corrected,' he says. 'But that was a long time ago. I'm done with all that, you know, Sigrid.'

I'm to know that. He wants me to know. He looks at me, I wonder what I look like in his eyes, how I looked nineteen years ago. I feel certain that he's never seen me through the same obsessive veil that elevates a person, the veil that bestows every action and expression and text message with meaning and uniqueness and beauty. It is the same veil that fades and disintegrates over time, revealing nothing but commonness and toenails in need of grooming. I've waited for it, the liberating realisation that he, too, is ordinary, but Jens remains beautiful and special. Perhaps he appears that way to the rest of the world too, I think to myself as I consider his long, well-proportioned body, from his well-groomed toes to his slim fingers as he reaches up to grab two mugs from the top shelf.

I try to regain a sense of seriousness once again.

'I want to talk to you about Mia. About how we talk to her about Mum's illness,' I say.

He nods. He pours loose tea leaves into two small tea strainers, placing one in each large mug.

'Sure, she's so grown up these days,' Jens says.

These days.

'She's somewhere in between,' I reply. 'She's still a child scared for her grandmother's sake, too.'

Jens smiles and nods.

'I've always thought that it's best to be upfront about things. Children are capable of dealing with more than we think, you know, as long as they're given enough information,' he says.

I can't respond, do my best not to focus on the fact that I'm standing in the midst of one of my own fantasies, Jens and I discussing our child's upbringing, one in which he reveals opinions and insights and hopes he has for Mia. I take the mug he passes me and blow gently on the tea, bringing it to my lips.

'But *we* don't have enough information in this case,' I reply eventually. 'And you know even less than us. Nobody knows what the outcome of all this will be,' I continue.

Jens moves closer to me.

'I know that you're scared for Anne, Sigrid,' he says. 'I know that this all feels unfair, and that you need to hold out hope. Especially given the relationship you two have had, you don't want to feel upset, you'd rather put off thinking about anything to do with it.'

Finally I feel my anger rise up.

'Impressive analysis. But listen, *Jens*, I don't want you talking to Mia about Mum. If she asks, send her to me. I know Mia better than you do,' I tell him. 'We need to set some boundaries.'

'Of course,' he says, shrugging, but he doesn't seem to be feeling any guilt, and there is something deeply disturbing about his natural state, his gaze never faltering, so free and easy, no regrets in life. 'You've always had a thing about boundaries,' he adds with a chuckle.

By the time I get home, Aslak has gone to bed. He wakes up at the sound of me opening the bedroom door, lifts his head and looks at me, but doesn't ask where I've been. I undress quickly, creeping under the covers and shuffling over to lie by his back, resting my cold hand between his thighs. He inhales, tenses, turns to face me. For the first time in years, I close my eyes and feel Jens' body against mine, Jens' skin beneath my fingertips, I know every inch of him by heart even now, freckles, iliac crest, knee tendons and all.

Frida turns up for her check-up in the third week of February. She's called me five times since she was discharged from the psychiatric unit, still high on the fact she was admitted in the first place, she's had a taste of blood after all the attention she's received. She's wept and made threats on the phone to me, expected and demanded an earlier appointment, but I've stood my ground. There's a long waiting list just after New Year, I've told her, and I've wanted to tell her that it's for the best, that the boundaries I've done what I can to maintain are the most effective form of treatment she could hope for. She knows that, and she gets it, she's also working hard to accept it, but for her the line between being well and being ill is so fine, and exists just there, between insight and the ability to trade it in for an appointment.

She's sitting in her usual spot; I catch sight of her as I emerge to fetch the patient before her. I lock eyes with her fleetingly and smile.

'Lucas?' I say, shifting my gaze to the mother sitting with a child covered from head to toe in chicken pox on her lap.

Out of the corner of my eye I see Frida sink in her seat.

The mother stands up with her son in her arms, a man beside her stands up too. As all three approach me, he places a hand on her back, as if to lead or support her.

'Oh, wait, would you mind grabbing his hat and mittens?' she says to him.

He turns around and picks up the hat and a pair of mittens that had been left on the chair beside Frida before returning and wrapping his free arm around the mother's shoulders. I open the door to my office, watch as Frida observes them, her expression almost ravenous.

❖

There are just four weeks until Frida's due date, and she's decided that she doesn't want to give birth.

'There's no way out now, Frida,' I tell her, remembering the way I woke up in the middle of the night calling for Mum and Jens in the lead up to my own due date with Mia.

'I'd rather die,' she says.

'You need to start preparing yourself,' I tell her. 'Is Kristoffer going to be at the birth, have you two spoken about it at all?'

She falls silent for a moment.

'You need to send me back to hospital,' she says. 'It was irresponsible of that doctor to discharge me so soon. Totally premature.'

'I've spoken to him,' I say, Frida looks suddenly enthusiastic at the idea of us talking about her, discussing her. 'We agreed that discharging you was the best course of action. Your own experiences have shown that being admitted to hospital doesn't benefit you in the scheme of things, haven't you even said so yourself?'

I can't recall if Frida has said it, but I do know that it's true, that admitting Frida to hospital only ever has the effect of pouring fuel on the fire. She swings between two conditions and worlds, too ill to be independent and too independent to be considered properly ill.

'I've never said that,' Frida replies. 'I mean it, I'm not going through labour, I want a C-section.'

'I understand that you're afraid, but do you think you could lie down for me so I can have a feel of your bump?'

She does as I ask, her stomach is enormous in comparison to her slight frame and narrow hips. In that moment I remember a conversation I had with Mum when I was pregnant with Viljar, when she had clearly decided to do better this time around, to be better than she had been last time with Mia; you're lucky to have my hips, we were made to birth children, she said with self-satisfaction, grasping her own hips. It took all my effort not to say that she might have been made to birth children, but she was in no way made to *have* them. But she's right that my own births were physically uncomplicated, so straightforward that I know I have to choose my words carefully when faced with fearful pregnant patients. At one time, I thought they were afraid of the pain, but after a while I realised that was too simple an explanation, that more than anything they were afraid of the overwhelming unknown, the loss of control. There have been more of them in recent years. Last year a man entered my office, staring at the floor from the moment he walked in to the moment he left again, mumbling that he needed help sleeping – it's very important that you're able to sleep, of course, I told him after a few introductory questions, he didn't look particularly reassured, but is there a specific reason that you're struggling to sleep, a problem you're having or something making you feel anxious? His voice cracked when he told me about his pregnant girlfriend and how afraid he was of the birth, of everything that could happen, everything that could go wrong, and what was he supposed to do, what's my role?

I'm fairly certain that Frida isn't afraid of the birth itself, that actually it's become something to which she can affix her fear of that which is *truly* frightening, something I'm equally afraid of myself – how on earth is she supposed to take care of a child?

'Great,' I say to her, she pulls her jumper up over her bump. 'You know, there are plenty of people ready and willing to help you out.'

She turns to face the wall, says nothing, she's got over ten years' experience receiving help from others, and even Frida must realise where exactly she sits on the ladder of needs where such help is concerned. Over the years, I've spoken to social security and district psychiatric services and the local council and various hospitals about Frida more times than I can count, and the answer is always the same, no space, nothing else to offer, starting from scratch in an endless vicious circle. There's no reason for us to keep her here any longer, the doctor on the psychiatric ward told me when he called. I wanted to tell them that there was no reason to discharge her, either.

I place my hands at the top of her abdomen, then carefully move them down, feel movement beneath the skin, shift my hands from one side to the other, I feel a tiny back flush against my right palm, I smile at Frida, she's still staring at the wall. Eventually I locate the head lower down, carefully press against it, no movement.

'Your little girl is ready to make her way into the world, at any rate,' I tell Frida, who sits up, shakes her head then starts to cry, I know so well how she feels that I can't help but wrap an arm around her, she sobs into my white coat.

Mum calls one Saturday morning in early March, when I'm out feeding the ducks at Bogstadvannet with Viljar, carrying out some sort of half-hearted exposure therapy to combat his fear of birds. The snow has melted, spring is already in the air. There's nothing out of the ordinary about Mum calling, we've spoken almost every other day since Christmas, every three days at least, and Aslak and I have booked an extra week's holiday after Easter to stay in the village. Magnus has just spent a week there, and one of my aunts visited at the end of January. You're lucky, I've told her, to have so many people around you. She's never responded, it's possible that she nodded on the other end of the phone line, and equally possible that she rolled her eyes. I don't know how else I could have dealt with it, I've said to Aslak, when my guilty conscience and a new, or perhaps long-standing, yearning has gained the upper hand. Well, we'd have to have moved out there, he said. Or she'd have to have moved here, he added quickly.

It was Mum who had insisted on managing by herself, she wanted to go it alone, the best thing for her was that we carried on with our lives. Let's take it one day at a time, she said just before we left on New Year's Day. I nodded; it was hard to leave, even more so given that she was being so brave and grateful while looking so frail.

We've brought an old loaf of bread with us, I break off small pieces and throw them for the ducks at the water's edge. Even though Viljar was excited at the prospect of feeding them this morning, he's run away and climbed up onto a bench behind me, tiptoeing around on it with a mixture of fear and exhilaration as he points out where I should throw the bread next.

'Do you think the ducks can't climb, Viljar?' I ask him, then laugh, both at him and how mean I am, pulling my mobile out of my pocket.

I brace myself, as usual.

'Hi, Mum,' I say.

11

'The cancer has spread to my lungs,' I say.

Sigrid falls silent.

'Are you still there?' I ask after a few seconds, I can hear Viljar in the background, the longing I feel for him, for them, it pulses throughout my body.

'Yes, I'm here,' Sigrid says. 'When did you find that out?'

'At my check-up yesterday,' I tell her.

'What did the doctor say?' she asks, her voice is just as monotone as it was when I first told her about the cancer, this time I feel more upset by it, why can't she react like any normal daughter, any normal person at the very least, why can't she raise her voice or cry or rage?

'What do you mean, what did he say? He said I'm going to die,' I say loudly.

'I'm sure he didn't say that, Mum,' Sigrid says.

No, he didn't say that, not exactly, but the message was clear, it lay there quivering behind the words he used – and those he didn't. I stared at his mouth, waited for a 'but' while he explained all about lung metastases, and then he came out with it: *But* we still believe you have a number of good years ahead of you, with the right treatment.

'He's stopped using words like "healthy" and "hope", in any case,' I tell Sigrid. 'Now he's talking about how many years I *could* have ahead of me.'

'That's just how they express things,' Sigrid says. 'I'll call them.'

'They? That's how you *all* express things,' I say. 'And it's humiliating to be talked down to in such a way.'

'Nobody is talking down to you,' Sigrid replies. 'But nobody can really *know* the outcome of all this, they can't tell you that you're going to die when they don't know that for certain.'

'Why not? Surely it's better to be pleasantly surprised when you survive than to be caught off guard by death,' I say.

'Listen, Viljar and I are out feeding the ducks just now, but I'll call you back once we get home, we're just setting off now, I'll call you soon,' Sigrid says quickly.

I hang up without saying goodbye.

'Never mind the fact that you've just been told your mother's going to die,' I say to Kant, currently curled up at the foot of the bed. I haven't found a reason to get out of bed today. 'What do you reckon to that, eh?'

Kant's left ear pricks up. Nobody reacts the way they're supposed to.

I was shown the CT scans of my lungs. You can see it quite clearly here, the doctor said, pointing at a few cloudy, white smudges that appeared to be growing from my spine. Are they on my spine? I asked. The doctor shook his head, no, these are your *lungs*, he said loudly and pointed, as if I were hard of hearing. Once again I felt shame rise up within me, but it was too much to take in, too much eluded me, I found myself unable to properly process the information.

I lie there and look at my arm, at the scar left from the time the doctor removed a suspect mole four years ago, just to be on the safe side. I was so unconcerned about it that I'd forgotten all about it when he called to let me know that it was nothing to worry about. The skin on the underside of my upper arm hangs loose, any fat or muscle gone, absorbed by my body on its hunt for nutrition to nurse me back to good health, as I've imagined to be the case, though in reality it has been gathering its strength to launch more excessive attacks. And now you're going to die, my slack, sallow skin tells me.

Kant hovers by the door after a short while, whimpering and scraping. He's old, his back slightly hunched, and I suspect that his hearing has started to go, but he's not going to die before I do, the realisation hits me as I drag myself out of bed to let him out. And with that insight, I am suddenly inundated with a stream of thoughts I've thus far managed to hold at bay, about what will happen to him, to the farm, to the tractor, the car, the curtains, the tablecloths, the flower pots, all the things that Sigrid and Magnus are guaranteed not to want. I text Magnus after letting Kant out, ask him if he thinks he'll want the old photos up in the loft, the ones that used to hang in my mother and father's drawing room. They're worthless old prints, but I didn't have the heart to throw them out after they'd both died and I was clearing out the old house, just as I now imagine Sigrid and Magnus doing here, throwing away everything they come across without a single thought. They're a bit kitsch, I add in a follow-up message. A small speech bubble appears under my last message, the three dots dancing there for an eternity before they disappear altogether. Then they pop up once again, before disappearing. Finally a message comes through from Magnus. Stop, it says.

Magnus has been to see me several times since Christmas, he's driven up from Stavanger, one evening he arrived without warning. I just wanted to see to you, he said. See *to* me, or *see* me, I replied, chuckling with some uncertainty. Both, he replied. When I told him about the cancer having spread, he told me he wanted to come over on Sunday. I think he's been here more often in the past three months than he has in the past three years.

❖

'It's strange, but I think one of the hardest things to get my head around is the fact that I'll never be well again, I'll never again have a normal, functioning body, I'm going to die of an illness,' I tell Gustav.

I haven't been to see him for a whole week, I've resisted; I haven't felt up to it, haven't had the energy to do anything other than make it through the days, as if my body were leaking strength, but it's also become more difficult to communicate with him. The idea that I'm going to disappear before he does, that he won't understand what's happened, where I've gone, that he might think I've abandoned him – or worse still, that he won't notice my absence – is impossible for me to remain rational about.

What exactly is going to kill me? I asked the doctor at the hospital. When all is said and done, your organs will begin to fail, but this isn't the kind of thing to focus on for now, Anne, for the moment you need to be thinking about making the most of the time you have left. It exasperates me that everyone I talk to, the doctors, Sigrid, Magnus, they all refuse to discuss the fact I'm going to die.

Even Gustav shies away from it, he rocks restlessly in his chair, shaking his head.

'You need to hear this,' I tell him. 'What if I should die before you do? You hadn't ever imagined that would be the case,' I continue.

I hadn't imagined it, in any case, I've long sought to prepare myself for him suffering a final, fatal stroke. It would be a good thing for him to slip away before too long, a friend said to me a few years ago. And for you too, she added. For me? I said, surprised. Well, yes, it would allow you to move on, she said. I don't plan on moving on, I said. No part of me wants him dead, quite the contrary, in fact, I've feared it for many years now.

I don't think I can remember how to live without you, I said to

Gustav as he lay in the hospital after his first stroke, he was sleep-ing, Sigrid and Magnus ran up and down the corridor outside the room, shouting. We'd been told that he was going to survive, but nobody could tell me how much damage he had suffered, if he would ever even recognise me again. Ever since I met him, I've steered my life to follow his, and even now there are no conceiv-able ways to live my life that don't revolve around him.

It would have been better for Sigrid and Magnus if it had been me who had suffered one stroke after another before gradually dis-appearing, Gustav would have handled it all so much better than I have, and he would have endured losing me so much more capably than I have endured losing him. That's not true, Mum, Sigrid said, she must have been about thirteen at the time, but what else could she possibly say.

You're lucky, only being remembered until the age of forty, I've told Gustav many a time. Everything that followed is exempt, at-tributed to something unjustified. Sigrid and Magnus's memories of him before he fell ill are gilt-edged, he remains the person he was back then. It occasionally feels unfair that I am the only one of the two of us to be subjected to their adult analysis and criti-cism. I've felt a need to provide nuance to their image of him, largely to justify my own reactions. My God, Sigrid, the things I could tell you, I once shouted. She was an adult by then, probably in her mid-twenties, I can no longer remember what I was re-sponding to, but it fell amid a whole host of comments along the lines of 'if Dad wasn't ill'.

'Sorry, we don't need to talk about this now, that was silly of me. I just get scared,' I say to Gustav, his gaze is fixed on the bath-room door. 'Do you want a bath?'

I wheel him into the bathroom, start running the tap, undress him bit by bit until he's sitting in his wheelchair with nothing on. There are still muscles visible beneath the skin of his upper body, but his legs are skinny, they look as if they belong to a different body altogether, or to no body at all. I call the carer for some help transferring Gustav into the hoist. I used to find it uncomfortable, Gustav sitting naked in the presence of myself and another person, I remember how awful it was when he got an erection on one of the first occasions that I was here when the carer was due to bathe him. The most awful part was just how angry I got with him, it was utterly instinctive, the way I scolded him once the carer had left, driven to madness by everything that was lost and yet which continued to exist.

I gently lower him into the water, he closes his eyes as I sponge his body.

Magnus has two weeks off, as it turns out. I've explained this to you so many times, he said when he arrived on Sunday. I don't understand his working patterns in the slightest, he doesn't seem to spend more than a few weeks every six months at work as far as I can tell, neither on the North Sea platform nor at the dockyard in South Korea, but he loses his temper when I comment on the fact. I work more hours than anyone else I know, he says. Your whole approach to work is warped, the idea that it has to involve physical labour or operate strictly from eight until four each day, nothing else seems to count in your eyes. It's very old-fashioned. It might be old-fashioned, but I *am* old-fashioned, I argue. No, you're not, Magnus replies, you just have out-dated views.

I haven't dared ask him if he's anticipated spending the entire fortnight here, but it's too much, I can't face the prospect. He's in a forcibly good mood, positively jovial, rebuffs any talk of the cancer or its spread unless the discussion is focused on one of the articles he carries around in his growing file. He stopped emailing them to me when he realised I wasn't reading them, and now he prints them out and appears with a new pile whenever he visits. It's silly, the idea that you shouldn't read something that might give you hope, he said when I told him that Sigrid and every other doctor I'd come across had warned me not to go online on the hunt for more information. That's typical of doctors, they just want to make sure they're in the clear, he said. I can't face opening the file he's left on the kitchen table, I can see through the trans-parent plastic where he's highlighted sections in yellow, presumably to emphasise particularly important information.

Sigrid calls me on Friday morning, a week after I first received the news of the cancer spreading to my lungs.

'I've spoken to your doctor,' she says. 'We both agree that you're going to need more help moving forwards.'

Still no change in intonation. Poor Aslak, I think to myself.

'What do you mean?' I ask.

'You've said yourself that you feel so unwell that you almost can't bring yourself to get out of bed on some days,' Sigrid says, 'so I've arranged for someone from the local council to call you to arrange a home visit, so that you can work out what happens next.'

It's true that I've felt worse over the past week, and that it's been harder for me to breathe, but that's all psychological, Magnus has declared, it's because you *think* that you can't breathe.

'Who needs someone from the local council when I have you,' I mumble.

'What was that?' Sigrid replies without skipping a beat.

'Can't you speak normally?' I ask. 'You're talking to me as if I were any old patient.'

'You *are* any old patient, Mum, you have cancer just like thou-sands of other people, and I'm trying my best to help you,' Sigrid says, finally a hint of engagement in her voice.

You'd be here if that were the case, I think to myself, surprising even myself at the thought. I don't want her here, I don't want anyone here, I just want her to *want* to be here, I want her to miss me and need me, to cry on my shoulder, to find the idea of my death unbearable.

Two weeks later, I spot one of the local authority's electric cars sweeping up the driveway, I stand at the window in the hallway, just by the front door, hide behind the curtains, filled with dread. Magnus and I spent two days cleaning the house from top to bottom, which hadn't been done since Christmas. Nobody cares about a bit of dust, Magnus said as I set to work, it's not the house they're coming to see. I'm going to do this whether you help me or not, I told him.

Sigrid thought I should make an appointment with the community nurse, that way you can arrange things for when it best suits you, but I want to know that someone is coming in during the day to see to you, she said. I remember when my grandmother was unwell, the fact that she moved in with my mother and father and was nursed by my mother until the day she died in the guest bedroom. The thought of dying in Sigrid and Aslak's house sends shivers down my spine, it feels remote and humiliating, not least the thought of saddling them with my body, my illness. Even so, Sigrid's dependable solution triggers something within me, in spite of the fact that I've never expressed any expectation that I should be cared for during old age or illness, whether by Sigrid or Magnus. We've never discussed it, not one of us has even mentioned it. I've heard friends and colleagues discussing their demands and expectations, I'm just saying, if they stick me in some home after all the time I've spent looking after their grandchildren while they've been at work and travelling and getting on with their lives, then I'm making my escape to Gran Canaria.

I had issues with the idea that a community nurse should gain an intimate picture of things, my home and my routine, all the things they'd see; I tried to remember who was working as a community nurse these days, no doubt one or more of my former students. Community nursing always reminds me of Gustav, or of the mountain of bureaucracy I found myself up against in my attempts to get more help for my father after he turned ninety and started getting lost in his own garden while functioning too well to be eligible for more assistance – the community nurse's visits are simply a small detour on the route towards the inevitable. I spent a week swallowing my pride and bracing myself for a phone call from the community oncology nurse before agreeing to meet with her; after that, I grabbed my mop and bucket.

Fine, but let me do it, Magnus said when he grasped that this wasn't something that was up for discussion. To my surprise, I found that Magnus is not only incapable of cleaning, but also helpless when it comes to the most fundamental of tasks. I stood in the kitchen doorway and watched as he attempted to attach a mop head to the mop handle, followed by the helpless, haphazard method he employed, which succeeded only in dragging dirty water all over the floor. I couldn't remember ever having taught him to clean, the same was true of Sigrid, but neither of them has ever confronted me about the fact, both must have cleaners at home. Perhaps this is the punishment I deserve, spending two days going back over the areas Magnus has attempted, mopping the floors and wiping down the mirrors all over again after he's gone to bed, my body aching all over, every joint throbbing, struggling to catch my breath, unable to draw the air deep down into my lungs, nursing a fever that leaves me shivering.

❖

The oncology nurse is named Hanne. We're the same age, we were in the same class at primary and secondary school, but we've never been close friends. One of her daughters was a pupil of mine many years ago now, she was in year eight, I remember it made for a difficult discussion at parents' evening when I was forced to bring up the fact that her daughter had been accused of bullying a classmate. Hanne felt that my handling of the situation had been dreadful, that we were biased and inattentive. With hindsight, I suspect she may have had a point.

I stand in the hallway with a blanket around my shoulders and watch as she parks her car, sitting there for a few minutes on her phone before opening the door and stepping out. She looks younger than I do, younger than most sixty-seven-year-olds, she's wearing jeans and trainers, a brown leather jacket, I wish she'd come wearing her nurse's tunic. I remove my blanket, adjust my headscarf, avoid my own gaze in the mirror.

When I open the door to her, I feel unsure how to greet her, unsure how well acquainted we are, the circumstances, our roles, everything has been turned on its head. Hanne gives me no choice, she smiles and embraces me warmly and efficiently, rests her hand on my upper arm for a moment, it feels as if her fingers extend all the way around. The pain leaves me dizzy, I cling to the doorframe.

'I'm sorry to be seeing you under these circumstances, Anne,' she says, kicking off her trainers in the hallway.

She doesn't say anything about it being unfair, surprising, inconceivable, not like everybody else, I catch myself missing it.

'I suppose that's life,' I say eventually, I can say no more.

'That's life, but it's sad all the same. Let's do what we can to sort things out for you,' she says, following me upstairs. 'Sigrid suggested we'd need to get a community nurse sorted as soon as possible.'

I've no idea what Sigrid has told anyone, but I don't have the breath in my body to respond to her, need to focus all my efforts on not toppling backwards down the stairs, the sweat trickles down the back of my neck, I have to stop. Hanne takes my arm and practically carries me up the rest of the stairs.

'How long has your breathing been like this?' she asks once she's lowered me onto the sofa, I try to inhale smoothly, hear a squeaking somewhere deep inside my chest.

'For a few weeks now,' I eventually manage to say, 'but it's been worse the past few days, since Magnus left, it feels like someone is sitting on my chest.'

Nobody at the hospital can tell me if it's the cancer or the pneumonia that's causing my breathing difficulties and the stabbing pain in my back. But it doesn't really matter, the doctor says, we'll treat it as if it's pneumonia regardless, given your high CRP levels. It matters to me, deep inside I hope it's pneumonia, that's easier to deal with, I had pneumonia thirty years ago, I know about pneumonia. I don't know about cancer in the same way, even now, no matter how familiar I've become with the technicalities, cell division and mutation and spread. I find myself wishing for bacteria or viruses, an external attack, anything but this self-sabotage, this ambush by my own organisms.

Hanne drove me straight to the medic on duty, one of the new junior doctors was on shift. I attempted to make small talk, to be a good patient so she'd see that this is how we do things here, we're easy and grateful patients, even if our cancer is spreading. So many ingrained patterns that refuse to fade, what does it matter to you if a junior doctor stays in the village or leaves, I thought to myself as I forced a smile through the fog of pain, what does it matter to you if she leaves for Oslo, what does any of it matter. Insight struck me, a brief glimmer, then disappeared once again, either way she was too nervous to listen to what I had to say, her hands were shaking as she pressed the stethoscope to my chest and back. I knew she was planning to admit me even before she heard the gurgling and squeaking from my lungs.

A doctor stops by on his rounds on my third day in hospital. He's satisfied that the antibiotics are working, he sounds like a proud father.

'We'll need to do something about your diet,' he says. 'Your body's got no reserves to draw on, nothing to help it fight, not with you being so malnourished.'

He's the first and only person, besides Magnus, to use the word 'fight' since the cancer spread to my lungs.

'Fight?' I repeat.

He looks as if he regrets his choice of words, or perhaps he's just mulling things over, I'm less certain these days whether doctors have any capacity for remorse, or whether their medical studies force that out of them, whether they train them not to engage with that feeling, never to explain or defend themselves. To face up to their mistakes, possibly, but never to express regret.

'Yes, it's important that your body is in better shape to fight off infections like the one in your lungs,' he says, I'm surprised to feel a stab of disappointment, 'and the more reserves you have to support you with that, the better,' he continues.

I fall silent. He gives me an encouraging if slightly impatient look. I get the feeling that I'm holding him up, that he has more important patients to see. I'm sure it's true, others who'll live and contribute, and it strikes me in that moment that I represent only a gaping, black abyss of time and care and funds from this point onwards.

'Is that really the case?' I ask.

After he's gone, I lie there looking through pictures on my

phone. I've taken more than I can count, pictures of the view from the veranda, sunrises and sunsets, Kant sitting against the glow of a misty morning sky, Kant's silhouette against pink clouds, water in every imaginable light, mountains green and brown and red and white. There is only the occasional picture of Magnus, Sigrid, Mia, Viljar. None of Gustav. If someone happened to find my phone, the camera roll would tell them very little about its owner. Or perhaps it would tell them of a life of monotony. Loneliness. I delete at least half of the pictures of water and mountain peaks.

I'm discharged from hospital four days later. It's easier to breathe, I can finally draw the air deep down into my lungs and think clearly. I walk the whole three hundred metres to my neighbour's house to collect Kant.

'You look well,' my neighbour says when she opens the door. 'Better than you have in a long while.'

She rarely ever visits, but I know she keeps an eye on me, checking to make sure the light is on and there's smoke coming from the chimney each morning, that she often sits at the kitchen window with her binoculars when I'm out swimming, watches my car as I drive past her. She's done it since long before I fell ill, all in plain sight, it's felt invasive on occasion. But no longer. I smile, thank her, let Kant out ahead of me.

The following day Sigrid calls me before I've got out of bed, she wants to make sure I'm not planning on going swimming.

'You know how it is, Mum. You can't go swimming now, promise me that you won't,' she says.

'I promise I won't go swimming today,' I tell her.

'You've just recovered from pneumonia, you can't go tomorrow either,' Sigrid says. 'It'll be a long time before you can go again, Mum,' she continues, more gently this time.

She hangs up. Our conversations these days are so frequent and brief that they're more reminiscent of text messages, we rarely say goodbye before hanging up, we both understand when the conversation is over. I lie there and gaze out of the bedroom window, the mountainside is beginning to turn so green up towards the cabin that I can no longer see the roof of it between the trees. I yearn to feel my legs, my thigh muscles on the ascent, my feet on the soft path covered in pine needles, I long to feel the straps of my rucksack on my shoulders, its weight on my back, sweat at my hairline, long to have a hairline to feel sweaty in the first place.

I almost can't bear to look at the water, the way the wind sends small, inviting ripples across its surface, it glitters and calls out to me in the morning light, come on, Gustav shouts. It feels like a betrayal to him, not swimming. I'm left gasping for air when I realise that I'll never again dive from the jetty, my entire understanding of the future becomes focused in the idea of this dive, I play it out over and over again in my mind as I lie there in bed, the feeling of the water as it envelops my body, the rushing in my ears, inhaling just above the surface, pulling air deep down into a healthy set of lungs.

I feel dizzy, grasp the phone, call Sigrid back without thinking, but I can't speak when I hear her voice.

'Mum?' she says gently after a few seconds.

'I'm not going to be any good at all this,' I say eventually, hear how shrill and angry and critical my voice sounds.

Sigrid is silent, but I can hear her breathing, the rhythm of it, irritable and impatient. Bored. It stokes everything already smouldering and aching within me.

'I'm not going to be able to set my expectations to one side, Sigrid, and I don't want to make the most of the time I have left,'

I shout, my efforts leave me gasping for air. 'I don't want to juggle grandchildren alongside my aches and pains, or morphine with my baking duties, I can't do it, I can't face it.'

I throw trousers and jumpers into my suitcase at random, under-wear and socks, enough to last me a few weeks, find ski boots and trainers, late Easter is an impossible season for packing lightly or sensibly. Without thinking I write a message to Mum, ask if the conditions are right for skiing. I regret it the moment I press send. The usual chaos of packing for Easter with Viljar and Aslak has momentarily erased the knowledge that I'm not packing for any ordinary Easter, it's erased the fear of what will greet us, what will greet *me*.

I pull out my black dress, hesitate before placing it on top of the items in my case. I remove it. Put it back. Take it out and hang it up in my wardrobe, close the sliding door. Check my phone, Mum hasn't replied. I place the dress back inside, close the suit-case.

Aslak is sitting in the car on the driveway, Viljar strapped into his car seat, already engrossed in his iPad. Aslak has left the engine running, he's trying to make a point, I'm surprised that he dares given that Mia is due to join us, but he's toughened up in her pres-ence since Christmas, perhaps especially so after finding out that I'd met up with Jens.

Why didn't I tell him, I thought to myself when he confronted me a few days after I'd been, I had no good reason. It's become more difficult to come up with reasonable explanations for my own actions, thoughts, opinions. Not because I'd otherwise never have hidden anything or lied to Aslak – his romantic notions about our relationship are a kind of lie in their own right, or an exaggeration at the very least – but because I can't compose myself, can't find my footing. My foundations are growing increasingly indistinct, unimportant.

Aslak was genuinely angry for once. Why are you so angry? I asked, I had to talk to him, he was telling Mia all sorts about Mum, God knows what else he says to her. You know he advised her to get a sick note when she hurt her ankle back in January, I continued, rolling my eyes. Aslak refused to take the bait. That's a straw man if ever I've heard one, I couldn't care less what he says to Mia, he said, but that's not true, and I realised this is one of the reasons he almost never loses his temper, he knows how stupid and illogical he becomes during any confrontation. You couldn't care less what he says to Mia? I repeated, seizing the moment, banking some time. Obviously that's not what I mean, Aslak replied, but that's not the point, the point is that you didn't tell me you were going to see him. That's because it wasn't important, I said, and fortunately I managed to stop myself before telling him that it had nothing to do with him. Are you alone in being allowed to decide what's important? What about me? No, of course not, but I thought it best not to involve you, for your own sake more than anything else. For *my* sake, he repeated, raising his voice, so it was for *my* sake that you decided to meet up with Jens to discuss Mia without telling me, without involving me. How do you think that makes me feel? he shouted, I can't remember ever seeing him like this, he was shaking.

There are queues of traffic winding their way out of the city, Aslak has decided to drive via Kongsberg to save time, but it takes us an hour and a half just to make it to Asker. Viljar has already polished off the sandwiches that I'd imagined he might have held off eating until we made it to Nesbyen, at the very least, and he's managed to drink almost an entire litre of juice. Now he needs a wee. Aslak sighs with irritation.

'Couldn't you have kept an eye on him a bit?' he asks, looking at Mia in the rear-view mirror, who's sitting beside Viljar in the back seat.

'An eye on what?' Mia asks, surprised.

She and I both look at Aslak.

'On your brother, he's managed to down a litre of juice without you even noticing,' Aslak replies.

'Sorry, but I didn't realise there were rules about how much Viljar was supposed to drink,' Mia replies, she's not angry, she seems surprised more than anything.

'You're allowed to engage your brain, rather than spending the entire journey glued to your bloody phone,' Aslak replies, craning his neck to see how far we are from the top of the hill, it's going to take us at least half an hour in this slow-moving traffic.

'She can't control how much he drinks, Aslak. It was my fault, I shouldn't have given him the whole bottle,' I say.

'Why are you defending her, she needs to take some responsibility every now and then,' Aslak says loudly. 'She's an adult, after all, she can think for herself,' he adds.

'I need a wee wee!' Viljar shouts.

'What the fuck is that supposed to mean?' Mia says to Aslak. 'He's your child, keep an eye on him yourself.'

Aslak falls silent. Mia falls silent. In the queue beside us is a Volvo with a ski box on the roof, an older couple are sitting in the front seats, both wearing white woolly jumpers and no doubt clad in matching suede breeches, they look as if they're singing along to something on the radio, laughing at themselves and each other. I long to be in the back seat of their car.

'I need a wee wee, now, now, now!' Viljar shouts again.

Aslak pulls the car into the hard shoulder and hits the hazard lights.

'There,' he says, looking over at me, throwing out one arm, 'knock yourself out.'

Once we've passed Lærdal, I call Mum to tell her where we are. No answer. I turn around and take a Snapchat picture of Mia and Viljar, both fast asleep, Mia with her head against his child seat. Their faces are dimly lit by the film still running on Viljar's iPad. I type *Lærdal*. Smiley face. Delete the smiley face. Send.

She looks like she's at death's door, Magnus said when he called from the hospital a few weeks ago, after Mum was admitted with pneumonia. But the doctors reckon she'll rally, he added. Honestly, you can't let her clean the house in her condition, Magnus, I shouted after she'd told me that she'd gone over the place from top to bottom before the community nurse turned up, in spite of the fact she could barely breathe at the time. How was I supposed to stop her? You know what she's like, Magnus replied. But how could you leave her when she was feeling as bad as she was? I said, my voice still loud, unrestrained. She didn't seem that bad to me, she said she felt OK, she managed the cleaning, for God's sake, I had no idea how bad it was until I got the call to say she'd been admitted, he replied. Silence fell for a few moments. It's bloody unfair for you to lay the blame at *my* door, Sigrid, it's not like *you* were here at the time, not like you've been here at all, he said, then hung up.

Even though I've witnessed more similar situations than I can count involving cancer patients moving from the point of diagnosis to death, and even though I know how strikingly and ruthlessly quickly things can unfold, how people can appear to deteriorate overnight, particularly after receiving news of any cancer having spread, it still surprises me that the same thing should happen to Mum. I've known it since November, I thought I was without hope, but the feeling I had when she told me the cancer had spread to her lungs revealed the fact that actually I'd been filled with hope. Filled with denial, at the very least. Were you really so surprised, you said yourself it was going to be the case, Aslak said when I told him. I was surprised, shocked, furious, that she should simply be one of many, a statistic, any old patient.

I'm dreading seeing her. Being at a distance, keeping myself at a distance, has made it possible to picture Mum as she's always looked, in her blue Viking boots, her yellow coat, her long, thick hair looped into a bun, always moving, swimming, walking, washing, weeding. She's stopped sending selfies to Mia and me. Mia taught her how to use Snapchat two years ago, they sat to-gether on the sofa at our house, Mum with her glasses perched on the end of her nose. And the picture disappears straight away? she asked. Yeah, that's the whole point, Mia said. Clever, Mum replied. Ever since then, pictures of her and Dad and Kant and the cabin and the house and the hens have streamed in, indiscriminate and unfiltered, occasionally it's been impossible to understand what she might think we'd gain from seeing them, but since she only has Aslak, Mia and myself on her contact list, I haven't bothered to ask. Now I miss waking up to five different views of the water and the mountains and her morning swim, selfies of Mum looking hale and hearty, red-cheeked, her hair wet.

I'm used to missing Mum, I've spent long periods of my life missing her, but the sense of longing that has flourished within me over these past few months has been unmanageable, it's popped up out of nowhere when I've been looking at Mia's face or cuddling Viljar or arguing with Aslak or seething about Jens.

I try calling her once again.

'Mum isn't picking up,' I tell Aslak after trying her for a third time.

'She never picks up,' he replies.

'She always picks up when I call,' Mia says from the back seat.

'Things are a bit up and down between us,' I say.

'Great, there's your answer, then, you try her, Mia,' Aslak says, 'since she always picks up when you call.'

Mia goes quiet. I'd rather not encourage any discord between them by picking a side, but my unease at Mum failing to pick up is making me feel queasy, I can't shake images of her body lying at the bottom of the stairs, on the bathroom floor, in the garden, can't keep them at a rational arm's length any longer. I turn to face Mia.

'Would you mind trying?' I ask, smiling at her.

For a moment, Mia looks as if she wants to object, but she sees something when she looks at me, something in my expression, and instead she nods. She puts the phone on loud speaker. I hear the click before Mum's answerphone kicks in, you've reached Anne's voicemail, I can't get to the phone right now.

Frida has just nursed her baby for the first time. I'd have felt all the happier about the picture, the calm pride in Frida's expression, had the anxiety over Mum's lack of contact not reared its ugly head. Aslak and Mia look at me as they hear the beep signalling an incoming message. I shake my head.

'Just a patient,' I say.

'Sending you messages at ten o'clock at night over the Easter holiday?' Aslak says, his suspicion is new, too.

I turn my screen to face him, show him the picture of Frida.

'Let me see,' Mia says, I show her the picture from a distance. 'Why is she sending you that?'

'Because I'm her doctor,' I reply.

'That's not exactly normal,' Mia says. 'Dad says you should never give your phone number to your patients, you'll never get a moment's peace.'

Aslak stares ahead of him.

'Well, the difference here is that Jens doesn't have patients, he has *clients*,' I reply, turning to look at the road, consider placing my hand on Aslak's where it rests on the gear stick, but I don't dare.

I decide to give Mum ten minutes to call back before ringing Magnus. I try to breathe calmly. I zoom in on the picture of Frida, she's pale and sweaty with big, dark circles under her eyes, but still she looks better than she has in a long time. The last time I saw her was four days ago, by that point she was so tired of being pregnant that she barely had the strength to uphold her ever-shifting outward sense of self. And maybe, just maybe, I've thought to myself, and I think it now too, gazing at the tiny, downy head peeping out of the pink blanket, maybe there's room for me to dare to hope that something in her will change with this new responsibility for a little life.

13

Gustav lost his voice mid-shout. He was standing at the top of the stairs, bellowing at me as I walked away from him, as he used to do several times a day back then, always with a fresh stream of curse words that I had no idea were in his vocabulary. I stopped at the bottom of the stairs as he fell silent mid-sentence. Heard him attempt to start anew, but the sounds, when they did emerge, were foreign, unintelligible, like pig Latin.

I wrote him a letter, sitting in the hospital in the corridor outside his room after watching the realisation dawn on him that words were no longer available to him, seeing the effort and despair whenever he tried to speak, the muscles that tensed at his throat and jawline – his wild eyes, the acknowledgement that he was trapped within his own body. I was still angry. So furious and exhausted that I thought it served him right, that it was what he deserved for allowing himself to surrender, to yield, to disappear.

I burn the letter I wrote him that evening, which he never received and which I haven't read since. I have a feeling that there must be more I should burn, but I can't think what – all the other paper-work in my desk is formal and unsentimental, bills and contracts and a few newspaper clippings from when Gustav led the protests against the development of cabins north of the water. A few letters and postcards from friends. Lists of Gustav's medication that I feel might be useful for Magnus and Sigrid to have if they should be faced with any questions from the nursing home, and which I leave in an obvious place on the kitchen table. I stand there for a moment, the palms of my hands on the table as I support myself there, staring at a greasy mark on one of the sheets of paper, it could be anything, could have been left there by anyone, Gustav, Sigrid, Magnus; I stroke the mark before heading up into the attic, checking the window is closed. I empty the bathroom and kitchen bins.

I call for Kant, put on his lead, my hands are shaking, I do my best not to catch his eye, drop him off with the neighbour. I lock the door for the first time in what must be two years, leave the key in Gustav's old boot. I sit in the car and fasten my seatbelt without thinking, turn out of the driveway, see a flash of March sunlight reflected in the window of Sigrid's old room.

14

I stand in a cold hospital room, so afraid I can't move. I look out of the window, my back to Mum. I recognise that hospital smell, so safe and familiar to me since the early days of my studies, but which now leaves me feeling sick, angered, scared, Mum lying in the bed behind me looking pale and weak.

Nobody would call an unsuccessful suicide attempt by a sixty-seven-year-old cancer patient a cry for help. Cries for help are reserved for the young, those looking for someone else to take the reins, to give them direction and help anchor them in the world and life in general. Mum doesn't cry, she doesn't say a word. She lies in the hospital bed in silence, just as she has for a fortnight since they discovered her in Thon Hotel in central Bergen.

'If you really wanted to kill yourself, you'd have succeeded. This is just a cry for help, and a terribly self-centred one at that,' I say, regretting the words as soon as they pass my lips, but I'm so scared and furious and overwhelmed by my guilty conscience that I don't know what to say, there's nothing *to* say.

I shouted it all at the top of my voice while alone in the car on my way to the hospital, everything on my mind, speeding to the hospital at 120km an hour, my God, she has to make it, please let her make it, I promise there's so much left to say.

When I opened the door and saw her lying in the hospital bed, thin, pale, bald, silent, something subsided within me, I couldn't utter a single word. I stood there and gazed at her, she was awake but wouldn't look me in the eye. In the car I'd imagined our embrace, felt her body against mine, the smell of her, nothing was more important during that four-mile journey than her at least living long enough to know that it was me, to sense the power and all that had gone unsaid in my embrace.

When I first met the doctor at the hospital, the one who said she was in better shape than I'd imagined she would be – that she was exhausted, but that she would pull through this, as he put it, with an emphasis on the *this* – I felt my anger flare up.

'My God, Mum, what were you thinking?' I exclaim when she hasn't answered me after a minute, my voice shaking.

I'm still standing with my back to her, looking out of the window.

'What about Mia,' I shout in the direction of the car park, the sun, the early signs of spring, and what about me, 'what about Viljar?'

When she still says nothing, I turn around and look at her, she's crying.

Before I have a chance to react, Magnus walks through the door, his eyes wide, his face red, he heads straight to Mum's bed and embraces her, holds her long and hard, sobbing at her neck, his broad shoulders shaking as Mum wraps her frail arms around him.

15

'I'd choose April any day,' Magnus says, he steps out onto the terrace in his pyjama bottoms and a wool jumper, squinting up at the sun and at me, stretching, smiling. 'What a gorgeous day.'

I say nothing, lean back against the wall of the house wrapped up in a blanket with a thick, woolly hat pulled over my headscarf. The air is clear and cold, but the brown stained panel behind me absorbs the heat of the sun's rays. I rest my head against it and close my eyes. I've been sitting here for an hour, gazing at the water, the flat calm, I can just about make out the thermometer by the jetty. Magnus sits beside me on the bench, I hear him pick up the newspaper I brought out, he leafs through it impatiently before setting it to one side.

'"In which the aged fall", I murmur after a while, without opening my eyes.

'What's that?' he says.

'"It causes uproar,"' I continue, slowly, quietly.

'What are you talking about?' Magnus asks.

'You were the one who quoted Bjørnson,' I reply, opening my eyes to look at him.

'Oh, I see, was it Bjørnstjerne Bjørnson who chose April?' Magnus asks.

Just how much is his lack of cleaning, literary-history and cooking knowledge my failure, and how much is a result of Gustav's restless genes? Gustav had a selective memory and poor concentration, which he would freely admit to when he came home from the supermarket without milk or potatoes or anything else on the shopping list, I forget things when they're not all that important, he said. They might not be important to you, I said. On the other hand, his ability to dig deep into certain subjects was out of this world, the way he taught himself entire piano sonatas by heart on the old piano without being able to read music, or vanished for an entire spring to cultivate Shetland cabbage and tomatoes behind the barn. I'm sure that his brain is wired differently to most, filled with unusual and divergent connections. I probably ought to donate it for research purposes when he dies, I've thought to myself.

'You know I want to be cremated,' I say to Magnus. 'God help you if you two have me buried.'

I'm pushing the boundaries, but I can't help myself, it's easier to be defiant than apologetic, more straightforward to run the risk of cold, hard detachment than to face shame and fear.

I know we've agreed not to talk about illness and death and burials before Viljar has gone to bed, but Sigrid has taken him into the garden to prune the apple trees, she's keeping him as far as she possibly can from me, she doesn't trust me. I understand that; I don't trust myself.

'Do you mind not talking about these things,' Magnus says. 'Please.'

'I'm just saying,' I reply.

'Did you see that article I left on the kitchen table,' she says. 'On immunotherapy, it's very promising.'

'There wasn't an article on the kitchen table this morning that I saw,' I say.

Silence falls, we watch Sigrid, the way she maims the apple trees, slicing off new growth with efficiency, determination. The trees look naked and deformed, she's safeguarding herself against having to come here and harvest apples this autumn, I think to myself. This autumn.

❖

We need to be able to talk about this, Mum, Magnus said on Easter Monday. He, Sigrid and I were sitting in the living room, the others were visiting Aslak's parents, no doubt under Sigrid's orders, and now she was sitting in Gustav's old wing chair, her arms crossed, avoiding eye contact with me. I understand that you feel a sense of despair, that things feel hopeless, Magnus said, but my God, Mum, what were you thinking? I couldn't answer, couldn't even look at him – it would have been so much easier for them to accept the fact that I had died, cleanly and efficiently, the whole affair over and done with, than to deal with a messy, unsuccessful suicide attempt. I wanted to tell them that I'd done it for them, so they wouldn't have to watch me wither away before their eyes, to feel as though they had to take care of me, to show up, for one year, two maybe, three, five, to witness me becoming more feeble, more demanding, more insistent.

Sorry, I whispered eventually, there was nothing else to say, it was out of the question that I should try to explain – Sigrid would call me egotistic, self-centred, what about *them*, as she said at the hospital, did I think *my* pain was the only valid consideration, the only thing that mattered?

No, Sigrid said loudly in the living room, that's not good enough, Mum, she continued. How could you? she shouted, slamming her fist against the wall. She stopped, turned around and left the room. Magnus followed her. I sat there, alone once again, breathless as I reflected on everything she hadn't said. How could you, and yes, how the hell *could* I, after my never-ending failures and absences, opt to disappear without a word, how could I choose the ultimate betrayal?

We need to draw up some rules, Magnus said the following day. You need to promise not to hurt yourself, he said, you have to promise to call us if you start thinking like that. Fine, I promise to call you both before I kill myself, I replied, then smiled, tried to lighten the mood. He stared at me. Sigrid had left this conversation to him, and I missed her part in it, missed her insistence on the same thing, that she might look me in the eye and beg me to choose life, choose life, choose to be part of *her* life. But I realised then that I'd destroyed more between us than any time left would allow us to repair. I've apologised, Magnus, and I promise not to kill myself, I said eventually, louder and more firmly than I'd intended.

Sigrid and Viljar join us on the terrace.

'I'm going to visit Dad,' Sigrid says, she hasn't been since she came home. 'Can Viljar stay here with you until Aslak gets back?' she asks Magnus.

'Of course he can stay with us,' I say.

Sigrid says nothing.

'Of course,' Magnus said, 'are you hungry, Viljar? Shall we make some breakfast?'

'I want Grandma to make breakfast,' Viljar says, running at me in his orange winter boots, letting himself fall once he's practically in my lap, so confident that I'll catch him.

Sigrid and Magnus exchange glances, quick and customary, doing their best not to let me see them, but my God, I made them both. I almost start laughing, they're so obvious, like children, but I say nothing, pull Viljar up onto my knee, my back aches from the effort.

'No, you and I can make breakfast,' Magnus says quickly. 'How about pancakes?'

Viljar abandons me without a moment's hesitation at the mention of pancakes, he wriggles free, jumps up into Magnus's arms. Magnus throws him up in the air before carrying him into the kitchen. He ought to have a child of his own, I once said to Sigrid many years ago now, she and I sitting in the kitchen and watching Magnus creating ski jumps for Mia on the slope leading down towards the water's edge. A child would do him good now, at the very least, or a girlfriend, a buffer of some sort to cushion him from everything to come. When they were teenagers, Sigrid often teased Magnus about his non-existent love life or secret girl-friend, the fact that he must be hiding her, or him, away from us. Magnus only ever responded once, suggesting that the opposite was true. At some point in time after Sigrid became a doctor, an understanding was formed – between them, or perhaps simply on Sigrid's part – that Magnus has issues when it comes to forming attachments, which she mentioned over breakfast once as she passed me the bread basket, she refused to let it go before I locked eyes with her.

Sigrid gets up, heads for the stairs leading down to the garage. The thought of what she might say to Gustav scares me, every-thing she could tell him about me. I recall the night I sat on the stairs outside Gustav's room and heard her telling him how she couldn't face dealing with me any longer, how self-centred and unreasonable I was, how much she missed him.

'Sigrid,' I say, she stops and turns around, 'please don't say any-thing to Gustav.'

She looks as if she's weighing things up, she stands there for a moment.

'Of course,' she says, I think she's smiling, but the light is so strong that I can't be sure.

Magnus returns to Stavanger the Sunday after Easter, Sigrid and the family are staying for a few more days. Nobody asked me, I've lost the right to an opinion on anything. I've been systematised, I haven't objected, I don't have the energy to do so. My back is really aching, I told Sigrid a few days ago, it feels as if it's in my bones, not my muscles. She examined me, her hands cold, practical, but even so, hers was such a welcome touch that I was on the verge of turning around and hugging her tight. She pulled my jumper back down before I had the chance to do so myself, it's your lungs, I should think, she said, you've inflicted an additional burden on your body and now it's expending energy it doesn't have on recovery, so it's hardly surprising that you're in pain.

I've spent almost the entire Easter holiday on the sofa or the sunlounger out on the terrace. Sigrid, often via Mia, frequently asks me to wear an extra scarf, to make sure I've taken my medication, wakes me at mealtimes. Have another potato, Grandma, Mia says. Another carrot, just another small spoonful, you can do it, there's some milk left in your glass. It's more difficult to accept these invitations when they come from Mia, but Sigrid keeps a safe distance, she operates behind the scenes. Whether she intends to punish me or protect me, I can't pretend to know, perhaps she's protecting herself. And Mia.

Mia doesn't know about what happened, Sigrid told me in the car on the way home from the hospital. She thinks you were in with pneumonia again, she continued, not looking at me. Fine, I said. And I don't want her to find out, either, Sigrid said, her voice thick. No, I reply, of course not.

I wondered about leaving a letter for Mia. But it would have been too difficult to leave a letter for one grandchild and not the other, I'd have had to write something for Viljar too, but a suicide note for a four-year-old is an impossible notion – even though I could obviously have written that he should only read it when he was older, but that would be difficult too, since he wouldn't remember a great deal about me when he was sixteen, seventeen, and opening a letter from a grandmother he didn't remember but who'd chosen to take her own life was an absurd idea. Leaving a note for Sigrid and Magnus was out of the question. I know that Sigrid needs an apology from me, she needs me to make amends, but I can't find the words, I don't know how. What about Mia? Sigrid shouted at the hospital. What about you? I'd wanted to shout back at her, what about you, Sigrid, what about you?

I've thought about the fact that an apology to Sigrid has to be sincere, that it has to echo my own thoughts and memories. That the fact she exaggerates things matters, the fact she anchors everything painful, everything in her life that causes her distress, in her childhood. That it matters that so many of her memories paint a distorted picture of me, that it's important to correct those, that I can't offer her an apology without the kind of caveats that ultimately mean it will hold very little value for her. She doesn't remember anything *good*, I told Gustav after Sigrid had confronted me about the waterproofs, she's forgotten all the little things, she's forgotten all about picking apples and watching films together and the way I'd skim the skin off her hot chocolate for her. She's forgotten all the nights I spent lying in her bed after Gustav's first stroke, when she had stomach ache every night for weeks on end and couldn't sleep unless I was tucked up beside her in her narrow bed – all the times I lay back down beside her as she woke up and clung to my arm just as I tried to sneak away.

As I swallowed one tablet after the next with four seconds in between each one in a hotel room in Bergen, I realised that I hadn't prepared myself for the fact that it would take time, that I would have time to think. After taking half of the tablets, I was still sufficiently clear-headed to recognise that I ought to have swallowed my pride, suppressed the need to be correct, that it was ultimately meaningless who was right. Neither of us was right.

Ever since Sigrid picked me up from the hospital, I've tried to recapture that sensation, but whenever I lay eyes on her, it eludes me.

Life remains a vacuum. Every touch, every gaze, every word and colour and smell and sensation hits me differently, filtered through something new, and is either stripped of all sentimentality and emotion, or quite the opposite. Very little resides in the space in between, I might find myself moved by the sight of a white wagtail darting back and forth on the terrace, or suddenly stirred by the smell of manure in the fields. All the while, I have a sense that I'm waiting for something while having missed something else altogether.

She can't have properly thought it through, I heard Aslak say to Sigrid down in the basement sitting room one morning when they thought I was sleeping, I pictured them standing and looking at the heap of rubbish under the stairs, all the things I've amassed over time. He was partly right, if I'd prepared myself sufficiently well then I'd be dead by now.

I didn't think things through well enough, not when it came to Sigrid and Magnus – I simply thought they might be spared all the waiting around, spared having to nurse me until the day I died. I didn't think it would come across as yet another failure, a final confirmation of just how inconsiderate and uncaring I am. After all Sigrid's reproaches, it's difficult to appreciate that she's still waiting for something from me, that she hasn't given up on me.

Suicide isn't always suicide, Magnus, I said during one of our many conversations that Easter, that was as much as I can remember, the last part, I was drowsy and muddled from the morphine and sleeping pills. Magnus had come up when he heard me trying to get up to go to the toilet, he helped me to the bathroom and was sitting on the edge of the bed when I re-emerged. I didn't have the energy to explain what I meant. Yes, it is, Mum, he replied, suicide is suicide.

Over the past week, he's come out with various statements and exclamations intended to make me feel happy to be alive, even Aslak has joined in to a degree, mentioning all sorts of things about the weather and Easter and food, and about Viljar, who's taught himself to play a song on the piano. Look at him, Magnus' expression seemed to say as Viljar turned to face me after gracing us with his version of 'Mary Had a Little Lamb', fit to burst with pride. Look at him, look at everything you could have missed out on, look at us, look at how lovely it is to be here, in this life, even in the face of intense pain and breathing difficulties and the prospect of more of the same until you die, how lovely.

'Could you manage a walk, do you think, Grandma?' Mia asks on the afternoon before they're due to return to Oslo.

I'm lying on the sofa, Sigrid, Aslak and Viljar are visiting Aslak's parents. I overheard the argument in the hallway when they were getting ready to leave, Mia objected to the visit. They've hardly seen you all year, Aslak said loudly. I was there four days ago, Mia replied. For half an hour, sure, do you realise how selfish you're being, Aslak said. I heard Sigrid say something, her voice low and disarming, but I couldn't make it out. They're not *my* family, Mia snapped. Silence fell until I heard the front door bang. Mia climbed the stairs alone, I could only see half her face through the crack in the doorway, she had a hand to her forehead, looking despondent.

'I can certainly try,' I reply, my back hurts so much that the mere idea of moving more than a few metres is painful.

Mia helps me up. She supports me as we make our way into the hallway, finds my coat and scarf, calls for Kant. Slowly we amble along the pathway down towards the water's edge, the sun is beginning to set, it lends the snow still clinging to the mountain peaks a golden glimmer; the air is mild and gentle on my lungs, tinged with the raw scent of spring, yet another spring.

Mia tells me about a new reality television series she's working on, I half follow what she's saying, it takes all my concentration to avoid tripping over, I can't rely upon my nerves or any sense of balance, but that's the medication, Sigrid said, not the cancer.

'So I think I'm going to put off going to university for another year,' Mia says.

'Put off going to university?' I repeat, stopping in my tracks.

'Yes, or maybe study in Oslo instead,' she says.

'But why?' I ask her.

'I just told you, I was offered a new position on the same project. I could study alongside work,' she says, sounding a little too nonchalant.

I feel sad and moved, take her by the arm.

'But you've been making up credits and working so hard to study in England,' I say.

Mia shrugs.

'Look at that,' she says, pointing at Kant, he's running in our direction with a dead hare clamped between his teeth. 'Oh no, God, poor thing, is that a rabbit?'

Sigrid comes into the living room after the others have gone to bed. I'm sitting in the chair in front of the television, watching news I've already seen. She stands and watches for a few minutes, a piece about a mother being reunited with her daughter in a flood-stricken region of East Africa, the rest of their family likely dead following a landslide. I brace myself several times, take a deep breath to say something, but still can't find the words to tell her that I know I've let her down, can't formulate any sentence that is sufficiently nuanced to make space for her while making sense to me.

'How are you feeling?' Sigrid asks, she's perched herself on the edge of the chair in the corner of the room, one leg twitching, she looks nervous.

'Fine,' I reply, turning off the television. 'My back hurts a bit, but it's better today than it was yesterday.'

'So, what's the plan from here on out?' she asks.

I smile. 'The plan?'

'Yes, when's your next round of chemo?'

'I can't recall, a few weeks, I think,' I reply, I've decided to stop the chemotherapy, but I can't tell Sigrid that, not now.

'I'll come back and see you then,' she says.

'You don't need to do that,' I reply.

Sigrid rests her head in her hands, leans forwards. I'm surprised, spend too long simply trying to rise to my feet, my stomach aches. I make my way over to her, sit on the arm of her chair and place my hand on her back, slowly stroke it, she's grown thinner, I can feel her ribs, they judder as she sobs beneath my touch. Neither of us speaks for a few minutes.

'I promise, Sigrid,' I say eventually.

16

As we unload the car, I see that Aslak has brought a small bureau back to Oslo. I lift it out of the boot of the car and set it down on the gravel driveway. I recognise it, even though it looks naked and unfamiliar here compared to when it's in its usual position between Magnus's bedroom and my own, where it's stood for as long as I can remember. I think it belonged to my grandmother, one of many items of furniture left behind when Mum and Dad inherited the farm. Mum is generally indifferent when it comes to interior design matters, the house looks just as it did when Dad fell ill, she hasn't even finished the painting she started in the basement sitting room. She got as far as painting one wall a deep shade of green, but the three remaining walls still have their fibreglass wallcoverings and pine wainscoting. I can't recall her ever buying or moving a single item of furniture or replacing a chair or sofa, the only exception being the day the house was adapted for Dad's wheelchair, when she moved a cupboard in the hallway a metre to the left to make room for the stairlift, leaving it blocking half the doorway leading down to the basement sitting room; even though the local council have since dismantled and removed the stairlift, the cupboard remains where it was left.

'Why did you bring this back?' I ask Aslak when he re-emerges after carrying Viljar and the first load of bags into the house.

'Anne wondered if we wanted it,' he replies.

'And do we?' I ask, try to smile, can't do it.

He says nothing, grabs my suitcase from the boot.

'You can't see what she's doing, can you?' I say.

He doesn't get it until now, I can see it dawn on him as he grabs Mia's bag, he pauses for a fleeting second before slinging it over his shoulder.

'It's just a bureau, Sigrid. I'm going to sand it and oil it, you'll see, it'll come up nicely.'

'That's not the point, Aslak,' I say, louder now. 'You can't go accepting things from Mum, not now, it's like giving her permission to give up.'

'Giving her permission?' Aslak repeats. 'Who exactly does she need permission from?'

He says no more. He picks up my suitcase with one hand, Mia's bag over his shoulder, the bureau in his other hand.

'Would you mind bringing Viljar's water bottle in,' he says as he passes me, still standing by the car, just as I have been since we parked up twenty minutes ago, unable to do anything else. I remain where I am.

Magnus calls me a few days later, he thinks we should take Mum to Germany for a second opinion, as he puts it. He's researched things thoroughly; his tone is just as enthusiastic as it was when he was thirteen years old, regaling me with the details of model airplanes.

'We think we've got the best healthcare system the world has to offer,' he says, 'but when it comes to cancer treatment, we're actually incredibly conservative compared to places like Germany and the US.'

I don't know what to say. As it happens, I needn't say anything, as any pause in Magnus's monologues are short-lived.

'They're much more innovative in Germany, the doctors are free to take advantage of unauthorised methods, they're able to use their own judgement to a much greater extent, and they're more experimental in their approach. I'm being serious, Sigrid, there's no end of alternative treatments that Norwegian doctors

I'd never been on a holiday like it, I'd barely been on holiday at all. We'll celebrate in London, no, Barcelona, he said two days before my birthday. The feeling I had en route to the airport, on my way to another country without having let Mum or Magnus or anyone else know, it was quite possibly the best thing about the entire trip. The rest of the break was dictated by Jens' whims and shifts in mood, but at his highest points he was infectiously joyous and impulsive. I feel my diaphragm jerk softly at the mere memory of the way he looked at me, saw me, even though I know now that he was as high as a kite and saw little more than himself wherever he happened to be looking.

I catch Aslak's eye across the table.

'Listen, I know it's hard to know where you stand when it comes to all this stuff with Jens,' I say.

I can't help but smile when I say his name, surprise even myself.

'He's not the one who leaves me unsure where I stand,' Aslak says.

He looks out of the window.

'No, no, but Mia and Jens, you know,' I reply.

'She's a grown adult, she makes her own decisions,' he says.

'Everyone says that, that she's a grown adult, but she's not, Aslak, not really, she's still a teenager,' I say.

'Everyone?' Aslak says, looking me in the eye, but fortunately at that moment a waiter arrives to pour us more wine, he takes his time, and afterwards we discuss whether or not Viljar needs a pair of football boots to join the kids' football club.

Frida turns up at my office on Monday morning, sits in the waiting room with the pram. It's not until I say her name and see a woman stand up beside her that I realise she's brought her mother with her. I shake her mother's hand and introduce myself. The only likeness they share is around the eyes and mouth, but otherwise they are polar opposites – Frida's mother is dark-haired, short and obese.

'Is it OK if my mum comes in?' Frida asks.

'That's up to you,' I reply.

Frida nods at her mother. I hold the door for them, fetch the extra chair pushed up against the wall. Frida parks the enormous pram in the middle of the room, fumbling slightly with the brake before managing to click it into place. Initially she sits in her usual chair, the one without armrests, but she quickly moves over to the other one when she sees her mother gazing at it with uncertainty, the slightly too narrow armrests.

'Happy belated birthday,' Frida says, smiling and looking at the floor.

I feel unexpectedly pleased, even though it's not surprising in the slightest that Frida has remembered my birthday.

'Thank you, but I should be the one congratulating you,' I say, making my way over to the pram. 'Can I take a look?'

Frida nods. I glance inside the pram, where a chubby baby in a pink hat and pink mittens lies under a pink blanket.

'She's lovely, Frida,' I say. 'I can see you in her,' I continue, even though it's not true.

Her mother chuckles. 'She doesn't look anything like either of us,' she says.

I take a seat at my desk.

'How are you both?' I ask.

Frida is different, she's not on her guard, she doesn't look as if she's constantly listening out for something between the lines of everything I say, not like usual. She seems calm, happy, almost, for the first time since I've known her.

'Things are fine, Mum's helping out a lot,' she replies, glancing at her mother. 'She's living with me for a while, just as an extra pair of hands.'

'That's great,' I say, can't recall all the details about Frida's mother, but know that Frida was removed from her care when she was five years old, and, as far as I know, they haven't had much contact since. 'It's good to have help in the early days.'

'But we wanted to talk to you about social services,' she says. 'I think we can get by without them from here on out.'

Her mother nods beside her.

'I thought we had agreed that you'd accept any help you could get?' I say.

'Yes, but she has me now,' her mother says.

The baby starts to cry. Frida gets up at once and picks her up, her gestures awkward. As she places the baby over her shoulder and goes to fish the blanket out of the pram with her free hand, I'm forced to bite my tongue to avoid blurting out that she needs to watch out for baby's head. Eventually she remembers this herself, catches my eye and smiles quickly as she wraps a hand around her head and neck and sits back down.

'I think it's a good idea having them there for some extra support in these early days. Let's take another look at things in the summer,' I say.

Her mother inhales as if to say something, but fortunately Frida nods.

'Do you want to hold her?' she asks, passing the baby to me.

I feel tears in my eyes as the weight and warmth of the tiny bundle is placed in my arms.

Mia has decided not to move to England to study after all, she's decided to stay in Oslo. Are you staying for Grandma's sake? I asked her when she told me, just over a week after we got back from Mum's. Her moment's hesitation before responding revealed that it wasn't the whole reason, but she nodded, yes, it feels wrong to leave now, she said. I asked no more, felt sure that it was Jens that had tempted her to remain in Oslo. I'd passed her room a few days earlier and had seen her looking up flats she couldn't afford by any means, she'd closed the lid of her laptop when she'd seen me standing in the doorway.

I've tried defending my instinctive resistance to Mia's increasingly close relationship with Jens by reminding myself that he's unstable, unreliable, that he'll leave her or hurt her. Part of me is convinced by it, the idea that I'm trying to protect her. But really, as I told Dad when I visited him over Easter, really I realise that it feels as though she's betraying *me* more than anything, that she's taking his side, that she forgives him. Is that really it? Dad's expression seemed to ask, or are you simply such an awful person, such a bad mother, that you feel jealous of Mia's close relationship with Jens, above all else?

The evening before I'm due to go back and see Mum, I hear Aslak and Mia down in the kitchen, I'm in my bedroom trying to pack, don't know what to take with me this time either, whether I should be preparing myself for an unexpectedly prolonged stay. I'm going alone this time, Aslak's staying here with Viljar, Mia's said she has to work tomorrow and that she's going away for the weekend with a few girlfriends to a cabin somewhere. I only have myself to thank for the fact she no longer tells me if she's going to stay with Jens, but holding back from interrogating her explanations is a challenge.

I haven't told Aslak that Mia has decided against going to England, he's been more encouraging of her studying abroad than I have. The spring she dropped out of high school, he sat with her and counted her credits, and helped her to apply for a place at a sixth form college, you can do it, he said, it'll be good for you to gain a different perspective on life, to experience a bit more of the world now, when you have the chance.

I wonder what she'll look like when she's twenty, Aslak said once when Mia was about three years old, we were sitting on the lawn in front of his house and watching her run around after a ball. And what she'll be like, you know? he continued. At best, I recall feeling ambivalence at his long-term view. When most people hear how Aslak and I got together, the responsibility he took on as a twenty-three-year-old, their voices and faces soften, think of everything he gave up, a friend of mine said, almost his entire young-adult life. Well, he was twenty-three, and it wasn't like he had that much to give up, to be quite honest, I replied laughing, I can't ever resist trying to add some nuance to people's impression of him, mostly because any such nuance is entirely lacking – other than Aslak's own true nuances, though he's never expressed those. I just wanted to be with you, he's replied if I've ever pressed him, is that so hard to understand? But it *is* hard to understand, and even harder to live up to.

I make up my mind to pack lightly, I need to head to the hallway to fetch the small bag in the cupboard there.

As I pass the kitchen doorway, I hear Aslak's voice.

'You're going to regret it, Mia,' he says, I stop, take a step back.

Aslak is standing with his back to me. I can't see Mia, but I can hear that she's sitting at the kitchen table.

'What do you know about it, you've barely left Norway,' Mia replies.

'Precisely,' Aslak says. 'My God, do you realise the kind of op-portunities you have, all the things you can do, how free you are at this point in your life?'

'Yes, free to choose what I want most, and that's to stay and work and maybe do a bit of studying, but here in Oslo,' Mia replies.

'Out of the question,' Aslak said loudly.

'Luckily that's not for you to decide,' Mia says. 'And I don't need your permission, I've got enough people around me who support my decision.'

Aslak slams a cupboard door, stands there.

'People,' he repeats loudly, and he falls silent for a few seconds. 'What's this about?' he asks quietly, more gently now.

I expect Mia to respond scornfully, perhaps in anger, I prepare to move out of the way so she won't storm out and catch sight of me. But then I hear her sniffling a few times. Aslak's back doesn't move.

'I can't leave Mum now,' Mia says, she's crying, 'you know that, not when she's struggling like this.'

There's something meditative about driving alone, in silence, without any radio or other voices, just the sound of the engine and the tyres on the asphalt. I have a tendency to break the speed limit, drive at around 116km per hour in an eighty zone. As long as I don't lose my licence, it's worth paying what it costs to speed, worth it for the feeling of driving to or from something or someone.

On the journey west to Mum's I drive slowly, reluctantly. I'm going to be spending several days alone with her for the first time in years, and I have no idea how things are going to play out, I no longer have the ability to predict or anticipate anything. What would you need to tell your mother if you knew she was going to die? I asked Aslak a few days ago. I don't know, maybe just that I love her, that I'm grateful, he replied. Now you're lying, I said. He shrugged. I can't think, he said, I can't think of anything else it'd be important for her to know. No, but that's not what I'm asking,

I'm asking what *you* would feel the need to say. Why is that any more important than what *she* needs if she's dying, he said. Now you're just trying to make a point, you're not that selfless. The needs of the person who'll go on living are more important than the needs of the person who's dying, they make their escape, I said.

I spend the entire car journey doing my best to think like Aslak. Mum's needs in the period leading up to her death are more important than any need I have for some sort of showdown with her – over Easter I found myself having to turn away from her on a daily basis, to walk away, to keep my distance, not to shake her, not to demand that she feel some pressing need to confess, apologise. It's still difficult to accept the fact that she was willing to leave us behind without having received any form of forgiveness.

It's May, lush green mountainsides and meltwater streams flank the road into the village, it's Mum's time of year, everything is beginning all over again, she says the same thing every year as she stands out on the terrace and looks out across the water or up at the mountains. It's not difficult to get my head around the fear of losing control, of gradually weakening and withering away, suffering with tumours and pain, but it is hard to get my head around the desire or ability to leave all of this behind, every sensation and nuance, to leave *us*, before she absolutely has to.

Mum is sitting on the terrace facing the water when I arrive. The first thing I notice is that she's put on some weight. She's a tad plumper around the jowls, her cheekbones are less pronounced. She's sitting with her back to the sun-drenched wall, wearing a yellow scarf wrapped around her head like some sort of turban, plus a pair of sunglasses I've never seen before and a suede coat that looks new and expensive. I've prepared myself for her looking worse than she did before, that she'd be wiped out by the chemotherapy – and even though the sight of her in this condition tells me that she clearly hasn't had any chemotherapy of late, I feel intuitively, childishly happy to see her looking so fit and well.

'You look like a film star,' I tell her, sitting down beside her. 'New coat?'

'Yes, I ordered it online. And these,' Mum says, pulling the sunglasses with their extravagant Gucci logo down over the bridge of her nose and peering at me over the rim, she smiles. 'Nice, eh?'

'Very nice,' I reply, leaning the back of my head against the wall and closing my eyes.

I carry my bag up to my old room, I haven't slept there in years, Aslak and I always sleep in the basement room with Viljar. The posters Dad bought me are still hanging on the walls, my old schoolbag is still by my desk. The school photo of me in year seven is on the edge of the bookshelf, unframed. I was so happy with that picture, thought I looked pretty, I was so excited to show it to Mum. When I got home with it, she was standing with her back to me doing the washing up, she turned to look at me and smiled as I stepped in the door, I held out the picture. Lovely, she said, glancing at it quickly before turning back to her washing up. Stick it on your shelf and I'll frame it and hang it up for you, she said. It's been lying there facing upwards ever since, but I notice that there's only the faintest gauzy layer of dust covering it.

I sit on the bed, hear Mum clattering pots and pans in the kitchen just below me, ten minutes later I smell garlic frying, and for a want of any other adequate feeling or reaction in the face of the new her, I'm struck with intense pangs of hunger.

'Unni at the off-licence recommended this one,' Mum says,

holding up a bottle of red wine as I step into the kitchen, 'have you tried it?'

I shake my head. Mum has always bought the same French red wine, it costs 120 kroner and she only ever drinks it on Saturdays or public holidays, and always after six o'clock.

'I bought three bottles on the spot,' Mum says. 'Would you mind opening it?'

I take the bottle, find the corkscrew on top of the pile in the drawer. I open the kitchen cupboard, where at least four wine glasses are missing from the shelf, I have to stand on my tiptoes to reach the ones furthest in. Mum is cooking two steaks, I take greedy slurps of my wine as I watch her back, she's moving more quickly and confidently than when I last saw her, surer of herself, steadier on her feet.

She seems restless as we eat, asks me about Viljar and Mia and Aslak, but interrupts almost every answer I give with more questions, constantly getting up to fetch more water, more sauce, salt, pepper, wine. Her nervous gestures give me hope, I brace myself, want to let her take the lead, not to throw around isolated memories and accusations, I'll listen, accept. But I grow impatient after just ten minutes of the same hectic behaviour without her coming anywhere close to uttering a single sentence of any significance. She appears manic compared to when I saw her last, I suddenly realise that she must be high on cortisone, of course.

'Mum, have you stopped chemotherapy?' I ask.

Mum interrupts my question:

17

'Sigrid, I need to ask you a favour,' I say.

'Oh?' Sigrid says. 'What kind of favour?'

It wasn't how I'd planned on initiating the conversation, but my nerves gain the upper hand and the wine has dulled my mind, it's made me imprecise, sloppy, I forget the fact that I can handle less of the stuff than I'm used to, but it also emboldens me.

'Or, not so much a favour, I need your help,' I say.

Sigrid has changed out of the clothes she arrived in; she's wearing the dark-green woolly turtleneck jumper that's been sitting in the wardrobe in her room since she moved out. I remember her back best in that jumper, leaving the kitchen, walking up the stairs, turning the corner down by the main road, framed by dusky light in the garden, climbing into an unfamiliar car or on the back of some moped or other. She's tied her hair up in a loose bun, removed her make-up, she looks young, just like she did when she was nineteen, suddenly it strikes me as so bizarre that I should have two children in their forties, two children approaching middle age.

I've been preparing myself for this conversation with Sigrid. I've planned what I want to say and how I want to say it. I'll start by telling her about my latest check-up. No, there's no cure, the doctor said. As things stand, he added. Do you think such a thing will materialise before I die, I asked. It's impossible to say, research is moving at such a rapid— he began, but I interrupted him. Pace, yes, I said, completing his train of thought, but I was asking for your opinion. He fell silent, thought for a moment. No, I don't think so, not when we consider the progress of your illness and the rate of its spread up until this point, he said. So, continuing with chemotherapy would, in practise, give me, say, two, three, six more months of illness than I otherwise might have, I said. We can't say how many months you have left, with or without chemotherapy, but we do know that it's more *with* the chemotherapy than without it, he replied, as if this ought to be uplifting information.

I've pictured this part of the conversation with Sigrid as being the least problematic, she's a doctor and knows what those extra months will entail, for me, for her and for everyone else involved. I think she'll understand my wish, feel sure that she'll agree. It's the apology that will be the most difficult part, the part I've thought most about and practised most often in advance. To do my best to confirm her version of events throughout our lives, or to at least confirm that I understand her version of events to be just as true and important as my own.

But when I catch Sigrid's eye across the table, her expression so open and childlike, my preparation fades to nothing, and a landslide of buried emotions and thoughts are unleashed, criticisms and defensive attitudes, I can't even hear the sound of my own voice as I say the words:

'I need help to die.'

18

I run down the path towards the water. The mountains are dark against the sky in the May twilight. I take a right just before the jetty, join the gravel path, pick up speed, feel my thighs beginning to sting after just a few hundred metres, my body feels heavy after the half-eaten meal and three glasses of wine, after hearing Mum's question.

I've witnessed the progression of more illnesses with the same outcome than I can count, patients who, when faced with an ailing body and certain death hanging over them, experience a gradually narrowing field of vision, until eventually all they can see is themselves, at which point they enter a terminal state of self-absorption. It's hardly surprising, I told the wife of one dying patient just last year, he doesn't have the energy required to be generous or humane, these things are a luxury. The same goes for empathy, it's a luxury reserved for the healthy among us, I said. Humane? He's not even human, she said, shaking her head, he's downright unreasonable, only ever thinks of himself.

What if we're only ever considerate when it serves a purpose, I remarked to Amir in the break room afterwards, when we want to reproduce or fit in? What if we cast aside all those superfluous traits when we know we're going to die? He shook his head, people are afraid of being alone, *especially* when they're going to die, it serves a purpose if it means you won't die alone. But every man dies alone, I parried; he didn't catch the reference.

There's nothing particularly unique about Mum's selfishness, but it's striking that I thought she'd be an exception, that the process would prompt her to feel some remorse, that it might soften her and lead to self-scrutiny, an apology. I stop on the gravel path, gasping for air, my hands on my knees to support me.

Mum looked me in the eye as she asked me for help to die. She held my gaze, but I looked away, I couldn't maintain eye contact. I'd subconsciously interpreted her anxious gestures and interruptions as the build-up to an entirely different conversation. What exactly are you asking me for, I asked after a long pause. I'm asking for your help, Mum replied, a little louder now. I lifted my gaze and looked at her, she was clutching her wine glass in one hand with her other arm across her chest, resting at a diagonal. She tried to smile, I felt my legs beginning to shake, my diaphragm, my hands, I had to grip my chair to prevent myself from hurrying her demise by throwing my plate or fork or knife at her face.

I couldn't find any way to start saying all that I wanted to say, and there's no end to it, so I got up, calmly made my way to my old bedroom, threw my school photo in the bin, changed into my leggings and trainers and ran out into the brisk spring air.

Summer arrives. I'm sitting outside a café in Paris on a scorching hot day in June, the place is gaudy and noisy, with American flags draped behind the bar. I didn't make it any further than halfway along the Champs-Élysées, but I can just about see the Arc de Triomphe if I turn around and crane my neck to peer past the rack of magnets on the pavement. That will have to do.

There must be something you've always wanted to do, to experience, Erik said. We were sitting in the living room in front of the fire one evening in May, just after Sigrid had left and the cold had set in. Perhaps, I said, felt a faint flicker of hope that an invitation or suggestion to do something together lay behind the statement. Well, it's high time to do something about it, he said, and still I found myself unable to interpret his tone or smile, his hand resting on my thigh; the unbearable physical longing for him to move it further up my inner thigh, that he should want me, yet simultaneously realising that for him, this was simply a caring gesture, a show of pity.

I've never been to Paris, I said. Then you should go to Paris, Erik said firmly, squeezing my thigh in a somewhat fatherly manner before withdrawing his hand and killing any remaining hope that he might see me as he once had, that he might want me as he once had.

He called me two hours before he showed up at my door, asked if I was at home, if he could pop by for a cup of tea. I stood at the window watching for his dark pick-up truck from the moment he called until he pulled up on the driveway, watched every move he made, the fact he sat there for a moment writing a message before grabbing a bouquet of orange tulips from the passenger seat and jumping out of the car, his body so agile, his movements so leisurely, a spring in his step as he landed. He opened the back door, letting out his two Irish setters, clipping leads onto them both and leading them into Gustav's old sheep pen just in front of the barn. Tulips aside, it was like recollecting an era and a body that sent waves of desire and guilt pulsating through me.

After stopping chemotherapy, it took only a few weeks for me to gradually regain the feeling in my body; flashes of sensations and desires long forgotten took me by surprise – watching Erik's hands as he stroked the glossy coat of his largest setter before letting it loose, his long strides as he made his way across the yard, the sound of his strong knuckles as they rapped at the front door.

His expression as I opened the door wasn't the same as it used to be, all the times I'd barely managed to open the door a few inches before he'd squeezed his way inside, greedy and impatient. When he knocked on that day in May, he stood outside politely and waited for me to open the door completely, offering me a serene smile and throwing out his arms to invite me to hug him – if I needed it. I'm not that delicate, I told him as he cautiously wrapped his arms around me. I'd changed three times, I was wearing the blue shirt he'd once ripped in his eagerness to whip it off me, a little extra blush on my cheeks, even though my complexion was almost back to normal. Erik looked me directly in the eye, didn't cast a single glance at my body, I felt his gaze rest somewhere on the back of my head as I led the way upstairs. I caught a glance of myself in the mirror at the top of the stairs, skinny and unfamiliar, pale and wearing too much make-up – the ambivalence I felt between ardent desire and disgust at the sight of my own body raged within me.

The rumour that my condition had deteriorated since seeing

him at Christmas had reached him at his cabin a few kilometres away, in the mountains on the north side of the water – I swam naked there on so many mornings I knew he was staying at his cabin, even long after things ended between us. Something has to have started in order for it to come to an end, I said as he sat on the terrace on the day I could no longer bear the gnawing guilt I felt whenever I thought of Gustav, and we haven't properly started anything, not really, I continued. We'll have to agree to disagree there, he said, we're a long way past the start line. He argued in favour of continuing things with a surprising degree of dedication, and part of me, the small part sitting alone in an American café on the Champs-Élysées, the part that has half-heartedly decided to choose *life* for as long as I have the option to do so, that part of me regrets standing firm, choosing loneliness.

I had a battle on my hands securing a few days to myself in Paris, I'm due to meet the others tomorrow at the airport in Nice. Absolutely no chance, I told Magnus when he suggested that he and I travel to Paris together, what's wrong with you lot? You've all been lecturing me about *joie de vivre* and making the best of the time I have left for months now, what says *joie de vivre* more than spending a few days alone in Paris eating croissants and drinking wine and seeing the Mona Lisa? I continued. I had no desire to travel to Paris, nor to the south of France with Magnus and Sigrid and the rest of the family, but when Magnus suggested that we go away in the summer, all of us together, I had neither the energy nor the heart to object. But I want a few days to myself in Paris first, I said, speaking mostly out of some sort of sense of duty, both to Erik, who had sent me numerous hotel recommendations, all within a cancer patient's manageable walking distance of the most significant sights since his visit in May, and also because I felt I ought to cross off at least some of the famous sights the world has to offer, some of the places that Gustav and I had planned to see together – though now I wasn't sure what I'd been thinking, hatching plans to see something for the first and last time in my life.

I am content with a glimpse of the Arc de Triomphe. Mona Lisa, Notre Dame and the Eiffel Tower are forced to make way for countless glasses of wine in the cool bar of the expensive hotel I booked upon Erik's recommendation. For three days straight, I spend much of my time at a table by the window, concealed behind a large plant, watching people come and go from an expensive clothing boutique across the road, before taking the lift up to my room, where I lie on the bed and watch French television while googling facts about the Louvre – in order to have some sort of response to Sigrid and Magnus's inevitable questions – and the criteria for consenting to assisted suicide in the Netherlands.

Sigrid, Aslak, Viljar, Mia and Magnus are waiting for me in the arrivals hall. They've sent thirteen messages between them since I woke this morning, the last one to inform me that they're waiting for me just outside customs. I've woken up this morning feeling worse, as if there is something lodged in my lungs, something my body wants to force out through violent coughing fits – all to no avail, other than to infuriate my fellow Air France passengers, who initially flash me resigned expressions, and who subsequently begin shushing me in French. I'd forgotten what it feels like to try to suppress the reflex to cough, the choking sensation it brings, and in the end, I gave in and pulled off my wig, exposing my downy, speckled scalp for all to see before coughing and spluttering all the way to Nice.

I haven't put my wig back on, can't be bothered tying a head-scarf in place either, to my surprise I find that I've stopped worrying about the looks others give me, what people must think, and as I stand by the baggage carousel awaiting my suitcase, it strikes me as utterly absurd that I've given more consideration to society's aversion to any sign of other people's illnesses than I have to my own feelings thus far, I've tried to spare those around me the visible, indelicate symptoms that reveal the fact that I'm dying.

Viljar points at me, or possibly at my head, as I enter the arrivals hall, he says something to Aslak. Aslak laughs, Mia flashes a re-signed look in his direction. Magnus smiles when he catches sight of me, Sigrid looks mostly nervous, but the sight of them fills me with a sense of generosity, I breathe more easily with every step I take.

Do you still feel joy? Sigrid asked me on the evening I asked her for help to end my life, after she'd returned from her run. She was wet through and red-faced, but I couldn't work out if that was the result of exertion or tears shed. I sat on the sofa as she stood in the doorway. Do you still feel joy? she repeated, louder this time after I gave no reply. Yes, I'm not depressed, Sigrid, I'm being per-fectly rational. Not all death wishes fit within your set of diagnoses, I said. Do you think everyone would be better off without you around? Sigrid continued. My God, give it a rest, please, don't talk to me as if I were one of your patients, I replied loudly. Isn't that exactly what you've asked to be, Mum, Sigrid replied, one of my patients?

The last time Magnus, Sigrid and I were on holiday together, Gustav was with us too. It was the summer after his second stroke, before language loss took hold. I had decided to drive us to

Lofoten, taking the same route Gustav and I had driven during our first spring together. I had thought the memories would help, that they'd make him stronger, happier. Neither the doctors nor I had given up hope that he might get better to some extent, and my denial filled me with energy and suggestions and ways to help the process along. He stared out of the window all the way to Lofoten, silent and stubborn. I tried in vain to point out places we'd stopped, swinging by the campsite we'd stayed at on the first night of our trip, where we'd sat at a Formica folding table in front of the kiosk and drank beer and eaten chips, and for the first time begun to hint at the prospect of a future together. Look, I said to Gustav, do you remember how many hours we spent sitting there? He shook his head. Of course you do, I insisted. He rolled down the window and lit a cigarette, no, I don't remember, he replied. I refused to give in, stopped by all our old holiday haunts, repeated myself time and time again, you remember this, Gustav, come on, you remember we came here, you remember our tent flooding, and this is where we were stopped by the police, you talked your way out of a speeding ticket, and here, the night we spent here, you remember that. Gustav refused to play along. I can only vaguely remember Sigrid and Magnus on that trip, the tops of their heads in the rear-view mirror.

At the airport Magnus walks over to greet me, hugging me and grabbing my suitcase in one fell swoop. Sigrid remains where she is, bottles of juice and water in both hands, but smiling warmly all the same.

'Where's your hair?' Viljar asks, running towards me.

'Can't you see it?' I reply, trying to lift him up, but he's too heavy, or I'm too weak, I crouch down instead, lean my head in his direction, he carefully rests a hand on top of my head.

'Eugh,' he says, pulling it back.

'Don't say that, Viljar,' Aslak says.

'It's OK,' I say. 'It'll grow out again before too long, now that I'm all done with that awful chemotherapy business,' I add in the slightly over-the-top, child-like tone reserved for Viljar, I hold his gaze, he nods with a degree of uncertainty at the message that was never intended for him.

Both Sigrid and Magnus turn away from me simultaneously.

'Now then, we need to get out of this airport,' Magnus says loudly. 'Who fancies a swim?'

We settle into our hotel on the Promenade des Anglais, I've squandered more money on this trip than I've spent over the past year. I'll be paying, of course, even though Sigrid and Magnus both earn far more than I do. They each made their own objections, strikingly half-hearted, no doubt we all thought the same thing, that there was no difference between my money and their inheritance at this point in time.

Sigrid booked the hotel, and without asking planned it such that Mia and I are to share a room. We've shared a room before, on short weekend trips we've taken together, and when she was young and slept in my bed. But now the prospect of an entire week without privacy is impossible, particularly when I consider all the uncontrolled, unfamiliar, painful and ugly aspects of my body these days, everything Mia would be exposed to. I don't dare speak up in reception, simply take the key card Aslak passes me while smiling at Sigrid.

'Oh, look, Grandma,' Mia says when we reach our room, setting her suitcase down and crossing the room to open the double doors onto a balcony looking out to sea.

All I see is the glass wall separating the bath and toilet from the rest of the spacious room, frosted and only vaguely see-through up to waist height. It's hard to imagine anyone, regardless of their relationship, swapping privacy on the loo for a view of the Mediterranean Sea while showering, but I don't have the energy to harbour any irritation at creative interior architects – I realise that I have to find a gentle way to break it to Mia that I need my own space. She stands on the balcony with her back to me, stretches her arms into the air before turning around and coming back inside.

'Oh,' she says, then giggles as she catches sight of the bathroom, glancing at me, still standing there grasping my suitcase.

She thinks for a moment before opening the glass door leading into the bathroom, stepping inside and peering all around the room in an exaggerated fashion before locking eyes with me through the wall, smiling.

'You know what, I think this might be just a tad *too* see-through, would you mind if I asked Mum if I could have my own room?' she says.

I haven't spent more than four days in a row away from Gustav since he moved into the nursing home. Even though I haven't visited him on a daily basis, it's felt necessary to be close by. I call the home and they always respond to my questions with the same friendly, patient tone. I have brief moments when I realise what they must think of me, what everyone must think of me. In the first years after Gustav became dependent on nursing, everyone was filled with admiration over what they called my efforts, my stamina, my bravery and kindness in nursing him at home. Nobody realised that it never felt like a choice, that it was me who clung to him rather than the other way around – but after I eventually moved him into a nursing home, most changed their tune.

Initially I was met with a liberating sense of understanding, as if they were exhaling with relief on my behalf, but after that there came a sense of expectation, I still don't understand quite what about, perhaps the fact that I would finally have the freedom to live my own life, as my sister put it. When I've continued to be so completely absorbed by Gustav, refusing to let go and free myself, when I've visited as often as possible, continued my dialogue with him and about him, when I've become involved in conversations about his care, when I've called on an almost daily basis to make sure they've shaved and showered him, cut his nails, chased up on everything I've feared they'd neglect, I'm met evermore frequently with disparaging amazement, impatience.

Mia has left to organise her own room, and I lie down on the bed, exhausted by the day before the clock has even struck three. I hear a knock at the door, take a long time getting up, glance at my phone only to see that an hour has passed since I first lay down, no sense of the time that has elapsed.

'You were lucky, they only had one room left,' Sigrid says, looking impatient when I open the door.

She looks as if she regrets her tone.

'Hopeless bathroom,' she adds with a smile. 'Is it OK for you?'

I nod. 'Do you want to come in?'

She hesitates.

'I'm just heading down to meet the others on the beach, actually,' she says, glancing at the time. 'Don't you want to join us? Aslak has reserved us sunbeds with parasols.'

Sigrid and I haven't properly spoken since she stayed with me in May, even though she's called me and sent messages on an almost daily basis. The morning she was due to leave, she came up to my room before I'd got up. Do you know what exactly you're asking for? she asked. I do, I replied. So, what *are* you asking for, then? she continued. I'm asking you for help, I replied. I got that much, but to do *what* exactly? Sigrid asked. Are you asking me to write you a prescription for a big load of tablets, so you can overdose again? Do you want me to inject you with something? Smother you with a pillow? What the hell is it you think you're asking me to do? she continued. In several US states, terminally ill patients can be prescribed tablets to take when it suits them, I replied. So you thought that I, as your daughter, could send a prescription to your local pharmacy so you could go and pick up a deadly cocktail of pills, just like that? I don't know, that's why I'm asking for your help, I replied, the whole conversation was going wrong, it felt absurd, as if our voices were ringing out from the top of our throats, no echo of emotion in our words, so different from how I'd imagined things. I'd felt sure she would show some reaction to my words, but first and foremost I'd pictured an accepting sense of grief, that I would comfort her, reassure her, that together, after several conversations, we'd both reach the conclusion that this was best for us both, for us all, the least painful way forward. Will you at least think about it, I said to her in the bedroom. She stared at me. Then she nodded slowly. I'll think about it, if you promise to try to think about anyone but yourself in return, think of Mia and Viljar, think of Magnus, Sigrid said, then hesitated, leaving herself out.

'Of course, I'll come down to the beach,' I tell her.

20

Nice in early July with a headstrong four-year-old, an unpredict-able nineteen-year-old, a suicidal, cancer-stricken sixty-seven-year-old and numerous criss-crossing, strained relationships between holiday-goers is an exceptionally awful idea.

I think it'll help her to spend time with us outside of the usual framework, Magnus said when he suggested the trip, and after dis-missing experimental treatments in Germany and the US, endless lists of diets, supplements and special acupuncture techniques – as well as a Greek YouTube homeopath who guaranteed promising results – it was finally a suggestion that I could support.

The framework is unusual enough, in any case, the city is hot and teeming with people, sunburnt and overweight Norwegians, Brits and Germans, I haven't heard a single word of French beyond the hotel reception. It's so busy that Mum and I have to walk one behind the other along the promenade, I let her go first and set the pace, follow along behind her, watching her back. I'm struck by fleeting memories of sitting in the yellow bicycle seat on the back of her bike, holding on to her blue coat, her long hair whipping my face.

Fortunately she's covered her head with a thin scarf, as she has done since she lost her hair six months ago – it was deeply un-comfortable seeing her downy scalp at the airport, I felt ill, embarrassed on her behalf, she looked more naked and exposed than she would have done had she turned up in the arrivals hall in the nude. You need to keep your head covered to avoid sunburn, I told her before we left her room. You should, anyway, I added when I caught sight of the little wrinkle at the corner of her mouth. Her neck is sweaty, her back hunched, the straps of her bag look as if they're digging into her shoulders, I come up beside her and remove it without a word, she nods.

'We need to cross here, Mum,' I say as I catch sight of the sign for the beach bar Aslak sent a photo of, just across the road.

We need to cross a busy four-lane road with a central reservation to get to the beach. Mum follows obediently and without a moment's hesitation, apparently without checking whether she's stepping out while the red man is still on show. Instinctively I grab her arm and pull her back before she is mowed down by one of those Hop-on-Hop-off buses.

Magnus has taken Viljar down to the water to paddle, I can just about see them through the mass of exposed flesh up ahead. Aslak is lying on a sunbed in the shade of a parasol, sipping on a beer and typing or playing on his phone, while Mia has pulled her sunbed out into the sun, where she now lies immediately in front of Aslak, topless in a tiny pair of black bikini bottoms. I don't know whether I ought to feel reassured or troubled, whether it's an expression of something secure and familiar, or something beyond my grasp altogether, but either way, Mum beats me to it.

'Honestly, Mia, you can't lie there like that,' she says loudly.

Mia pulls out one of her headphones, turns her head and squints up at us apathetically.

'Look around you, Grandma, everyone sunbathes topless here,' she says.

Aslak keeps his gaze locked on his phone. I feel as if his entire pose radiates something triumphant; that's what you get for being so over the top about Mia and Viljar having a healthy relationship with their own bodies.

Mum says nothing in response, looks at me with a degree of uncertainty, no doubt hesitant to get involved, after previous attempts at concerning herself with my children's upbringing, but on this occasion I nod at her, this is one discussion she's welcome to have with Mia.

I perch myself on the edge of Aslak's sunbed, leave Mia and Mum to get on with things, smile at him. Somehow his chest has already started to turn a tell-tale shade of pink, even beneath the shade of his parasol.

'Hi there,' I say when he looks up.

'Hi,' he says, looking at me.

'Shall I rub some sun cream on your chest? You've caught the sun a little,' I say.

'No, I'm OK,' he says. 'Thanks.'

'OK, but would you mind doing my back?' I ask him, holding the bottle of sun cream up.

He puts down his phone and takes the sun cream. I pull my t-shirt over my head and turn away from him. I can't get enough of looking at your back, Jens told me on one of the first mornings after we'd moved in together, when you lie like that, my God, he said, running a finger lightly from the nape of my neck all the way down my spine, between my shoulder blades, down towards the small of my back, my bum, a touch I can still recall, a touch I *do* still recall, as Aslak rubs his flat palms erratically all over my back; it feels like he's pushing me away.

It was hard work persuading Aslak to join us on this trip. Isn't it better if you and Magnus and Anne go, so you can spend a bit of time together, just the three of you? he said. I couldn't imagine anything less appealing than a trip with Mum and Magnus without Aslak and the children joining us. He was evasive, offered up half-hearted arguments, forced me to spend several days convincing him. Please, I said on the day before I needed to book our tickets, I can't do this without you. I was sitting in the kitchen as he searched for a stripping machine in the cupboard just off the hallway, a door between us. I need you there, I said, he looked around the door at me, what did you just say? he asked, he seemed sincere. I need you, I said.

I haven't told him that Mum asked for my help to end her life. I don't know whether that's in order to protect her or him or myself. The only person I've told is Jens. I sent him a message in the car on the way back from Mum's, texted him one-handed at 110km per hour as I made my way over the mountains. Of course, Sigrid, he replied after five minutes when I asked if we could meet. He seemed to be the only option, the only person I could talk to, the only person who could help me, the only person who could offer any relief.

We met for dinner two evenings later. I told Aslak I was going to meet a friend, immediately regretted failing to give a name, but the lie would only have been more substantial then, and my guilty conscience all the heavier to bear. A friend, Aslak repeated, but he didn't deign to enquire any further than that. I couldn't make eye contact with him before stepping out of the front door, don't know if he watched me leave.

Jens didn't seem surprised that I wanted to see him, he was already seated at a table when I arrived five minutes early, he waved and smiled, I've ordered you a glass of wine, he said as I sat down. I didn't have the energy to reflect on the fact he allowed himself to act so casually in such a situation, so relaxed, not after our previous discussion. I hope you're hungry, he said, passing me a menu. We sat there talking for more than two hours without him once asking why I'd wanted to meet with him in the first place, and without me feeling able to face any talk of Mum.

Do you remember when I tried to fix up that veranda we had? he remarked with a chuckle at one point in our conversation. He

was referring to the decking he'd started work on the spring before
he walked out, and which he never did complete. To think, it's actually possible to take such a casual approach to life, I thought to
myself. You can refuse to allow half-finished verandas and other
memories to assume any greater significance than is strictly necessary, you can simply carry on with your life and drop them into
conversation twenty years later, seemingly unaware and unmoved
by the effect they might have on anyone else. I nodded, started
chuckling, ended up buckled over with laughter.

It's easy to see where Anne's coming from, Jens said eventually,
after two hours and several glasses of wine, when I'd finally told
him about Mum, I think I'd do the same if those were my chances.
But you wouldn't ask your own daughter ... you wouldn't ask Mia
to take your life, I replied, forgetting for a moment that I should
avoid nurturing any paternal feelings on his part. No, maybe not,
he said, but still, who else are you supposed to ask when it comes
to something like that? She's just so selfish, I said, as always, I
added.

I'd never have dared to call Mum selfish in the presence of
anyone other than Jens – everyone who knows her has seen how
self-sacrificing she is, they've seen her pushing Dad's wheelchair
on the way to the supermarket, the school, the cinema, they've
seen her stop and tuck his blanket around him, wipe his face,
they've seen her wheeling him along while talking and laughing,
all while Dad has stared into the distance, they've seen her stroke
his cheek, kiss the back of his head. They know that she cared for
him at home until it became irresponsible not to provide him with
continuous medical supervision, they've seen her love him uncon-
ditionally, then and now.

She seems totally brainwashed, Jens said after we'd been together for six months, he was the first and only person to see
things through my eyes, my narrative, I embraced him instinc-

tively as he uttered the words, guilt and relief clashing within me, pressed myself against him, couldn't get close enough. He noticed the sense of surrender in my reaction, and in the years that followed he continued to offer nuance to people's image of her, never overstepping the mark, expressing more than enough sympathy for her as he gradually granted me long-awaited validation of my explanations and experiences.

Sitting together over dinner a few weeks ago, I'd felt the same yearning. Of course it's selfish, Jens replied, she hasn't given any thought to what this would mean for you, for your feelings, but then that's always been the case, he continued. I felt a familiar relaxation of my neck muscles, even though I've no idea what it actually means for me and my feelings, I haven't been able to bring myself to think things through from start to finish, my thoughts and emotions come to an abrupt halt, faltering and retreating whenever I try to imagine helping Mum to end her life.

It's an impossible dilemma, Sigrid, I can see that, Jens said. I didn't catch what he said at first. Dilemma? I repeated.

'Don't you think Grandma seems better?' Mia says.

She and I are sitting on the balcony of her room before heading out for dinner. We're sharing a bottle of rosé, it still feels odd drinking with her, even though we've done it plenty of times over the past year. Too many times, if you ask Aslak, you're plying her with the stuff, you don't need to pass on your own bad habits, he said when Mia and I had spent much of one Wednesday night at the end of May sitting up together.

'She's in good shape at the moment, but it'll pass, just like we talked about, it's because she's not having any more chemotherapy for the time being,' I reply, can't face any more talk of Mum, I feel exhausted by anything to do with her, the fact that she invades every sphere, takes up every inch of available space.

Mia's phone rings, she reaches over to check the screen, rejects the call without answering. Smiles at me.

'It was just Filip,' she says.

'Filip?' I reply, I don't believe her, Mia is as bad a liar as Aslak, her eyes flit from side to side in the same way his do.

'I've told you about Filip,' she says.

'I don't think so,' I say.

'I did, I told you over a month ago I'd met a guy called Filip, the one who's moving to the States this autumn,' she says.

I try trawling my memory for any trace of the conversation but can't recall a thing, can't remember Mia saying anything about a new boyfriend.

'Oh yes, I remember, of course,' I say. 'But don't you want to talk to him?'

When Mia was in seventh grade, she became utterly infatuated with a boy in her class, and I started to worry that she was like me, that she'd inherited my tendency to become besotted, as I had been with Jens. Over the next few years she drifted in and out of several unsettled relationships in a carefree manner, and I became more concerned that she was actually like Jens, that she'd inherited his irresponsible inability to connect to others.

'Well, sure, but I don't need to talk to him right this minute, I just want to sit with you for now,' Mia says with a shrug, and regardless of whether she talks about Jens or Filip, I feel happiness permeate every inch of me.

We've agreed to meet by reception at seven. Mia and I are wearing similar summer dresses, but in different shades, bought in Italy the previous year. She was the first to catch sight of it in the window and went in to try it on. You look beautiful, you almost make me want one, I said when she emerged from the changing room to show it off. Try it on, Mia said. I promise I won't wear it at the same time you do, I said as I paid for them both. Mia just shrugged, it doesn't matter, she said.

Mum still hasn't appeared by ten past seven. I'm too tipsy and lightheaded to feel any concern, even when she fails to answer Magnus's calls.

'I think you should go and get her,' Aslak says eventually, he seems more worried than Magnus and me.

Magnus makes for the lift, stopping before he reaches the doors and turning around before making his way back in our direction.

'Can you come with me?' he asks me, his voice low.

Mum opens the door with surprising speed. She's wearing the hotel dressing gown and a pair of slippers, nothing on her head, and is holding a glass of wine in one hand, her gaze steady.

'Aren't you ready?' Magnus says.

'Do you know, I'm a bit too tired to go out this evening,' Mum says, 'I think I'll just stay here and order room service.'

'You don't really mean that,' Magnus says, looking at me, but I've got nothing to offer.

'I certainly do, but have a lovely time, we'll see each other in the morning,' Mum says breezily, then closes the door in our faces.

Both Magnus and I stand there for a moment without saying anything, before turning around and heading to the lift.

Dinner is cut abruptly short by Viljar. It ought to come as no surprise that he's far too tired for a meal out after the long journey here followed by several hours on the beach, I had tried explaining as much to Aslak before we left. He can nap for an hour now, Aslak said, nodding at Viljar, who was lying flat out in the middle of the double bed, where I guess and hope that he'll spend every night of this holiday.

Viljar finishes his chips in a few short minutes and is impatient and restless even before the rest of us have been served our main dishes. Aslak is initially determined to prove to me that bringing him out like this wasn't an error of judgment, set on demonstrating that we can be as refined and cosmopolitan as he thinks I want us to be. At first he does his best to entertain Viljar, and thereafter to ignore him, but when Viljar eventually collapses in a heap on the floor, face down on tiles sticky with grease and salt and other people's leftovers after a long day of tourists filing in and out of the premises, Aslak picks him up and sits him on his lap, passing him his mobile phone without looking over at me. He eats quickly and returns to the hotel with Viljar as I'm still making my way through my pan-fried sea bream.

'I think I'll head off too,' Mia says after dinner.

'Head off where, exactly?' I ask her.

'I'm going to meet up with a few people I know,' she says.

'You're going to meet up with a few people you know *here*, in Nice?' I ask her. 'Who?'

'A colleague from another department is sailing nearby, we're going to meet at a club down by the old port,' Mia says.

I want to tell her no, that she can't go, primarily because I don't want to be left alone with Magnus and more talk of Mum and the future. But Mia is of age, I can't stand in her way, don't want to ruin things between us, to push her away – and I certainly want to avoid any unnecessary discussions that might fuel what I imagine to be her continuous comparison of Jens and me.

Magnus watches her as she kisses my cheek and skips out of the restaurant in her overly short shorts.

'Oh, to be nineteen again,' he says.

'You were a miserable nineteen-year-old,' I reply with a laugh.

'What do you know about it?' Magnus replies.

I say nothing, realise that I don't know a thing, I've only ever taken it for granted that Magnus at nineteen, and throughout his teenage years for that matter, was having just as bad a time of it as I was, worse perhaps, since I had Jens, at the very least.

'You were so lonely,' I say.

Magnus starts laughing.

'Lonely? That's news to me,' he says.

I grow irritated, convinced that he's putting it on. Even though I don't recall much about Magnus at that time, I do know that he was compulsive and controlled, punctual to the point of obsessiveness, that he'd iron his clothes over and over again, and would exclaim in frustration if he discovered even the tiniest stain on the sleeve of his jumper on the way to catch the school bus; nothing in his life could be left to chance.

'You spent almost every weekend at home alone,' I say.

'Yeah, helping Mum,' he says, shrugging, he doesn't sound accusatory or upset about it. 'Anyway, someone had to be around to pick you up.'

After he passed his driving test, Magnus would collect me in the early hours of the morning, long past when we'd agreed I'd be home. Don't slam the door behind you, he always said when we got back, and I'd slam it aggressively to wake Mum, just so she'd realise she ought to care. Magnus was the one who paid attention, he was the one to set boundaries for me between the ages of twelve and eighteen, he was the one to tell me I had to be home by midnight, and the one to discover when I wasn't.

I say nothing, feel too hot and tipsy to face up to the idea that Magnus and I don't share the same feelings about our upbringings, that he doesn't feel as angry as I do, as despondent, as betrayed.

I split the remainder of the bottle of wine between us.

'Should we call and see how Mum's doing?' he asks after a while.

'No, she'll let us know if she needs anything,' I say.

'She seems much better if you ask me, it's been good for her to get away, to indulge new impulses,' Magnus says.

'It's only because she's stopped the chemotherapy,' I reply. 'It won't last.'

'I'm not sure that's true,' Magnus says.

'Magnus—' I begin.

He interrupts me. 'I know what you're going to say.' He raises his palms to stop me asserting what he believes to be several condescending arguments against alternative medicine. 'But I have to be allowed to believe in something that doesn't necessarily feature in the general practitioner's handbook, I need to be allowed to see things differently to you.'

I nod, even though that wasn't what I'd been planning on saying at all.

'I need to have my own sense of hope,' he adds, swallowing, his eyes shining.

'You're right,' I reply, and he *is* right, and has his own right to hope, and to avoid hearing about Mum's wishes and the anger I feel at him.

21

They're standing around me in a horseshoe shape, I feel like a trapped animal, but it's not triumph or aggression I see in Sigrid and Mia and Aslak and Magnus and Viljar's faces, but surprise.

'I mean it,' I tell them, 'I want to stay here,' I repeat loudly.

We're standing in the hotel lobby, fortunately it's our last day in Nice. Magnus has hired a minivan to drive us further along the coast. We're going to Cannes, Mia said excitedly over breakfast. Nobody's raised the idea with me, it was no doubt decided during one of the many dinners I've steered clear of.

'You've spent almost the whole holiday in the hotel,' Magnus says. 'Won't you come with us?'

The entire horseshoe nods in unison, even Viljar loyally nods along with them, I feel my stress levels increasing with the mounting pressure, step away from them, feel my back against the wall.

'Nobody asked me,' I say.

'It was supposed to be a surprise,' Mia says.

'And who exactly thought that surprises were high on the wish list of a cancer-stricken old woman?' I say, trying my best to smile to conceal my anger, which is threatening to overwhelm me.

'God, Mum,' Sigrid says, trying to wrap an arm around Mia, who pulls away with tears in her eyes before running towards the lift.

I don't have the energy to feel anything but the tiniest sting of guilt, almost imperceptible, when it strikes me that it was, of course, Mia's idea.

'What the hell's wrong with you?' Magnus says before turning around and walking away.

It's the heat. Thirty-six degrees in the shade melts away any sense of self-control, all week I've been surprised by some of the things I've come out with, some of the things I've done, almost every feeling I've had. I've felt endlessly irritated by Viljar, his whining, by Aslak and Sigrid's incessant pedagogical attention and interest, by how impatient Mia can make me feel, her self-centred and individualistic understanding of the world, her lack of any real interests – or how furious I find myself feeling at Sigrid, who has truly perfected the art of pretending as if nothing is amiss.

Aren't you going to say anything, I said yesterday, when I decided to skip yet another dinner. I've spent most of my time holed up here in the hotel, either in my room or in the air-conditioned hotel bar just beyond reception. I realised it on that first day on the beach, that the constant presence and company was too oppressive – the feeling was only intensified by too much skin, even Sigrid and Magnus's half-naked bodies felt invasive and un-relenting. For the fifth evening in a row, Sigrid had come to my hotel room to ask if I wanted to join them for dinner. She was just about to go her own way once again when I took hold of her arm, it was just as surprising for me as it was for her, she flinched. Quickly I let her go. Say something about what? she asked. I said nothing, turned around and headed into my room. Say something about what? she asked again, coming after me. I knew that I was the one who ought to say something, that I ought to tell her that I realised how inconsiderate it was to ask her for help, that out of sheer desperation I hadn't properly grasped what it even was that I was asking her to do, that I felt remorse. But the list of things that required an apology, things that demanded my repentance and which needed making up for, it's too long, it's impossible to strike a balance between the weight of myself and my actions on one hand, and Sigrid's experiences on the other, and I short-circuited, I deferred to defensiveness and thereafter to attack, as I had so many times before. Don't play dumb, I said, you've spent the entire holiday avoiding me. Is that what this behaviour is about, Sigrid said, are you making yet another point? I shook my head; not even I knew what it was all about.

Norway is living and lush and green, it glides by outside the window of the train, I'm relieved to never again be leaving this country. To never again be leaving the huge oak tree in the yard at home, the view of the mountains, the water, the scent of corn and grass from the fields, wood and sheep from the sun-warmed wall of the cowshed, the landscape that has made me who I am, that's shaped me, held me.

We got off at Oslo Central Station, everyone in a noticeably better mood than the last few days in Nice, relieved at the prospect of some time apart. Sigrid gave me a fleeting hug, we'll keep in touch, she said. I raised my arm to wrap it around her, to reciprocate, to hold her tight for a brief moment, but I was too slow, she'd already pulled away, turned to face Aslak. Shall we go, then, she said to him, and I stood there and watched Sigrid, Mia, Aslak and Viljar disappear down the escalator leading to the underground platform before taking a seat on a bench, it took all my might not to fall asleep before my train left, taking me west just half an hour later.

I fetch Kant, take him down to visit Gustav. Sitting in the car, I'm surprised by just how impatient I feel to see him again, I'm filled with an old sense of expectation and enthusiasm as I drive down to the nursing home, feel a familiar pull to be in his presence, close to him.

He's sitting by the window in his wheelchair, in the very same place I left him, he's sleeping with his chin resting on his chest. I stop a few metres away, check to see whether his upper body is rising and falling, don't want to risk reaching out only to find his cheek or hand cold to my touch. His head moves visibly with every breath he takes, I step closer and carefully run a finger along the hairline at the nape of his neck.

'Gustav?' I say.

He's always been a light, restless sleeper, I felt fearful on the mornings I woke without him, when he'd left me and our bed in the restless search for sleep somewhere else in the house, on the sofa, in the guest room, on the living-room floor, in the armchair in front of the television. It's not you, he assured me early on, when I was afraid of what sort of sounds I might have come out with or movements I might have made in my deep, unbroken sleep. All the same, he appeared to sleep so much better and more reliably after he fell ill and had to move into the guest room, alarmingly so.

'Gustav,' I repeat, louder this time.

He's snoring lightly, but still doesn't wake.

'Hi, Anne,' a carer says as he appears in the doorway of the communal lounge.

He's new, I've never seen him before, it vexes me that he feels entitled to use my first name so casually all the same.

'I can't wake him,' I say.

'No, we've given him a sedative,' the carer tells me in a neutral tone. 'That'll be why.'

I shake my head. 'A sedative? Why?' I ask.

The carer, whose badge suggests his name is Thomas, smiles at me.

'It's nothing to worry about, Anne, lots of dementia patients feel agitated from time to time,' he says.

I want to punch him.

'I realise that,' I say, 'but we have an explicit agreement that someone here will call me if he becomes agitated.'

'I was told that you were on holiday, not to mention that you're not very well yourself,' he says, giving a shameless nod at the top of my head, 'that we should give you a break.'

I don't feel touched by his consideration, don't feel the slightest hint of gratitude, I look around to see if I can see Janne, the head of the unit. She always comes across as well intentioned and kind, and in her bid to prove just how kind and well intentioned she is, she has decided to break our agreement, to undermine me.

'And for how long has he been *agitated*?' I ask, I'm struggling to control my tone.

Thomas glances down at his watch, his eyes finally flitting from side to side as my voice increases in volume.

'Well, he's been quite distressed for the past two weeks, more or less,' he replies.

Autumn begins. I dive from the jetty, feel the cold, fresh water against my skin, I haven't been swimming for several weeks. I tried bathing in the Mediterranean Sea twice when I was in France, but the lukewarm water repulsed me, its surface oily with sun cream and grease from the various tourists.

Since I stopped poisoning the cells in my body, I've been feeling relatively well. The biggest difference I've noticed is with my breathing – the air feels thick and hard to draw down into my lungs, even the clear air here at home feels thicker than ever before – and then there's the cough that won't budge. What if you have a coughing fit in the water, Sigrid said after one of the three dinners we'd had together in Nice. You swim at home every day, Mia said as we ate, why don't you want to swim here? Do you still bathe every morning? Aslak asked, smiling and looking impressed. Not *every* morning, I said, quickly glancing over at Sigrid, but occasionally. Sigrid cut Viljar's pizza for him, she didn't look at me and said nothing until we were on our way home. You're all alone, totally helpless if anything were to happen, she said. To happen? I replied. Like I said, you could have a seizure, or pain, cramps, you name it, you could drown, she replied, stopping herself all of a sudden, realising perhaps that this conversation, like most others we had, sounded absurd in light of everything that was already said and done.

As I make my fourth stroke out towards the first buoy, the pain on the left side of my abdomen strikes, somewhere I can't remember having felt it before, I try to picture the anatomical model in my classroom, which of my organs is causing the sensation I feel. The cancer has prompted an agonising mapping of my own body, I feel aware of nerves and organs I'd never previously offered a single thought. I swim further out, defying the pain in what I presume to be my spleen, but the lack of air and aches all over leave me weary. I'm forced to flip onto my back just to stay afloat, arms outstretched like the Vitruvian man. The sunlight blinds me, I have to close my eyes, I lose my balance, end up with water in my mouth. I don't remember where it was that I read or heard that drowning is the best way to die, but I do recall an old Faroese folk tale that says those that commit suicide are reincarnated as seals, was that intended as some sort of moral punishment, I wonder, I allow myself to sink.

But the promise I made Sigrid and Magnus weighs more heavily on me than my own body in the water, it fills me with sufficient adrenaline to bring me floundering to the jetty, grasping the ladder, regaining my breath.

❖

Both have kept their distance since our trip to Nice. Now our contact is limited to two text messages a day, almost as if to prove that I'm alive each morning and evening. Magnus has called me a few times, says he wants to come and see me during his free weeks in September. Sigrid hasn't called, hasn't mentioned visiting, but on the one evening I neglected to send her a message by nine o'clock, Mia called me half an hour later.

Shall I save you a lock of hair? my hairdresser asked me when I had my head shaved back in January. No, thank you, I replied as I stared into the distance, into the mirror, past myself and my bare scalp. It'll grow back, I added with a smile. Of course, she replied, but when it was time for me to pay and leave, she placed a little lock of my hair tied with a purple ribbon on the counter top. Just a little inspiration while you wait, she said.

That lock of hair is still lying on top of the chest of drawers. Thick, blonde strands of hair with an unmistakeable reddish tinge. Magnus's hair is the same colour, but it was almost entirely red when he was born, something Mum was sure was the result of a genetic error, red hair symbolised something weak and sickly in her eyes.

My hair has lost any colour, it's growing out grey, almost white. Now it's four centimetres long and, in addition to having become grey and fine, it also stands up on end. You look like a punk, one of my students told me when I met him out and about a few days ago. It's not a particularly good match given your fondness for practicality and comfort, Mia remarked, what with your impressive array of wool and Gore-Tex. I'm surprised that I still care about my appearance, that I catch myself standing in front of the mirror, for instance, trying to do something, anything, with my hair before heading to see the doctor.

'You look good,' he says as we sit together in his office.

I smile.

'You do. Different, but good,' he says.

The last time I was here, just before the summer holiday, I told him I didn't want to attend any more check-ups. It's pointless, other than to track my own decline, I said. It gives us the chance to make sure the time you have left is as good as it possibly can be, he said, but his attempts to persuade me were half-hearted at best, since we both knew that I was right. We compromised on an hour's appointment to be held now, at the end of August, just in order to arrange any further pain relief.

'I'm in pain,' I tell him, I've set aside any ambitions I once had of being a good, long-suffering patient. 'But half the time I don't understand where the pain is coming from or what's actually hurting,' I continue.

'That's quite a common experience when cancer spreads and enlarges, there's less space,' he says.

'Less space? Inside me, you mean?' I ask, the images are unsettling.

'Well yes, when it begins to put pressure on your organs, many nerves are compressed in the process,' he says, touching his own stomach, something about his gesture strikes me as provocative.

'I need more painkillers,' I say.

'Of course,' he says, 'I've already talked it over with Sigrid, we spoke yesterday.'

22

'See, there's another one, Viljar,' Aslak says.

'Don't catch it,' Viljar shouts.

'Look,' Aslak says.

'No,' Viljar wails.

I don't need to open my eyes to know what's happening, I lie there motionless on the warm, smooth coastal rock, count the seconds until Viljar's wet body presses itself against mine. I make it to four before he throws himself upon me where I lie on the towel, I wrap my arms around him in his orange life vest, it smells of the sea and the boathouse.

'It's coming to get you,' Aslak says, making his way up from the water with the afternoon sun on his back, I can only make out his silhouette in the light.

Viljar presses himself closer to me, but I can't decide if he's playing along or genuinely fearful. Aslak stops in front of us, holding a large, dripping wet jellyfish in his right hand. The long tentacles drape down to the ground like a glossy veil. Aslak looks proud, he holds the jellyfish high in the air, as if in triumph.

'Look, Viljar,' Aslak says.

Viljar lies with his back to him, curled up against my chest, refuses to turn around.

'It's not going to do you any harm, look how long the tentacles are,' Aslak says, he refuses to give up.

Viljar still won't turn around. Aslak doesn't look at me, he stands there for a moment looking confused, and only when he eventually turns around and makes his way back to the water's edge do I loosen my grip on Viljar.

❖

Aslak's parents' cabin is located by a campsite a quarter of a mile outside Svinesund. It was here, at the small beach below the smooth, sloping coastal rocks, that Mia first learned to swim fourteen summers ago. Aslak's father walked patiently back and forth with his hand under her tummy for several hours every day, right up until she eventually managed to coordinate the movements of her arms and legs, finally grasping the relationship between forward thrust and buoyancy.

This is the first summer we've come here without Mia. Even though both Aslak and I have given her the choice in previous years, she's always wanted to come with us. You're not a normal teenager, do you know that, Aslak said in the car, laughing on our way here a few years ago when Mia had chosen to join us instead of staying at home alone. My God, if I were seventeen years old and had to decide between a trip to the cabin with my parents and a week at home alone, Aslak continued, and failed to complete his train of thought. Mia just shrugged. I tried not to think about the decisions I made as a seventeen-year-old, decisions I was never confronted about.

I've tried to convince her to come down here with us ever since we got back from France, I've tried bribing her with shopping trips, told her she can bring Filip or a friend, I just can't face it this year, Mum, she replied, it doesn't feel right. I get it, I've said to her, it's just going to feel a little bit emptier without you there this summer, what with everything being the way it is, things with Grandma, you know, I continued, and I hated myself for playing on her guilty conscience. Mia hesitated. Can't you stay at home instead, she said, and let him and Viljar go? For want of any better options when it comes to referring to Aslak, she's simply started using the word *him*, since it would be too conspicuous if she were to begin calling him Aslak and no longer to refer to him as Dad. I'd gladly have stayed at home with Mia, escaped Aslak's clutches, his gaze, I regret convincing him to come to Nice with us, regret my debts to him, great and small.

Mia's absence fills the empty space more than if she'd been here with us, I miss her between Aslak and me, miss her over dinners eaten in silence with Aslak's parents, miss her between me and my own thoughts, between me and my distance to Mum, I miss her.

Frida rings me over and over again. She's called several times a day over the past week. I picked up the first two calls. I just wondered when you'd be back at work, Frida said during our first conversation. I've told you, Frida, we've got an appointment at the end of August, they texted you, I replied. I've lost my phone, Frida replied. But even then, you should call the surgery, I said, you can't call me unless it's an emergency, I continued. No need to get so angry about it, Frida said. I'm not angry, I said as Viljar tugged at the sleeve of my jumper, nagging me to be allowed to download some game or other, he started whinging when I failed to give him the attention he craved. I tried to catch Aslak's eye, he was sitting on the sofa on the iPad, I pointed at Viljar exaggeratedly. Come here, Viljar, Aslak said eventually, without lifting his gaze. Who was that? Frida asked, quick as a flash. Did you hear what I said, Frida? I asked her, ignoring her question. Yes, I heard you, but surely you can just let me know when you'll be back? No, I'm sorry but if you've forgotten when your appointment is, you need to call the surgery and ask them, I said, certain that she hadn't forgotten at all. I'll see you in August, I said, then hung up.

She called me the following day at the same time. I was hungover, I'd spent every evening of the holiday sitting up long after the others had gone to bed, drinking as I used to do years ago, quickly and consistently and without too much thought, focused on a clear goal, that I might feel sufficiently numb and intoxicated to fall asleep without my mind beginning to race. I sent an overly sentimental message to Jens on one of our first nights there, woke up to feel my heart pounding, the rest of the nights I turned my phone off after my fourth glass.

On the second morning that Frida rang, Aslak had opened the door to Viljar's bedroom to wake me at ten, breakfast time, he said, but you really ought to shower and brush your teeth first, he added, leaving the door wide open to make a point. Feeling shame and guilt, I joined Viljar in a game of croquet in the baking heat. I hadn't eaten, I felt sweaty and nauseous and dizzy when Frida called. Nobody's picking up at the surgery, she said. Frida, we agreed yesterday that you wouldn't call me unless it was something serious, I said loudly, impatient and irritated, didn't have it in me to control my tone. But I can't find out when my appointment is, Frida said, beginning to cry. Her tears served only to stir up further feelings of annoyance. Try them again, I replied. Can't you just tell me? Frida said. No, stop it Frida, I don't memorise my appointment list, I said.

I consider blocking her number, but I can't bring myself to do it. I leave the phone to ring, make my way down to the water, dive in from the rocks without hesitation. The water is cool and forgiving, I lie on my back, stretch my arms and legs out and float on the surface.

I think you like my parents more than you like me, Aslak said a few years after we got together. I think you're right, I said. I thought they were boring at first, with their barbecues and nights in front of the TV and bookshelves filled with chinaware instead of books, but that was before I discovered the security to be found in every gaze and gesture and routine, the matching slippers and reclining chairs, the concurring conversations, the way his mother laughed at Mia's every little hiccup, the way she stroked my cheek before she even really knew me.

I still feel flashes of affection for them, perhaps it's gratitude, but this summer I can't help but feel annoyed by the tediousness, the conversations lacking any substance. On several occasions I catch myself thinking that they should have the sense to leave the cabin to Aslak and me sooner rather than later, I feel frustrated that they take it for granted that we'll spend every single summer holiday with them.

'How's Anne today?' Aslak's mother asks once we've made our way back up to the cabin.

She asks me about Mum every day, but Mum hasn't called since we got back from France, she sends brief text messages lacking any punctuation that tell me nothing other than the fact that she's survived another day. Still alive, she wrote yesterday morning. Still alive, she wrote again yesterday evening. Twenty-six degrees, her message first thing today had read.

'About the same as yesterday,' I reply.

'Good to hear,' Aslak's mother replies, 'she's strong to hold out for this long.'

I smile and nod. 'Well, what's the alternative?' I reply.

'What do you mean?' she asks, pausing her washing up, I can barely remember having seen her anywhere but at the sink all week long, the thought of that enrages me too. I look out of the window, down towards the boathouse, where Aslak and his father are leaning over an engine they've been repairing for years, a ridiculous endeavour.

'Holding out for this long,' I say.

She looks uncertain.

'I'm not sure I know what you're getting at,' she says, smiling.

It's obvious that she knows exactly what I'm getting at, but she doesn't understand why I'm asking, why I'm standing with my back to the door, my expression firm, I don't understand it myself.

'You said Mum's tough, holding out for this long,' I said, 'but what alternative do you see to holding out?'

'Well, giving up, I suppose,' she replies with a slight chuckle.

Nothing in me is appeased by her laughter, by her eyes flitting back and forth in her round face. Quite the contrary.

'Giving up? What does that mean, exactly? Dying?'

She says nothing, looks genuinely despondent.

'Do you really think she has any choice in the matter? Holding out or giving up? Do you think she's free to decide?' I continue, hearing my own voice, loud and unfamiliar.

She shakes her head slightly, still saying nothing. I stand there and look at her, don't know how to continue without any antagonism to push back against. I don't know how to continue without Mum. We stand there for a few long seconds, staring at one another until she removes her rubber gloves and makes her way towards me, wrapping her arms around me.

We arrive back to an empty house in Oslo, the air thick and stale, Mia can hardly have spent any time here at all. Aslak swears loudly in the kitchen, emerges with a half-full bag of rubbish in an outstretched hand.

'How does she manage to forget to take out the bin *every single time* we go away?' he asks as he walks past.

It sounds like an honest question rather than a rhetorical one, like so many questions and comments about Mia over the past few weeks. The void between us leaves me uneasy.

'You know what she's like, she forgets all sorts,' I say quickly, following him out of the door. 'Not unlike some other people I know,' I say, trying to laugh as he opens the outside bin.

Aslak gives a fleeting smile as he pushes past me to come back inside.

'But I agree, it's a pain,' I say, following him, feeling like a dog, 'we can talk to her this evening, tell her that if she's going to have the house to herself then she's going to have to learn to look after it.'

Aslak says nothing, making his way upstairs with our suitcases. I stop myself following him up, but don't know quite what to do with myself, hate those hours just after returning from holiday, the nothingness that reveals itself. I make my way out to Viljar, who's playing on the swing set outside, I push him without him asking me to, don't register how hard I'm pushing until he starts shrieking, the entire swing set almost flips over.

Mia doesn't come home, she texts me to tell me she'll be back tomorrow. She doesn't mention where she is. You forgot to take out the rubbish, I write out of loyalty to Aslak, but I delete it again. I'm no longer bothered by the thought of her staying with Jens, instead I'm on a kind of high, happy, at least when I imagine them without Zadie in the picture. I see Aslak through the bedroom window, he's trying to slot my suitcase into place on the highest shelf in the wardrobe.

I offer to pick Mia up the following day, message her before I get out of bed. It takes three impossibly long hours for her to reply, first thanking me, then sending a link to Google Maps, I open it and a red pin appears in Torshov. Filip's address, she explains in her next message. I'm so disappointed that I reply telling her she doesn't need to send three messages when one would do, but Mia has argued in the past that text messages aren't like letters or emails, they're more like an actual conversation. But that's silly, I replied, you could just ring if that were really the case.

After driving by Jens and Zadie's house, where nobody was outside or visible through the windows, I stop outside the apartment block in Torshov where Filip lives. I call Mia, who naturally fails to pick up the phone, but who texts me a thumbs up as I hang up. I crane my neck to get a better view of the apartment block, realise I know nothing about Filip, whether he lives alone and if so, why, how he can afford it, where he's from, what he looks like. The answer to the last question is revealed when Mia opens the door; behind her is a tall boy with blond hair, he makes his way over to the car with one arm around her. He's carrying a bag slung over one shoulder, I don't have the chance to wonder why until he opens the back door of the car and climbs inside as Mia slides into the front passenger seat.

'Hi,' Mia says, leaning in and kissing me on the cheek. 'This is Filip,' she says, smiling proudly.

I turn to look at the boy in the back seat, he offers me a hand and as I squeeze it, I realise he reminds me of Aslak.

'Filip's apartment is being redecorated,' Mia explains out of the blue in the car on the way home. 'It's OK if he stays with us for a few days, right?' she continues.

I don't have a chance to respond.

'You said you'd already asked her,' Filip says in the back seat. 'She can't say no now.'

Mia laughs.

'I knew it would be fine,' she says. 'Right, Mum?'

Filip's right, it's difficult to say anything but yes, but it's not immediately appealing to invite a new, unfamiliar individual into our home to witness the tension simmering between Aslak and me, not to mention the strain between Aslak and Mia, everything I've tried so hard to hold together and which is now coming undone. At the same time, there's something about the way Mia asks, the fact she isn't asking at all, the way she's chosen to introduce her family to a new boyfriend, so self-assured, so natural. Without any fear of being a burden, an extra weight to carry. This carefree sense of assurance is something Aslak and I have done our best to foster in Mia, and I want to retain that at the very least, to uphold it.

'Of course,' I say, smiling at Filip in the rear-view mirror. 'That's no problem.'

'We were thinking of going to see Grandma this weekend,' Mia says.

Instinctively I hit the brakes, the car jerks.

'Have you spoken to her?' I ask Mia.

'Of course. She said I was to ask you if we could borrow the car,' Mia says. 'Filip can drive.'

'Of course,' I say, as breezily as I can. 'But did Grandma call you?'

'What do you mean?' Mia asks.

'I just wondered if you'd spoken to her on the phone or if you'd just arranged it via message,' I say, hearing the fact that I'm struggling to maintain a normal tone of voice.

Mia turns to look at Filip for a moment, I don't catch the look they exchange.

'I spoke to her on the phone,' Mia says, pausing for a moment. 'Maybe you'd like to come with us?'

❖

I sit in the back seat of the car on the way over the mountain, behind Mia and Filip. They're both loudly singing along to the song playing on the radio, Mia's hand on the back of his neck or his leg or on his hand where it rests on the gearstick. Although Filip is a good driver, I feel stressed, perhaps by the resolutely un-embarrassed nature of their behaviour more than anything else. Or perhaps it's the prospect of Mia readying herself to disappear into her own adult life, into Filip, into everything that has nothing to do with me.

I think that's a good idea, Aslak said when I told him I was thinking about going to see Mum with Mia and Filip. He was standing in the workshop he's fitted out in the garage, planing something I guessed was going to be a cupboard door. Beside the pile of wood and planks and old items of furniture was the bureau from Mum, still with its old, peeling white paint. Yes, probably a good idea, I said, leaning against the doorframe. Aslak paused for a moment, lifted his safety goggles slightly, looked at me inquisi-tively. Sorry, there wasn't anything else, but is it OK if Viljar stays here with you? I said, mostly just to say something, anything. OK? Aslak repeated. Yes, you know what I mean, I said. No, he said, I don't know what you mean, but yes, Viljar can stay here with me.

I waited until yesterday evening to tell Mum that I would be coming, I wanted to give myself as long as possible to change my mind. I sent her a message, asked if it would be OK for me to join Mia and Filip. I must have composed and deleted the message four times, just so it wouldn't seem as if I was underlining her absence after our French trip by asking if it would be OK for me to come, all while trying to give her the opportunity to tell me that it *wasn't* OK, to let her know that she could be left in peace with Mia and Filip if that was what she wanted. I gave up. Is it OK with you if I come back home for a visit this weekend? I wrote, chucking a smiley face in for good measure. Mum replied two hours later.

That'd be lovely, she wrote, no exclamation mark or full stop, but still.

Lovely is bound to be an exaggeration, but I'm going to do my best this time too. You don't always *have* to focus on the difficult things, Jens said when I spoke to him on the phone yesterday morning, it's possible to change your memories, to change the way you *experience* them, or at least to add some nuance to them. I don't know how to do that, I said. Well, you just have to make up your mind to feel something else when a memory of Anne crops up, and repeat that over and over, he replied, it's about willpower more than anything else, forcing the memories along different emotional pathways; it's not like they represent the truth of things, anyway, he added, at the same time providing an answer to three thousand questions about us.

Mum looks unfamiliar with her grey crew-cut. She's standing on the driveway when we pull up, using a crutch to support her weight. She's thinner than she was when I last saw her in France, unexpectedly so, she had looked much more herself then, at least when her head was covered.

Mia inhales sharply when she catches sight of her, brings a hand to her mouth.

'It's OK, Mia,' I say, squeezing her shoulders, 'it's mostly the hair that makes her look so different.'

There are tears in Mia's eyes, she shakes her head with her hand over her mouth. Filip looks confused, but parks the car and turns off the engine. I concentrate on Mia, delay my own reaction to the fact that Mum hasn't told me how much she's deteriorated in the space of just a few short weeks. When I discussed pain relief with her doctor, it was in order to be better prepared for when she became properly ill. After the trip to Nice, where Mum came across as unreasonable and angry rather than unwell, I thought that was a long way off, that we had time to spare. Now it seems that time has swallowed up half of her, her clothing is loosely draped on her frame, her throat is sinewy under her pointed chin, her wrists and fingers clutching her crutch are bony, her hand looks more like a rotting twig.

'Let's get out and say hello,' I say, letting go of her shoulders, 'you'll get used to it soon enough, she looks worse than she is,' I continue, even though I know and can see that it isn't the case, not really.

Mia nods, dries her tears. I sit in the back seat and watch as she makes her way towards Mum, who readies herself, leaning her crutch against the fence post, smiling gently at Mia; I see Mia unable to hold back her tears in Mum's embrace, and Mum holds her tight, strokes her back, then holds her out in front of her, saying something as she nods and smiles, wiping Mia's cheeks with a crooked hand, again and again, all while smiling and chatting, wiping away tear after tear.

23

It's good to see you. It's good of you to come, I'm so glad you decided to join them, I've missed you, I said to Kant earlier this morning.

Sigrid opens the car door, slowly stepping out and stretching. She smiles at me, nods at Filip.

'Hi there,' she says, standing beside the car. 'This is Filip,' she says, sending him ahead of her in my direction.

I've spent far too much of this morning, and of my energy, trying to make both the house and myself look as inviting as possible; I've put flowers from the garden in Sigrid's room and the basement sitting room, I've brushed the dog hair off the sofa and my clothes, I've covered the stained kitchen table with a tablecloth and applied foundation to my face. I regret the latter, feel embarrassed by my pathetic attempts to improve my appearance, the overly dark foundation coating my pale, paper-thin skin, the line at my jaw, embarrassed that Mia and Sigrid will see.

Sigrid makes straight for the boot of the car, she hauls out the bags as I greet Filip. After setting the three small bags on the steps outside the front door, she eventually makes her way towards us.

'Have you hurt yourself?' she asks, pointing at the crutch, still keeping her distance.

I shake my head.

'It's just my back, or my hip, maybe,' I say, 'not that it matters all that much, but it's good to have some sort of assistance, a little something to support me,' I continue.

Sigrid looks at me. Already I regret my choice of words, I can see her interpreting them as yet another declaration of failure.

'It makes a difference where the pain is coming from,' she says.

'Well, yes,' I reply quickly, 'I didn't mean it like that, but neither the doctor nor I can figure it out,' I continue, taking a step in her direction.

'Hi,' I say, giving her a hug. 'It's good to see you.'

I was so happy when Sigrid messaged to say she wanted to come, so much so that in spite of the pain I drove straight down to see Gustav, I had to tell someone, to share the news with another person, with him. This time, I said, things will be different, I won't allow myself to become caught up in myself and her and our old habits.

Sigrid and I sit on the terrace and watch Mia and Filip swim out from the jetty.

'Look how in love Mia is,' I say, smiling at Sigrid.

'Yes, smitten at the very least,' Sigrid says. 'But she's always found it easy to fall for people, it's not necessarily as serious as it looks,' she adds.

She rests her head against the wall behind her, I feel for her, how afraid she is of Mia breaking free, but I daren't say anything.

'He seems like a nice lad, in any case,' I say.

'He is, he's very nice,' Sigrid says.

'He looks a bit like Gustav as a young man,' I add.

Sigrid shakes her head. 'He reminds me more of Aslak,' she says.

'Aslak isn't the worst person to resemble,' I say.

Sigrid says nothing, peers down at Mia and Filip, she looks tired, small. I detect a possibility, an opening, there's something in Sigrid's uncertain expression, the slight twitch around her eyes, I seize the moment:

'Are things difficult at the moment, between you two, I mean?' I ask.

She shakes her head. 'Is that what Mia says?' she asks, she doesn't sound too reserved, her tone is inviting.

'No, no, not at all,' I reply, 'things just seemed a little tense between you in France,' I continue.

'There was a lot of tension in France full stop,' Sigrid replies, turning to look at me, but then she composes herself once more, 'but you're right, things are difficult, perhaps most of all between Mia and Aslak.'

Sigrid has never spoken to me about her relationship with Aslak. Isn't it a little soon? I asked when she decided to move in with him just six months after Mia was born. I was sitting with Mia on my lap, watching as Sigrid deconstructed the cot in the living room. She stood up and looked at me. You should be glad, she said eventually. I can't remember what I said, but I do recall that Sigrid took Mia from me on her own initiative for the first time. I *was* glad, the extra responsibility and care was wearing me out, the changing of Mia's nappies and Gustav's bibs, Sigrid's pleading looks whenever Mia cried – I was worn out by Sigrid's helplessness, the fear of how things were going to work out for her and Mia when she could barely take care of herself.

I can't remember the last time Sigrid and I spoke about something so intimate without the conversation simply spiralling into an exchange of criticisms and defensive comments.

'Yes,' I say, 'but perhaps it's more to do with you than Aslak,' I continue without giving much thought to what I'm saying.

Sigrid straightens herself up.

'What do you mean? she asks.

This is where the line is, I know that, but I don't have the time to be cautious.

'Don't you think it might have more to do with your own relationship with Aslak, the fact that Mia comes to your defence in such a way?'

I look at Sigrid. She says nothing, looks down at Mia, who runs along the jetty at that same moment, leaping out into the water with her arms wrapped around her knees. I laugh.

'She's wonderful, you got a lot right with that one,' I say.

I've written a list of everything I need to say, everything I need to do, everything I need to explain. Much has changed in the period between Easter and now – initially I had been prepared to leave any clear-ups and conflicts and disclosures for Sigrid and Magnus to deal with in the wake of my death, but the urge to tidy up after myself has intensified since then. The list grows longer and more chaotic with every passing day: the hot water tank that needs changing, the things I haven't told Sigrid or Magnus about my own mother, things I think they ought to hear, all of Gustav's mother's recipes that I've being meaning to write down.

I've tried writing something for Sigrid, but I come to a halt as soon as I've written her name. I still don't know how to apologise for not having been better, for not having managed to *do* better, I explained to Gustav as I sat by his bed and tried to conjure up the right words, it just feels so lacking in substance, so hollow, so devoid of responsibility, I continue. I remember Gustav shouting at me across the living room once after an argument, telling me that I was terrible at apologising, that my apologies always came with caveats. An apology is worth nothing if it comes with anything but the unreserved promise of improvement, he said.

I awaken the following day to the sound of Sigrid talking to the community nurse. Her voice sounds strained as she asks why nobody has called her, I don't hear what the nurse says in reply, just catch the word 'holiday'. That's not the point, Sigrid says loudly, we had an agreement in place that you'd call me if her condition deteriorated. I lie there and listen to their discussion, Sigrid's questioning and reprimands regarding medication and escalation, equipment and plans in place, it's so soothing that it sends me back to sleep.

Are you in much pain? she asked me yesterday evening as she helped me into bed. I can manage, I said, I do this by myself every night. She said nothing, just continued to help me upstairs, finding my nightgown, making her way into the bathroom and filling my glass of water as I got changed, reappearing and perching herself on the edge of the bed. Yes, I'm in pain, but I've got painkillers, I replied, they help. You must say if you find that you need more of them, she said as she smoothed my bedcovers. I smiled. How many more, I said, even though I couldn't be sure if this new, fragile intimacy between us could stand up to such a quip. Sigrid fell silent for a few unbearable seconds, but then she smiled at me, chuckled to herself. 'Too soon', that's what Mia would have said to that, she replied. I laughed, held my hands in the air. Fine, I said. I waited for her to get up and leave, but she stayed where she was. Are you scared? she asked me eventually. No, I replied, and in that moment, it was true for the first time in a year.

'There's another one right above your head,' I tell Mia, I'm sitting in a deckchair in the garden, watching her and Filip pick apples.

She picks the last one, placing it on top of the pile in the bucket which, in spite of Sigrid's overly zealous pruning last year, is full of reddish-gold Gravenstein apples.

'Where do you want them?' Mia asks.

'Just pop them on the bench on the terrace for now,' I say. 'But make sure you leave them in the shade.'

'For now?' Mia says.

'You'll have to take them with you this year,' I say.

Mia starts crying once again. In the three days they've spent here, she's cried so often and so openly that it's left me feeling uneasy. It was manageable and understandable on the day she arrived, when one glance at my unfamiliar appearance was enough to see that my condition had deteriorated since she'd seen me last. It was straightforward enough to console her, to reassure her. It was more difficult by the second day, with Mia already in tears by breakfast time when I couldn't get the lid off the jam. In spite of the fact that it was on so tight that Sigrid was equally unable to open it, Mia continued to weep. Yesterday evening, when her tears began to fall as she caught sight of me reaching for my pill dispenser, Filip once again hurried to her aid, holding her and comforting her and hushing her sympathetically. Sigrid and I exchanged a look, and Sigrid rolled her eyes knowingly. It was enough to bring tears to my own eyes.

'I'll see you in a few weeks,' Sigrid says as they prepare to leave.

She hugs me, holding me for longer than I'm prepared for, then sits in the back seat. Mia bids me a tearful farewell, I see Sigrid place a hand on her shoulder as she climbs into the car, she says something and laughs, and Mia laughs through her tears too, then Filip reverses the car down the driveway and they toot the horn and wave as they drive away.

I haven't managed to say half of what I wanted to, the weekend has exposed the fact that it's simply impossible to say everything I thought needed saying, everything that needed making up for.

24

For the first time I feel uncertain whether Frida is going to show up for her appointment, I spend all morning feeling nervous and uneasy, afraid I might emerge to an empty chair in the waiting room at eleven – and just as afraid that she might be sitting there, afraid of being confronted by my own failure and the consequences of that.

It took a week for her to give up trying to contact me in the summer, I thrust her to the back of my mind, to the back of the queue of people and problems that required my attention, that's where she belongs after all, Jens said yesterday as we wandered along by the Aker River, you can't let your patients take up so much of your life, it's enough to wear you out.

Frida is sitting in her usual spot, in the middle of the row of chairs lined up along the wall, capable of seeing everything and impossible to overlook when I come out to fetch her. I'm relieved to see her even though she's sitting there with her arms crossed, both legs shaking impatiently, making her entire body tremble as she stares directly ahead of her.

'Hi Frida,' I say, smiling at her.

She says nothing, but gets up and follows me into my office. She removes her denim jacket without encouragement, she is wearing only a white vest top with fine straps underneath, her left lower arm is bandaged and the right is covered in sore-looking, recent scars. She lays her arms conspicuously on the armrests of the chair, her eyes locked on me as I take a seat, ready to absorb the reaction that I don't have the heart to deny her today.

'Oh gosh, you poor thing,' I say, cocking my head to one side, looking down at her arms. 'Has something happened?'

She doesn't reply but instead holds eye contact, she looks as if she's challenging me. The relief I felt at seeing her sitting in the waiting room, at her familiar acts of self-harm, at the fact she's fallen back into old habits in spite of everything else going on, the fact that she's found an outlet and is actively seeking attention, it all fades away when I'm met with silence and her steely expression. She carries on staring at me without saying a word.

'Has something in particular happened?' I ask, making another attempt. 'Is everything going OK with Emma, is she at home with your mother?'

Frida remains silent. She breaks eye contact and her gaze roams around the room, as if this were her first visit here.

'I tried calling you,' she says eventually, her tone neutral.

'I know, we spoke,' I say.

She falls silent again, looks down at her arms.

'How are things going with Emma?' I ask.

'Who were you on holiday with?' Frida asks casually, catching my eye once again.

I hesitate, don't know where I stand with her, her seemingly innocent expression as she asks the question, combined with something else I can't quite put my finger on.

'My family,' I reply after a brief pause, 'but—'

'Your husband?' she asks, interrupting me, but still with the same casual, carefree tone.

'We're not married, but yes,' I reply, realise that something is wrong, I've known it ever since she called me in the summer, 'but Frida, can you answer my question. Where's Emma?'

'Why aren't you two married, haven't you been together for, like, a hundred years? Are you waiting for someone better to come along?'

She smiles. I say nothing. We sit there looking at one another for a few seconds.

'Shall I take a look at your cuts?' I ask eventually, realising that I need to take a different approach to things.

Frida willingly stretches her arms out in my direction, I carefully unravel the bandage on one of them. Beneath the innermost layer is a cut that has been carefully sutured with at least five stitches. It's fresh, a few days old at most.

'Did you go to the hospital for these stitches?' I ask.

She nods, can't help but reveal something resembling a look of triumph.

'Are you taking your medication?' I ask her as I clean the wound with a piece of cotton wool, even though it looks perfectly clean, I just want to keep myself busy as I try to talk to her.

'Aren't you happy with him, your partner?' Frida says. 'Since you clearly don't want to marry him?'

I feel my cheeks growing warm, turn away from her to dispose of the piece of cotton wool I've been using. I can't seem to get through to her, there's something unsettling about the way she's acting, so direct and confrontational.

'Frida, I don't want to discuss my private life with you, we've talked about this,' I say.

She smiles again, raising her eyebrows. I avoid making eye contact with her, wrap a fresh bandage around her arm.

'Maybe you two just aren't having enough sex,' Frida suggests as I clean the wounds on her other arm. 'The day the sex stops, that's when you're fucked.'

I collect Viljar from preschool on my way home from the surgery. He doesn't want to go home, writhes around in the hallway, crawls so far under a bench that I'm eventually forced to get down on my hands and knees to haul him out, he grabs the leg of the bench, I pull so hard that I could probably have broken his wrists in my attempts to pull him out, I've got no patience, and had there not been an employee standing there smiling at us, I'd have sworn at him loudly.

Frida's baby has been taken into care. I called her social worker after Frida left my office. You know I can't talk to you about this, the social worker said. Come on, I almost shouted down the phone, I'm all she's got. Eventually she told me that someone had called to raise concerns at the beginning of the summer. Who was it? I asked, I knew she wouldn't tell me, and I continued without waiting: She was having weekly supervision sessions, I said. Everyone agreed it was for the best, at least in the meantime, she replied, it was based on an overall assessment. Everyone agreed? I repeated. Everyone, she confirmed. My sense of indignation in the face of a personal defeat was replaced with sympathy when I realised that Frida had willingly given up her child.

I tried calling her immediately afterwards, but her phone was off. I messaged her asking her to call me, telling her we could bring forward her next appointment. I still haven't heard back, either from her or from Jens, who I also messaged several hours ago, I check my phone every other minute in the car on the way home, almost crash straight into a roundabout, brake hard.

'You're not supposed to look at your phone when you're driving,' Viljar shouts from the back seat.

'I know,' I reply. 'Don't tell Daddy.'

Viljar smiles, looking animated, I hope at the thought of the secret we now share, rather than the prospect of telling on me.

Ever since I went for dinner with Jens in May, I've had the feeling that we're heading somewhere together – or perhaps he is the somewhere, and Mia is the road leading to him. Mia is, in any case, the bond that connects us, the argument, the explanation, the excuse, depending on how guilty I feel when I think about Aslak, it changes from day to day, hour to hour. But it's important for Mia that I have a good relationship with her father, I explained to a friend a few days ago. Is it important for Mia? she asked with a smile.

It's easy to defend our conversations, messages, meetings. It's more difficult to defend the pull I feel towards him, the fact that our interaction has become a critical point in my day. The fact I breathe more easily and think more clearly after a message or a conversation with him, that my feelings about everything are so much more straightforward, about Mum, Aslak, everything.

We take our usual stroll that evening, meeting at Nydalen just a few hundred metres from his house. We walk along the banks of the Aker River, just as we have done every other week at least over the past few months, just as we did yesterday – I'm afraid of using him up, meeting him two evenings in a row, using *us* up, but I couldn't resist when he suggested that we meet. We sit on a bench on the upper side of Grünerløkka. Sometimes, like now, he lights a cigarette as we sit here. He takes a few drags before holding it in my direction, I lean in, feel his fingers against my lips.

'There's nothing more you can do now, in any case,' he says once I've told him about Frida ignoring my attempts to get in touch, 'you did what you could, and either way, this sounds like the best solution all round. People like that can't take care of a baby, it never works out.'

'I knew it in the summer,' I say, 'when she wouldn't stop calling me, I knew there was something wrong.'

He shrugs.

'She's not your responsibility,' he says.

'But then whose responsibility is she, in your view?' I reply. 'She has no one else.'

'She's responsible for herself, just like the rest of us,' he replies.

'You need to learn to put some distance between yourself and your patients if you're going to survive in this job, Sigrid.'

'But she voluntarily gave up her own child, can you imagine?' I say without thinking.

'It's a good sign, it means she's got some sort of insight into her own nature,' he replies quickly.

Fortunately, Jens' phone rings a second later.

'Hi Zadie, no, I'm in Grünerløkka,' he says.

A high-pitched voice responds in English on the other end of the phone. Jens smiles expectantly, looks at me, finishes listening before laughing out loud.

'Not at all, I'm just sitting on a bench by the Aker River with Sigrid,' he says, 'again,' he adds.

The shame I feel over not having told Aslak about my meetings with Jens flares up within me, I feel myself growing warm, my cheeks red as I listen in to Jens' conversation with Zadie, the way he talks about me, the chirping sounds in reply. I'd taken it for granted that ours was a clandestine contract between the two of us, a secret exchange, that we were in this together to protect ourselves, at least for now.

He hangs up, lights another cigarette. He holds it out towards me, I shake my head.

'She's getting restless,' he says, smiling at me proudly.

'Restless?'

'Yes, everybody who's been out in the field grows restless, it's unavoidable, everything here at home feels so small and insignificant in comparison,' he says. 'I feel it myself, too, people's privileged first-world problems drive me up the wall.'

'But your patients have deep enough pockets to skip to the front of the queue, of course they're privileged,' I object.

'You know what I mean,' Jens says. 'Nothing compares to being out there.'

No one.

'No, I don't know what you mean.'

I'm surprised how much hope has existed within me as I feel him crush it, how physical it's become for me.

'But we do need to stick around for a few more months, maybe even up until Christmas,' he says.

When I get home, Mia is on the sofa reading a book for once. The house is silent, I sit down beside her, stroke her cheek.

'Hi there, my girl,' I say.

She looks up for a moment, smiles at me, then turns her gaze back to the page. The light from the lamp behind her casts a shadow across her face, she looks young, like a child. She stayed in Oslo for your sake, I shouted at Jens as we sat on the bench by the Aker River, she stayed here for you, what are you thinking, how could you do this to her?

I hear something from upstairs in the bedroom, Aslak, the wardrobe's sliding doors being opened and closed several times, the door to the bathroom creaking, water running through the pipes as he brushes his teeth and flushes the toilet, then several minutes of silence, what's he doing in such silence? Looking in the mirror? Sitting on the closed lid of the toilet, thinking? Flossing, helping himself to my moisturisers? I feel a fleeting sense of fondness until I hear the bathroom door open once again, his slippers on the floor, the bedroom door. I go into the kitchen, pour myself a glass of white wine as I wait for him to fall asleep. I stand at the kitchen worktop and drink it, gaze at the fridge door covered in postcards and magnets and Viljar's preschool calendar. Below it is the magnet Mum gave me: *My mother went to Paris and all I got was this lousy magnet*. Her strange and aggressive behaviour had irritated me more than anything else when she'd handed it to me in Nice; really I felt that she owed me an apology over anything else. Now the magnet appears to be exactly that, an admission, an apology. Self-deprecating. I start to laugh, realise that Mum, too, can be amusing in her own way.

She can't die alone, I told Magnus on the phone when Mia and I got back after visiting her last weekend. Magnus cried, no, of course not, he replied, he sounded inquisitive, as if he wondered why my tone was so firm, my voice steady as I made no attempt to console him. I feel calm, calmer than I have in a long time. When the fear had first gripped me in the face of Mum's deterioration, the anger I'd felt for half the year, half my life, suddenly eased. Perhaps it had something to do with her body, that the fact of her illness appeared to be a form of surrender in its own right, a self-sacrificing gesture. Perhaps it seemed unreasonable to demand anything, to rage against a body so plainly in the process of disintegrating. Perhaps it was mostly related to something fresh and new in our conversations, which were laden with self-scrutiny and understanding on her part. Don't you think that Mia feels she has to come to your defence, look after you, Mum said gently, holding eye contact with me. I had to look away, turned my gaze towards the water. I couldn't respond. She's wonderful, Sigrid, you did everything right with that one, Mum said, you're a good mother.

Our growing closeness and conversations made it more straightforward to feel at ease in Mum's company, to spend time with her. In spite of everything, it's a good thing that she'll avoid suffering a long and complicated process of deterioration, I said to Magnus, it'll be quick. I could hear him shaking his head. That's what she wants, too, I continued. Surely you don't regard that half-hearted suicide attempt as some sort of genuine desire to die, he said loudly. I was about to tell him that I hadn't been referring to that, but thought twice and decided against it. No, but everything she's said and done over the past year has demonstrated as much, I said. I don't know how you can be so cynical, he said. I was about to object, but perhaps he's right, perhaps I *am* cynical – not least due to the relief I feel at having been freed from having to respond to her wish to die for several more months or years, freed from having to meet her gaze through her various aches and pains, through hospital doors, freed from being the one who demands that she live, that she *wants* to live, for me and for us.

But we, or at least one of us, has to be there when she dies, I repeated to Magnus, that's the most important thing now. That's not the most important thing, Magnus replied, the most important thing is to be there for her *until* she dies. I smiled, true, of course, I said. He chuckled. Since spring I've feared the prospect of Mum dying alone. But I live alone, I *am* alone, it's natural that I should die alone, she said when I was there, unsentimental. We were sitting side by side on the jetty, the legs of our trousers rolled up, both dipping our toes in the cold water. You're not alone, not in life, I argued, you've got more people around you than many others do. I shan't die alone in that respect, Mum argued. But I'll try to time it so it works around yours and Magnus's schedules, how about that? she continued, laughing. I kicked her lightly, her leg against mine, yes, make sure you do, I said. She laid an arm around my shoulders.

Frida appears at the surgery the following day, turning up just after lunch without an appointment. We can hear her shouting all the way from my office, where I'm finishing writing a sick note for a student with the flu. He looks at me, raises his eyebrows. I smile, about to say something reassuring when Frida bursts through the door into my office. The medical secretary is standing behind her and flashes me a look of desperation, throwing out her arms in despair.

'You have to send me to hospital,' Frida shouts.

'OK, we can certainly talk about that, but I'm with another patient just now,' I say, nodding at the young man, who looks afraid. 'I'll come and get you when we're done.'

'I was just leaving,' he says, doing his best to smile, half standing up, but I still haven't finished his note.

'No, you need to wait until I'm ready to see you, Frida,' I say, feel my pulse thrumming in my neck, 'just take a seat,' I say to the student.

He takes a seat once again, looking uncertain, staring at the floor – in that moment I recall Magnus as a child, teaching me that I should never make eye contact with wolves or lunatics.

Frida shakes her head, makes her way into the office, sits on the examination table and grabs one of the footrests. The student, the medical secretary and Frida all look at me expectantly, I feel like I need to prove something now that I've asked Frida to wait, to exercise the authority they all expect from me, the authority the situation demands. I concede defeat without even trying, sign the sick note and send the student out with the medical secretary, who closes the door behind her.

'This isn't appropriate,' I say to Frida. 'You can't just barge your way in like this.'

She remains seated. After a while she lies down on the examination table, still gripping the footrest with one hand.

'I heard about Emma,' I say, making my way over to her, hesitating for a moment before resting a hand on her arm. 'I'm so sorry, Frida.'

'I'm going to kill myself,' she says with her eyes closed. 'You need to have me admitted.'

'Can we talk about this properly first? Could you sit up for me?'

She sits up, starts scratching her cuts as she holds my gaze.

'Frida,' I say, imploringly.

'I'm not going until you send me to the hospital,' she says.

I take a moment to compose myself to keep from shedding tears of sheer frustration, throw out my hands.

'Alright then,' I say, picking up the phone.

After ten minutes on the phone with the hospital, Frida eagerly hanging on every word from where she sits behind me, I'm required to explicitly assert my right to hospitalise her to the doctor on duty, who doesn't want to admit her. He tells me they don't have anything to offer her, no help they can give, no room for her.

'Fine, send her in, she can stay the night, but no longer,' he says eventually.

I press the phone close to my ear to keep his words from leaking to Frida and turn to look at her with a nod. For a fleeting moment, she looks happy.

I get home from work one day at the end of September to find the bureau from Mum's house in the middle of the living room. Aslak has sanded and varnished it and replaced its handles. I walk through the door to find him admiring it from a distance, walking around it to observe it from all angles.

'It's looking lovely,' I say.

He nods without looking at me, his eyes locked on the bureau.

'Though its position in the room could do with a little work,' I say with a smile.

He smiles briefly without looking over, says nothing. I step closer, reach out to touch it.

'Don't,' Aslak says quickly. 'It'll get greasy.'

I pull my hand away.

'Ah. Well in that case, good luck introducing this new member of the family to Viljar,' I say.

Aslak still doesn't laugh.

'I'm not leaving it here, I've sold it,' he says.

Finally he looks at me.

'You've sold Mum's bureau?' I say.

'It's not Anne's bureau anymore, she gave it to us,' Aslak says.

'To us, yes, not to you in order that you could sell it,' I say.

I don't care about the bureau, Aslak can flog it to anyone he likes for all I care, but finally an opportunity for conflict has arisen between us, an opportunity to react, to invite a reaction, after so many months of fleeting smiles and nods, months spent with nothing to cling to.

'You didn't want it,' Aslak says, louder now.

'I never said that,' I reply.

'You certainly made that out to be the case,' Aslak says.

'Well, I do want it,' I say, locking eyes with him.

25

In Gustav's old desk I find his almanacs, the first dating back to 1966. It's impossible to decipher what he's written in his final entry, the day before he lost his grasp on language. My guess is that it has something to do with the apples, but it could just as easily be a quote, a verse of poetry. I've never understood quite why, but I continued to add entries two days after he stopped doing so. I've written a line or two each day, carrying his project onwards, carrying him onwards.

A year ago, I noted down the temperature of the water, eleven degrees, and that I'd carried some planks of wood that day. A year ago, I hiked up to the mountain pasture with the planks over my shoulder, I was set to start replacing the back wall of the outdoor toilet, but I was so tired when I eventually made it up there, I had to lie down then and there. As I lay there and looked down upon the village below, the wood burner crackling, I remember thinking that it wouldn't be such a terrible time to be under the weather, as it meant I'd get out of attending a seminar in Trondheim a few days later.

I lie in Gustav's old room at home, gaze out of the window, up towards the mountain pasture. Scattered around me on the bed are the almanacs I've pulled out, I've read several of them from cover to cover for the very first time. There isn't a single thing of interest in what I've read thus far, nothing about me, nothing about Magnus or Sigrid, just temperatures and fertiliser blends, quotes and titles, one after another, filling the pages. On our first wedding anniversary, he'd written 'combustion vs. bokashi'. On

Magnus's seventeenth birthday, when Gustav had already been ill for a number of years, he'd written a quote in Swedish, a poetic verse I don't recognise.

I don't have the desire or energy to begin trying to decipher any of it, to once again be left with the feeling that I'm standing on the outside looking in, looking up at something out of my reach, as I had always felt until he fell ill.

On the bedside table, underneath three of the almanacs, is my personal plan for how I'll spend the days until I die. My wishes and aims. My assets. The needs and wishes of my next of kin. I filled it in with the help of my doctor after the diagnosis and treatment of my third chest infection in the space of two months. Sigrid joined us via FaceTime, her face filling the entire screen as she did her best to lead the conversation from Oslo. Of course there are things you want, Mum, she said loudly as we reached the section about my wishes and aims, and I found myself at a loss as to what sort of wishes and aims they could possibly be referring to. You want to stay at home, don't you? Sigrid continued. I nodded, that's true, I told my doctor, I do want to stay at home. And you want to take advantage of as much help as is available to you, Sigrid said. Yes, or, well, I don't want anything outside the norm, I tried saying, I don't want to be a drain on resources, I said, smiling at him. He nodded, did his best to note everything down. And she wants as much pain relief as possible, Sigrid said. Of course, the doctor said. Magnus and I would like to be kept informed as her closest next of kin, she continued, her cheeks had turned pink. After the doctor had held the sheet of paper up to the phone on Sigrid's request and she had corrected a few points, I ended the call. Sorry about that,

I said to him. He laughed, I'm sure I'd be the same if it was my mother, he said.

I don't want any more life-prolonging treatment, I said.

Sigrid is on her way over the mountains. I picture her in the car, her profile against the side window, as if I'm sitting in the passenger seat. She's driving fast, her eyes on the road. She runs her fingers through her hair, her thoughts settle on me.

I wake up to her smile.

26

I drive back and forth between Mum and Oslo, three days at home, two days with her, three days, four days, two weeks, driving through morning fog and a surprising flicker of hope over Geilo, through autumn rain and paralysing anxiety in Hønefoss, through blinding afternoon sunshine and grief in Lærdal, through the nights, the mornings, the days, the emotions, back and forth to Mum.

One of the community nurses told me yesterday that Mum calls for me in the mornings on the days he lets himself in when I'm not around. I was on the commuter train on my way home from the office, he called to tell me that they had finally decided to insert a pain pump. What do you mean she calls for me? I asked. She just calls for you, he replied. But I don't understand what you mean, I said, so loudly that a woman sitting beside me jumped, I got up before continuing: Is she angry, is she afraid? He fell silent. She sounds more curious than anything else, hopeful, maybe, as if she hopes it might be you arriving, he said eventually.

The idea of it leaves me feeling upset, yet there's also something positive about the fact that I'm the one she calls out for, the one she misses. I console myself with the idea that her medication leaves her sleepy and confused by the time morning rolls around, she doesn't remember it later in the day, she doesn't remember waking up and hoping that it might be me arriving.

It was Jens who recommended a pain pump. The sooner the better, he said a week ago. Cancer patients shouldn't need to suffer any pain, not in this day and age, he continued. Have you been reading up on palliative care? I asked. He laughed. Believe it or not, I know a fair bit about pain relief, he said. I had to bite my tongue to keep myself from saying that he also knew more than a fair bit about inflicting pain, I haven't met up with him since the evening we walked by the Aker River, when I couldn't stop myself begging him to stay. Don't do this to Mia, I shouted eventually. The fact he'd looked genuinely surprised, that he hadn't anticipated such a reaction, or any reaction at all, that ought to be enough in itself. The thought of what he's doing to Mia ought to be enough. Still, I can't get enough.

When I visit Mum a week later, she's had a tiny needle inserted in her stomach, with a tube leading to the pump she carries around in a small bag. She's sitting in the kitchen, eating soup when I arrive, pulls up her jumper to show me the needle and tube without any prompting.

'And if I press here,' she says, showing me the kit, 'I get an extra dose of morphine.'

'Have they given you permission to control it yourself?' I ask her.

'Yes, weren't they supposed to?' Mum asks. 'I'm the only one who knows how much pain I'm in.'

I say no more, make my way over to the stove.

'I hope you're not still eating the broth Magnus made two weeks ago,' I say, peering into the pan.

'No, this is good old meals on wheels,' Mum says, raising a spoon in my direction. 'Is it just you this time, too?'

I nod. Mia and Aslak have offered to join me on several occasions over the past month, but I haven't wanted them here with me, haven't desired their company, I want to be alone with Mum, there isn't enough time left to share it with others. How long does she really have left? Magnus asked me the last time our stays overlapped. I don't know, I replied, maybe a few months if she doesn't become ill. Ill? he repeated. Well, worse, if she doesn't catch an infection, I said, correcting myself. He looked relieved. Good, he said.

'The others are coming next time,' I tell Mum, taking a seat at the table beside her, watching as she struggles to consume the bland-looking soup. 'Do you want me to make you something else?' I ask.

She shakes her head.

'Then shall we have a glass of wine?' I suggest eventually.

She looks relieved, smiles at me. When Mum's condition started deteriorating a few months ago, I initially tried to throw together all manner of meals she might enjoy, anything I could think of, I spent hours making dishes that might tempt her. She put far too much effort into trying to avoid disappointing me by forcing herself to take a few bites of whatever I served up. You need to eat, Mum, I told her all the while, you need to take your pills, you need to keep moving, you need to sleep, you need to shower, you need to do this, you need to do that.

Last time I was here, she finally lost her temper. Why? she shouted, sounding desperate. I had no answer, and the following day I went out and came back with several bottles of expensive red wine. There, I said, placing them on the kitchen countertop. Mum hesitated, no doubt wondering whether I was trying to make a point, she checked the time, it was two o'clock in the afternoon. Let's have a drink, I said.

She grows sleepy after just one glass. Half dozes in her chair. I sit here and watch her for at least an hour before helping her up to bed. She grumbles, she's aching all over, she can no longer point at the pain chart to show where the discomfort is coming from, it's everywhere, she says when I ask. But she doesn't complain, she's stopped talking about illness and death altogether, she's stopped trying to give away her belongings, she's stopped asking what we're planning on doing with the farm, with Kant, with the cabin, whether I know how to wash the linen drapes, if we know all we need to know about Dad's medication. Her face seems softer, more serene, at least when it's not wincing in pain; I can no longer see fear and anger and reproach in the lines around her mouth and eyes, no hidden message in every expression.

I help her to undress, layer upon layer of wool. I chuckle as I reach the third and final woollen garment.

'Woollen base layer first,' I say.

'I've taught you one of the most important things in life, then,' Mum mumbles in her half-sleep, lying back in the bed.

I pull the covers up over her, she's breathing heavily and groaning ever so slightly.

'More,' she whispers.

I press the pump, she falls silent, the tiny muscles in her face letting go, smoothing out her features. I press it once more. She opens her eyes slightly before disappearing into sleep. I sit with my hand on the pump for a while, my gaze resting on the ampoules of morphine on her bedside table.

'No,' Magnus says when he arrives on Sunday evening.

'I told you not to answer until you'd had a chance to think about it,' I say.

'I don't need to think about it,' he says.

'She's so tired, Magnus,' I say.

'No,' he repeats.

'Think about it,' I say.

I get back to Oslo on Monday night. Mia's shoes are in the hallway, the sight moves me to tears, I'm so touched that she's here with Aslak and Viljar, that they're all lying in their beds, fast asleep.

Aslak turns the light on as I creep into the bedroom, sits up in bed. He peers over at me.

'Not sleeping?' I say.

'No, I thought you'd be back hours ago,' he says.

'Sorry, I had to stop for a nap on the way,' I say. 'Has everything been OK here?'

'What do you mean by OK?' Aslak asks.

'Have you had a nice few days?' I ask.

Aslak says nothing, just sits there and watches me as I undress, letting my clothes fall to the floor.

'I want us to move back home,' Aslak says. 'I want us to move into Anne's house.'

I'm surprised only by the fact that he says so now, that he still harbours any desires for us at all.

'She's not dead yet, Aslak,' I say, lying down beside him.

'I've made up my mind,' he says, his voice low, soft, he doesn't need to explain the fact that he's going, regardless of what I decide.

'I hear what you're saying,' I tell him.

I hear what he's saying, turn off the light, go to sleep.

Mia asks if she can come with me when I go back to see Mum in a few weeks. I can't deny her that, even though I still harbour an almost overwhelming urge to have Mum all to myself. Don't you have classes to attend? I ask. She shakes her head. Aslak suspects that Mia isn't doing any studying at all, that she's simply signed up for subjects she has no plan to take exams in, still, I'm not the one paying for it, he says.

'Have you seen Jens lately?' I ask Mia in the car on our way to Mum's.

She's no longer on her guard when I ask her about him, but nor does she seem particularly pleased at the interest I'm taking in him, not in the same way she had earlier in the autumn, before she realised I'd been seeing him without her. Jens was the one who mentioned it, just dropped it into conversation quite casually, that he'd also told Mia about the fact we were in touch. That might not have been such a good idea, I said. Why not? he asked breezily, surely any child would be glad to know their parents are friends, especially if they're divorced. I was on the brink of shouting that we weren't divorced, and nor were we friends. Mia hasn't said a word to me about it, but she came home from Jens' one evening a few weeks ago looking sullen, almost scornful.

'I was there last weekend,' she says. 'How about you?' she adds, in a tone I can't decipher.

I shake my head. I long to tell her that Jens is moving away, leaving her once again, letting her down, I long for her to prevent him, stop him, hold on to him.

Mia's phone is lying between us, we both look down at it when it rings, the sound on for once. *Dad*, it says on the screen. I feel the same soft lurch in my gut at Jens' presence before hearing Aslak's voice when Mia picks up.

❖

Mum's condition has deteriorated. She's weaker now. She doesn't want any more life-prolonging treatment, but her immune system is fighting to keep her alive – even against her will. In the last month alone, she's successfully fought off two infections without intervention.

When we arrive, she still seems in better shape than I've braced myself and Mia for, she's sitting in the living room listening to one of Dad's old CDs. Last time I was here, we had to turn around on our way to the nursing home, she'd felt dizzy and generally unwell, she was in pain, the morphine had sent her to sleep in the car, and I had decided to turn the car around. She started to cry when she awoke to find us pulling up at home. No, she said, we have to go back down to see Gustav, he'll be wondering where I am, please, Sigrid. I'll tell him, I said, helping her into bed, I'll drive down there and tell him.

Mia doesn't cry this time. She sits beside Mum on the sofa, resting her head on Mum's shoulder, it's so slender and bony that it can't possibly be very comfortable for either of them, but both sit there as I let Kant out and fetch the bags from the car.

I wake before Mum and Mia the following day. I grab Mum's down jacket and pull it on over my T-shirt, then step into her boots, which are a little too big for me. The ground is frosty, it's a dusky morning, I wander down the path towards the water. I've never understood Mum's urge to swim in the mornings, I shiver as I remove her jacket, gaze at the tranquil landscape, feel an intimacy and sense of belonging to the familiar elements all around me, to rocks and moors and mountains and water, to Mum, then I remove my T-shirt. I stand there naked but for Mum's boots for a few seconds, then make my way onto the jetty. I remove the boots, the boards are icy cold against the soles of my feet, the water beneath me is black and still. I brace myself, ready to jump at least five times, my body jerks but refuses to follow through, I change my mind at the last moment every single time.

'Coward,' Mum says as I open her bedroom door, she's raised the head of her bed to allow her to see out of the window, she's sitting upright, smiling.

'Agreed,' I say.

'Mia will have to be the one to carry on the bathing tradition,' Mum says.

I nod, perch on the edge of her bed. She rests a hand on my leg, we sit there in silence, looking out of the window until Mia calls to us from the kitchen.

After breakfast, Mum falls asleep again, I feel restless, wander aimlessly around the house, studying the furniture, the books, the junk, overwhelmed by memories one minute and subdued at the thought of everything that needs doing the next, everything that needs sorting out. I make a start on a pile of things Mum's stacked up under the stairs, but I stop when I realise that she'll see, that it will seem impatient. I make my way out to the cowshed, remember the sheep, the neighbour who accused Dad of ill-treatment because he never wanted to butcher them. I try to imagine the farm as home to animals once again, home to Aslak and me, Viljar, Mia, but the thought is so unfamiliar and intolerable, the images only appear in my mind by force, I find myself interrupted by a vision of Jens and Zadie's backs as they walk away, making their way through the departure lounge at Gardermoen airport.

In the cowshed are two of Mum's old chest freezers, one filled to the brim with labelled and unlabelled packages, berries and meat and vegetables, old iceboxes, their contents impossible to identify, and the other freezer filled with poorly-cleaned chicken carcasses. Feeling resolute, I make my way into the hallway and fetch some bin bags, sort the contents of one freezer into blue and green bags, throw out anything without a label and anything more than two years old, hesitate before disposing of the chickens one by one.

I roll Mum across the car park in a wheelchair we've been loaned by the local authority. We don't really need it today, she said as I carried it out to the car. You can barely walk from the living room to the bedroom, I said, we need to take it, just in case. But Gustav, she began, couldn't finish her sentence. You can get out of it at the front door, I suggested as we parked outside the nursing home and Mum could barely make it out of the car without help.

I take her arm through the hallway, she looks impatient. Dad is sitting by the window of the communal lounge, as usual, Mum lets go of my arm when she catches sight of him.

I let her cross the room alone, stand in the doorway and watch Dad and Mum, the way she gently brushes something from his shoulder, saying something and smiling before taking a seat beside him.

'I think you need to start using that dandruff shampoo again,' I say to Gustav, the shoulders of his dark jumper are covered in a sprinkling of white flakes.

I sit down beside him, and we remain there in silence for a while, gazing out at the village, I can just about make out the top of the highest peak north of the farm.

'The water temperature was just ten degrees today,' I tell him, taking his hand, the skin of his palms still leathery, I squeeze his rough fingers.

He turns his head and looks at me, makes eye contact.

'There you are,' I say.

It's snowing so heavily that we can't see the mountains outside the windows. Aslak and Magnus go out and clear the driveway every other hour to prevent us from ending up snowed in, to allow us to get the car out if anything were to happen. Nothing is going to happen that means we end up needing the car, Magnus, I tell him. Still they clear the driveway, perhaps just to keep themselves occupied, more than anything else.

Mum slips in and out of consciousness, lying in Dad's room just beyond the kitchen with the door open so she can hear us. I mostly sit in the chair at the end of the bed, monitoring her breathing, watching her chest as it rises and falls. I speak to her, tell her everything that comes to mind, regardless of whether she's asleep or awake.

Last week, Magnus found a book under the pillow in her room upstairs. I didn't ask how he stumbled across it, what he was doing in her bed. He came in to Mum and me yesterday evening, after the others had gone to bed, handed it to me. An old notebook like the kind we used to use at school, filled with Mum's beautiful handwriting, all cursive loops and curves and lines. Recipes, to-do lists, the odd word that made no sense, mixing ratios. Apologise, it says at the top of the last page. Underneath is a bullet point, a name, my name.

On Christmas Eve, Mum wakes up as I'm changing her bedding.

'Hi,' I say.

'Hi,' she says. 'I can smell ribs.'

I laugh.

'Aslak has made an early start on Christmas preparations, we had ribs yesterday,' I reply. 'Would you like some?'

She shakes her head. I pass her the glass of squash, she takes the end of the straw in her mouth, lifts her gaze to look out of the window behind me, closes her eyes for several minutes, I feel certain she's fallen asleep again.

'Swim,' she says.

'Do you want to swim?' I ask her.

The pathway is wet, I tread carefully to prevent myself from slipping on the smooth stones underfoot. The air smells raw and springlike. Kant runs ahead of me in the drizzle, the sun breaks through the clouds and morning mist once I've made it halfway down to the water. The wet landscape around me glitters in the sunlight, I can just about feel the warmth of the sun on my face.

Kant sniffs around behind a bush, God help you if you're eating a lemming, I shout, don't even think about it, I untie the knot of my dressing gown, take it off, drape it over the fence.

I fill the bathtub. Sit on the edge and watch the water rising, leave the room to turn up the central heating. I test the water again, add more hot before turning the tap off.

I make my way into Mum's room, fetch her dressing gown, which is hanging on a hook by the window. I hold it to my face for a moment, breathe in the soft towelling, smell it, stand there without being able to recall what I'm supposed to be doing for a few seconds before heading back down to Mum.

Carefully I remove her nightgown, she wakes up and helps me as I attempt to pull it over her head. I smile at her, I'm not sure whether she can see me.

'Can I sit you up a little?' I ask, lifting the head of the bed using the remote control.

I drape the dressing gown around her shoulders, carefully pull it underneath her, loosely tie it around her waist. I detach the pain pump. Then I call for Aslak.

I brace myself, leap from the jetty, dive into the dark water. I hear a rushing sound in my ears, the water is soft and cool, I am weightless, but the resistance makes my arms and legs feel heavy, at least until I get into a rhythm. I synchronise their movements, long, strong strokes, glide out towards the red buoy.

Aslak holds Mum tight as he carries her up the stairs, be careful, I say, be careful, there's no hurry, he says nothing, but I see him tighten his grip, her head resting on his shoulder.

I test the water once again before untying her dressing gown. I think you'll need to put her down first, I say to Aslak, I can't get it off when you hold her like that, he laughs quietly at my attempts, I join in, Mum wakes up once again, makes eye contact with me. Eventually I manage to coax her out of her dressing gown, Aslak looks her in the eye as he carefully lowers her into the water. She smiles, are you OK lying with your head like that, Mum? I ask her. She says nothing, but lies there quite peacefully, her head resting on the edge as Aslak lets go of her, he squeezes my shoulders as he walks past on his way out of the bathroom.

Quickly I swim out, around the fourth buoy, I'm on my way back when I catch sight of Sigrid standing on the jetty. She's wearing her green jumper, one hand covering her eyes to shield them from the sun, she looks as though she's searching for me in the water. I stop halfway, call out to her, come on, I'm not going anywhere until you join me.

ACKNOWLEDGEMENTS

A thousand thank-yous to my and newly retired editor Øyvind Pharo, for his invaluable reading, suggestions and conversations while I worked on this book. And thank you to my new editor, Jon Krog Pedersen, for our inspiring and motivating new partnership.

Thanks also to my Norwegian publisher's head of communications, Vidar Strøm Fallø, for his dedication and for tirelessly endorsing my books. And thank you to everyone at Aschehoug Publishing House and Oslo Literary Agency for believing in my books and bringing them to readers in Norway and worldwide.

I am very grateful to each of my international publishers and translators. Having my books translated into English has been a major milestone for me, and I would like to thank Orenda Books, and in particular publisher Karen Sullivan for her dedication, patience and never-ending efforts to introduce my novels to English readers. An equally warm thanks to translator Rosie Hedger for her thorough and beautiful work.

Last, but not least: a thousand thanks to all my dedicated readers.